The Jackson Jinx

Vincent Armstrong

Published by Magic Rainbow, 2022.

THE JACKSON JINX

First edition. November 10, 2022.

ISBN: 978-1735311074

Written by Vincent Armstrong.

Chapter 1

Not since the Atlanta child killings had an arrest created such a stir in the ATL. The melodrama and excitement that surrounded the Atlanta jail continued to build by the minute as everyone awaited the arrival of the most hyped suspect since Wayne Williams. Media from CNN, MSNBC, FoxNews, along with local and national press, crowded the rear entrance of the jail as they readied their cameras, microphones, and questions for the accused about to be ushered into the jail. The Memorial Day weekend in the ATL had been a hot sizzling affair. However, on this day, the first day of June, the temperature and tension couldn't rise any higher as everyone waited; waited for the prime suspect to finally arrive.

News of the murder of Joletta Anderson swept through the streets of Atlanta faster than the winning numbers of the Georgia Lottery. Everyone knew that Joletta, a former Miss Black America beauty queen and prominent business woman, wasn't your usual murder victim. She also happened to be the twenty-eight-year-old daughter of Hobskin Anderson, mayor of Atlanta.

The discovery of her body slumped over the steering wheel of her Mercedes with her throat slashed came as a shock to the city. Inquiries quickly went out for the perpetrator of this vicious murder, and in no time an investigation was under way. For two days since that early Sunday morning when the police found Joletta slumped over her steering wheel, the city of Atlanta had waited for answers about the story of her killer. Tension ran high as everyone was on edge. There was no illusion that this murder wouldn't take place under the microscope of the public's eye, and the police chief, seeing the magnitude of this case, personally vowed that the felon of this horrible crime would be quickly apprehended.

The tragic murder of Mayor Anderson's daughter, however, wasn't the sole reason for such a stir around the city and for such an imminent widespread investigation. Joletta Anderson wasn't only the daughter of Atlanta's highly popular mayor, but this talented, former Miss Black America beauty queen was a powerful player in her own right in Atlanta's thriving business, social, and entertainment community.

What Joletta had accomplished in her limited years was almost astounding. She owned and ran one of Atlanta's most prosperous and most talked about hip hop nightclubs known as Seven Flavors. She started her own music company and was on the verge of becoming one of Atlanta's next major music moguls. She also owned a popular sports bar, a car dealership, a state-of-the-art exercise gym, was the owner of one of Atlanta's most swank upscale restaurants, and had even opened up a number of small boutique shops all around the city as she began to market and distribute her own line of women clothes.

Despite Joletta's success in her many professional endeavors at the young age of twenty-eight, what really made her admired and loved around Atlanta was her commitment and dedication to the people of the community.

Joletta became a committed champion and a constant advocate for social causes and issues that plagued and ailed the city. She was a devoted stalwart for Aids Awareness, an advocate against teen pregnancy, a patron for young single black mothers, and a strong supporter for voter registration drives throughout the black community. With the help of her father's administration, she helped organize scholarship funds for underprivileged minorities, solicited endlessly for better access for the handicap, and became a spokesperson for those suffering in mental institutions. Joletta had an insatiable drive and a passion to help those who needed help, and her drive and passion quickly caught on and became the passion of others around the city.

There was absolutely nothing standing in the way of this shooting star and the future only looked brighter. Joletta was a pioneer and a trailblazer for the hip hop generation. She was a lady of many facets, and there seemed that it was nothing that she couldn't do. The recipient of a good family name and having the know-with-all of how to use it for the betterment of society, made her unique and loved. Joletta embodied the word excellence like a trophy given solely to her. Now the life of this young entrepreneurial, socially conscious, hip hop progressive diva had been cut short; cut short by an unexplained murder that had left the city of Atlanta in a state of shock.

THE JACKSON JINX

BY NOON, THE SCENE around the jail was about to erupt. Several hours had passed since the first reports of the apprehension of Joletta's murderer, but the suspect, still hadn't arrived. The press and the overflow of media, crammed together for hours under the hot sweltering sun, now grew impatient. They anxiously and eagerly wanted to report something—*anything*—on the status of Joletta's murderer. However, the media, with all of its ability to probe the unknown, were simply clueless. They, just like the rest of the city of Atlanta, would have to wait for their story.

Suddenly the wait was over. A line of patrol cars slowly approached the rear of the jail as the media and the press came alive. The excitement turned to near pandemonium as the procession of patrol cars came to a stop. Without further delay, the police jumped out as the suspect from the middle patrol car was quickly brought out, surrounded, and hurried toward the jail.

The flood of questions, barbs, and accusations that crackled through the air from the media directed toward the handcuffed suspect went unanswered. The suspect, six-feet-one black male with cornrows, wouldn't take the bait from the press as he lowered his head and ignored the excitement. Within seconds, it was all over as the apprehended suspect was whisked away into the jail, leaving the media hungry and salivating for a story.

The media, however, didn't have to wait long for its story. Moments after the suspect was hustled into the jail, a police spokesman stepped from the jail and addressed the throng of media that had pushed around him. With their microphones ready and their cameras rolling, the spokesman calmly and slowly announced that the person they had in custody was one Terrence Jackson, a twenty-three-year-old local DJ who worked at Joletta's prominent hip hop nightclub, Seven Flavors.

With the preliminaries of the story now set, the media began to fire question after question as they linked Terrence Jackson and Joletta Anderson in the most sensational crime Atlanta had witnessed in decades.

Chapter 2

Frances' Soul Food Restaurant on Auburn Avenue simmered with gossip. The gossip swirling around the investigation of Joletta Anderson's murder was a hot topic down at the busy restaurant as the midday lunch rush was in high gear. The down-home southern style cafeteria, which brought in hundreds of hungry customers every day, was a debating ground for nothing but rumors into the latest news of Joletta's murder since her body was found slumped over the steering wheel of her Mercedes over the weekend.

Besides the savory taste of Frances' famous collard greens, corn bread, black-eyed peas, pork chops, meat loaf, fried chicken, and fresh baked sweet potato pie, a steady dose of gossip surrounding the death of the mayor's daughter was as appetizing as any soulful dish that the restaurant had to offer. It was an insatiable habit to talk about Joletta's murder, and anyone who ventured through the doors of Atlanta's most popular soul food restaurant, was bound to get caught up in the hysteria. About the only people not constantly obsessed with the minute-by-minute details of the investigation was the restaurant staff; who today, as every day around noon, was too busy trying to serve the steady growing lunch crowd that continued to flood through the door.

By one o'clock, when the hectic lunch rush began to finally die down, Frances Jackson, the renowned owner and operator of Frances' Soul Food Restaurant, came from out of the kitchen to check on things out front. She approached Ernestine, her forty-year-old daughter working the cash register, as she rung up the few remaining customers still in line.

Frances, wiping the perspiration from her face with a rag, looked as if the busy lunch rush had gotten the best of her. Her plump frame, padded from years of eating her own good cooking, looked tired and slumped as she stood next to her daughter's slender body. However, at age sixty-seven, Frances' face and eyes still had the vitality and vigor of a woman who was on a mission to succeed. With one look at Frances, it was clear that she was a dedicated, proud black woman who'd never surrender to the word retirement.

"Curtis, you and Ronnie didn't come in last Thursday night for dinner." Frances bantered with two of her loyal customers still in line. "You know I have catfish every Thursday."

"Ah, now, Mrs. Frances, you know my wife would have a fit if I didn't come home to eat on Thursdays," Curtis spoke quickly. "Every Thursday night she makes her special beef stew."

"And I got a feeling if you have another Thursday night of your wife's beef stew, your tail will be running down to the corner store buying every bottle of Pepto-Bismol and ex-lax they have on the shelve."

Curtis and Ronnie appeared too amused to comment as they paid for their lunch and headed for the dining area. When Ernestine finally took the money from the last customer, Frances slowly looked at her with apprehension.

Frances knew her daughter could be difficult to deal with at times, and she knew whenever it came to confronting her about issues of running the cash register, that a nasty argument was bound to break out between the two of them. But since Ernestine had come to join her staff at the restaurant over nine months ago, Frances had learned to be patient. She wasn't expecting big things from Ernestine, just a little competence and dedication to her job. Simply put, after a long road of Ernestine recovering from drugs, dealing with unscrupulous men, and simply making bad life decisions, Frances was just satisfied to have her daughter's life finally turned around and headed in the right direction.

"Are you getting ready to count the till?" Frances asked when Ernestine closed the register.

"Yeah, Franny." She hissed angrily. "And don't start sweating me either. The till don't come up short, now do it?"

"No, that's just it. You've been over lately. And some of the customers are complaining that you're not giving them back their right amount of money. I don't want you cheating the people out of their proper change."

"Don't worry, I can *count*!"

"Some days I wonder," Frances mumbled to herself. "Look I'm going to check out in the dining area. Tell Earl to start boiling that water and getting some more food out for the next wave that's about to come in."

When Frances entered the dining area of her packed restaurant, she was immediately at home with her customers. Everyone knew Frances was a woman of God whose faith was as strong as any apostle in the Bible. She proclaimed her faith with an unabashed fervor that could put to shame even the most hell fire storming preacher.

Plastered all across the walls of her restaurant in big, black bold letters was her famous motto: GOD WILL MAKE A WAY. Her restaurant was more than just a place of business, it was more like a sanctuary where hungry souls from all around Atlanta came to her establishment not only to feast on Frances' mouth-watering soul food, but to listen to the wisdom that she bestowed.

To add to that, Frances had the gift of gab that would make anyone who entered through the doors of her establishment sit up and take notice, and at times, she'd even have them in stitches with her colorful humor. She was definitely the main attraction of her restaurant. She was part preacher, social worker, comedian, and a full-time cook better than any man or woman who ever ventured into a kitchen. Today, as she mingled through the packed dining area, she was in full stride as she greeted her old regulars and first-timers alike.

"What you say there Mingo?" Frances said in a hearty voice.

"Doing just fine, Mrs. Frances."

"You make it to church last Sunday?"

"Naw, Mrs. Frances. That new boss lady had me working to the grind down at the plant Sunday."

"Now that make four Sundays in a row. You sure that new *boss lady* ain't got you alone down there breaking your back."

Mingo simply smiled as Frances spotted another one of her regulars sitting across from him.

"Cecil, did y'all finally get your uncle's will settled?" She gibed.

"Sure did," he said with a huge grin. "And he left me with a nice hunk of dough, too, Mrs. Frances."

"I guess that's why that pretty young thang you came in with the other day finally paid you some mind." Frances laughed.

"Hey, Frances," another group called from across the dining room. "Turn on the overhead TV. Chuck said he passed by the jail about an hour ago and said the media was all camped out there. He heard there's been some kind of arrest in that Joletta Anderson murder."

"Yeah, let me turn on the television so we can all see what's going on."

Frances went over to the location of the TV as she reached up and turned on the set from the shelf. She flicked on CNN as a female reporter at the site of the jail commentated about the murder. The scene at the jail looked chaotic with all sorts of media, police, and spectators all mixed and jammed together. Everyone in the packed dining area suddenly became glued to the set as the reporter jabbered on. Frances turned up the sound on the set as the reporter's words came through loud and clear.

"Today there was an arrest in Atlanta in the murder of Joletta Anderson, the daughter of Mayor Hobskin Anderson who's currently running for a seat in the U.S. House of Representatives in this upcoming November general election," the reporter said. "The murder of the mayor's daughter over the weekend has been a shock to the city of Atlanta, and just moments ago police arrested this man—" The news flipped to a quick shot as the police hustled the apprehended suspect into the jail. "The man is named Terrence Jackson, a twenty-three-year-old local DJ who worked at the nightclub Seven Flavors which was owned by Joletta Anderson, has now been arrested for her murder."

Stunned silence suddenly choked the entire dining room as everyone watched in horror. Frances literally stared at the TV screen with a frozen dazed look. She couldn't even speak, but when the words finally did come out, they were loud enough to virtually shatter every window in the place.

"Oh, my goodness," Frances said with a shuddering tremble. "OH, MY GOODNESS! ERNESTINE, GET OUT HERE! QUICK!"

Frances' panic scream made Ernestine hurry into the dining area in a flash. The rest of the staff came running also. They stood behind Ernestine and Frances as everyone watched the breaking news report televised on CNN.

Ernestine nearly bit her lip as she watched the replay of the police escorting her son into the jail. Appearing too nervous and frightened to even speak, she could only look around at the others who were silent and glued to the TV. Frances, who was always strong and supportive in times of crises, was of no help. She could only watch in utter disbelief as her grandson was displayed to the world as the murderer of Joletta Anderson.

Chapter 3

Frances and Ernestine Jackson bolted from the restaurant as soon as they heard the shocking news of Terrence's arrest. They drove quickly to the jail hoping that Terrence's arrest was just some kind of big mistake, and that he really wasn't the accused murderer that the city, and the entire nation, had just seen. Neither Ernestine nor Frances said a word to the other as they drove in silence. It seemed the fear and tension that they both felt were literally unbearable.

When Frances finally found a parking space near the jail, she and Ernestine got out of the car and headed quickly toward the building. An assembly of reporters and various news crews were camped out in front of the jail as they went about the business of trying to attain more facts on the arrest of Terrence Jackson. Frances and Ernestine ignored the encampment of media and reporters as they rushed past them and made their way inside the jail.

The hustle and bustle of a big city jail immediately overtook the nervous women as they tried to make heads or tails of the situation. The myriad of police officers, apprehended felons, lawyers, administrators, desk clerks, and all sorts of other law officials hurrying back and forth in a furious manner, made the place seem like a maze of confusion. Ernestine and Frances quickly discovered that getting any kind of information on Terrence's status would be anything but easy. After pointed in all sorts of directions and getting the run-around for almost an hour, their tension and stress only seemed to grow worse.

Finally, after waiting over an hour for Terrence to be properly booked into the jail, Frances and Ernestine were allowed to see him. They sat in a huge visitation room, along with the other visitors who were busy talking on phones to their loved ones across a thick glass window. The thick glass window separated those who were in jail from those who were not.

Frances and Ernestine waited nervously for Terrence to be brought in as they listened to the other visitors around them ramble on with their conversations. The wait, which seemed like an eternity, soon became downright excruciating. But no sooner had they looked around, Terrence was suddenly brought into the room.

A heavy-set guard with large, powerful biceps escorted him down to the empty seat directly across the glass window from Frances and Ernestine. All eyes around the room immediately stared and gawked at this tall, lean young black man with cornrows. Terrence had on the same orange issued jumpsuit as everyone else in jail. However, it seemed that everyone, from visitor to incarcerated alike, knew that this inmate was different. Everyone had seen and heard the news, and it appeared everyone knew that he was the one arrested for the murder of Joletta Anderson.

When the guard unlocked Terrence's handcuffs and departed from the room, Terrence slowly had a seat as he stared across the glass window at Ernestine and Frances as they sat on the other side. Terrence, handsome with an air of hip swagger about him, appeared composed and at ease despite the extraordinary circumstances that surrounded him. It seemed that he could feel the burning, blatant stares of the others around him as they got a look at the new famous inmate.

Terrence quickly ignored the stares as he reached for the phone on the wall and picked it up. Ernestine, determined to be the good strong supportive mother that she was not, quickly picked up the phone on the other end. She stared across the glass at her twenty-three-year-old son, and it was clear the two had never been close. They looked at one another like two cars getting ready to collide head on.

"We just heard the news over the television," Ernestine said in a panic voice. "What happened?"

"What do you mean what happened?" Terrence said with an edge. "I got arrested—what the hell you think happened!"

"You didn't do it . . . did you?"

"What kind of dumb ass question is that?"

"It's a kind of question you going to have to stand up and answer in court!" Ernestine flared.

"Well, the answer is no!" Terrence flared back. "Hell, no I didn't kill Joletta."

"Well, what happened? What did you tell the police when they arrested you?"

"I didn't tell them bastards nothing! You think I'm going to give them a chance to try to pin this mess on me."

"Well, they must've had their reasons for arresting you. Where did they pick you up at?"

"At my apartment this morning. They came banging on my door saying they had a warrant for my arrest."

"When did you find out Joletta had been murdered?"

"The same as everyone else around the city. Sunday morning when I woke up and turned on the TV. Hell, me and Joletta were just together that Saturday night. We'd just come back from that Hip Hop Summit late Saturday night downtown at the Civic Center. After it was over, we headed back out Buckhead to work the club for a little while. We left there around 1 a.m. and she gave me a ride back to my apartment. She left from my place around three that morning, and that was the last I saw of her."

"Were you two still seeing one another?"

Terrence looked away for a second as his rough exterior began to melt. "We weren't as tight as we used to be in the past," he said slowly. "But that night before she left my apartment . . . we did sort of spend some time together."

Ernestine slowly looked over at Frances who sat only inches from her. Frances didn't say a word while Ernestine took control of the conversation. She only kept her compassionate stare straight through the glass window at her grandson.

"Terrence, this is not sounding good," Ernestine said as she shook her head and stared across the window. "The police said they found Joletta dead in her car around three-thirty that morning, and you're telling me you were with her till 3 a.m. This ain't sounding good at all."

"I said I didn't kill her," Terrence said as he glared through the window.

"Maybe you didn't. But you were probably the last person seen with her right up until she was killed, and I'm just saying it doesn't look good."

"I told you I didn't kill her!" Terrence roared.

"So, you say!" Ernestine flared. "But everyone *thinks* you did. The media has literally made you the scapegoat for murdering the mayor's daughter. This is going to go hard Terrence, not only for you, but for me and the whole family."

"For *you*." Terrence glowered. "What the hell is *you* got to be worried about? You ain't the one that's sitting over here."

"I'm your mother, Terrence. We're in this together. Whatever affects you, affect us all."

"Please, don't give me that crap." Terrence sneered. "You ain't never been concerned for nothing."

"I am concerned!"

"The only one that's ever been concerned for any of us is Franny. Hell, I don't know why you're even here."

"Terrence, don't start this here." Ernestine fumed. "I'm your mother and I'm always concerned whether you like it or not."

"The only thing my so-called crackhead mother has ever been concerned about was where she was going to get her next fix—or is it starring in your next porno flick, I forget?"

"Boy, how dare you talk to me that way!" Ernestine gritted through the phone. "How dare you!"

Frances quickly intervened as she put a restraining hand on Ernestine's shoulder. She slowly took the phone from her as Ernestine relinquished it like a contestant at a talent show giving back a microphone to the judge after failing so miserably. Ernestine looked around the room and caught the probing stares of the others and she appeared humiliated and embarrassed. Frances, however, wasn't concerned over her daughter's humiliation; at the moment, she was only focused on the serious predicament that her grandson was in.

"How you feeling, Terrence?" Frances said in a motherly voice.

"I'm fine, Franny," Terrence answered slowly as he still had his unforgiving glare dead on Ernestine.

"Have they set your bail yet?"

"No, and I don't know if they will, either, considering all the commotion this is causing."

"Well, you just hold on, child. We're going to try to get you out of here. And I'm going to see to it that you get a good lawyer, cause we all know you didn't do what they say you did. But you just hold on and stay strong. You hear me?"

"Yeah, I hear you Franny," Terrence said as he looked into Frances' strong, comforting face.

When the conversation went silent, Terrence threw a peace sign to Frances and hung up the phone. The muscular guard returned and immediately slapped the cuffs back onto Terrence's wrists and quickly whisked him away.

Frances slowly hung up the phone when Terrence was taken away as she and Ernestine began to head out of the visitation room. No sooner when they'd made it out of the jail, a horde of reporters quickly surrounded them.

Somehow word had spread among the media that they were related to the accused arrested for the murder of Joletta Anderson, and now the reporters and press were hungry for an interview. Frances was hellbent on ignoring the intrusion from these aggressive news people as she grabbed Ernestine's hand and led the way. However, despite Frances' refusal to acknowledge the horde that surrounded them, the questions kept coming.

"Are you related to Terrence Jackson?" a reporter asked.

"Yes, we are," Frances answered as they kept walking.

"What are your names?" another reporter asked.

"I'm his grandmother, this is his mother."

"Did you just come from visiting Terrence?"

"Yes."

"What did he have to say?"

No answer.

"Were Terrence and Joletta lovers?"

No answer.

"Is it true Joletta had signed Terrence as a rap artist to her new music label?"

No answer.

"Did Terrence murder Joletta Anderson?" a reporter boldly asked.

Frances suddenly stopped as she looked around at all the reporters and news cameras that were aimed directly at her and Ernestine. Frances had a defiant look in her eyes that seemed to make the reporters wonder what this stern, fearless woman was about to say. She held the reporters captivated, waiting for her to speak.

"I say with all the conviction in me," Frances' voice rose. "I say with all the absolute sincerity down deep in my soul, that my grandson, Terrence Jackson, did not murder this girl."

Frances and Ernestine headed on toward their car, leaving the reporters and press to grapple over their story.

Chapter 4

When Frances and Ernestine returned home from jail, Frances' house immediately became besieged with all sorts of visitors. The house quickly became filled with family, friends, church members, customers and co-workers from Frances' restaurant, and other concerned folk as they began to drop by to give their support for Terrence in his time of trouble.

The contention and debate that roared in Frances' living room among everyone quickly turned to the subject of who had killed Joletta Anderson. Everyone had their varied opinions and scenarios of who killed her and why, but absolutely no one believed Terrence was the culprit that the police and the media made him out to be. The constant news coverage and reporting on Terrence's arrest shown on TV as everyone in Frances' living room watched, only added to the speculation and debate. Everyone, filled with memories of past injustices, began to think there was a conspiracy brewing, and the city of Atlanta was behind it.

By late afternoon, the crowd that had besieged Frances' house slowly began to disperse. The few who still remained were Frances' best friend, Ermma; Frances' pastor, Reverend Speight; her daughter-in-law, Patricia; Frances' oldest daughter, Carolyn; and Ernestine. Ermma, Reverend Speight, and Patricia were on their way out as Frances saw them to the door.

"Frances, it seems like you're holding up pretty well through all this," Ermma said with concern before she headed out the door. "Don't try to put too much pressure on yourself. It's not good for you."

"I have to stay strong, Ermma," Frances said pointedly. "Terrence is going to need his family now more than ever."

"You think they're going to set bail for him?"

"I don't know," Frances suddenly said in a somber voice. "When we saw Terrence today, he didn't seem to think that he'd get bail."

"Yeah, that's probably true," Reverend Speight quickly answered. "No judge will probably set bail for a case like this. It's already been all in the media. It's too high profile. And after all," he said reluctantly, "it just happens to be the mayor's daughter who was killed."

"It's a shame what happened to that girl, but I know Terrence wasn't the one who killed her."

"We all know that, Sister Frances." Reverend Speight added reassuringly. "And we're all going to be praying for Terrence down at the church."

"Thank you, Reverend. You do that."

"Will you still be at choir rehearsal this Thursday?"

"Now, Reverend Speight, I haven't missed choir rehearsal in twenty years, and I ain't about to start now. Yes, Reverend," Frances said with conviction. "As God and His angels as my witness, I'll most certainly be there this Thursday."

Reverend Speight laughed. "Alright, Sister, we'll see you then."

When Ermma and Reverend Speight left out the door, Patricia gave Frances a huge hug.

"Thanks for coming by, Patricia," Frances said when they finally let go. "You've been a big comfort."

"I was just so shocked when I heard it on the news. I couldn't believe it. I just came right over when my shift at the hospital was over. I knew you and Ernestine had to be just tore up about it."

"We were all shocked when we heard the news down at the restaurant. It came as a blow to us all."

"Well, I know this is going to be tough on you, and you certainly can count on me for all the support you need."

"Thank you, baby. I know you really mean that," Frances said as she patted Patricia on the hand. "How's Willie Joe doing?"

"Not too good." Patricia sighed. "We still have our fights, and he's still hitting the bottle every day. I can just only hope that it gets better soon."

Frances shook her head as she scratched her brow. "I hope so too, baby. I'll try to get by soon and see how he's doing."

When Patricia left, Frances closed the door and headed back into the living room. Frances' oldest daughter, Carolyn, and Ernestine both sat on the couch as they watched the continuing news coverage of Terrence's arrest.

Carolyn and Ernestine were about as different as two sisters could get. Carolyn was a well-educated college professor married to a successful doctor and had two kids doing well in college. Ernestine, on the other hand, was a high school dropout riddled from a life full of bad mistakes and had three unruly kids who'd grown up out in the streets.

The love between these two opposite sisters was nowhere to be found, and whenever they were together, the contention and dislike for one another always flared up. Frances dreaded when these two opposing daughters of hers were together, hating the strife and friction that it created. And after a day full of nothing but friction and strife, Frances wasn't up for another one of their explosive battles.

Frances finally grew tired of listening to all of the negative coverage of Terrence's arrest as she turned down the TV and had a seat in her favorite recliner. She leaned back and closed her eyes as she tried to relax her tired, weary body.

"Franny, what are we going to do about getting Terrence a lawyer?" Ernestine implored. "They're already saying his case is going to go before the grand jury this Friday."

"I'll call around the first thing in the morning." Frances sighed. "We'll see if we can get an appointment to see a lawyer tomorrow. And Terrence is *definitely* going to need a good lawyer."

"You going to let Franny just mortgage away the restaurant again for a lawyer like she did the last time for Travis?" Carolyn said in a facetious tone.

Ernestine looked over at Carolyn with fight in her eyes. "Look, no one is asking you and George to help. So, you can just cut out all of the contemptuous bull."

"I'm just saying whenever your side of the family gets into trouble, you want to run to Franny and use her up. You want to make her put everything in jeopardy that she's worked so hard for."

"My *side* of the family!" Ernestine exploded.

"Carolyn, we're all one whole family." Frances quickly intervened. "Please don't start on that."

"Franny, all I'm saying is every time one of her wayward kids gets into trouble, she expects you to come to the rescue and bail them out. The last time you mortgaged the restaurant to get Travis a lawyer, it almost took you under. Now Travis is back in the streets selling drugs even more than ever."

"This is different, Carolyn," Frances said softly. "Terrence didn't kill that girl, and he's going to need a lawyer."

"How do we really know that?" Carolyn boldly said.

"Because Terrence didn't do it!" Ernestine roared.

"And how do you know that?"

"Cause I know my kids."

Carolyn let out a sarcastic laugh. "You don't know a flip about those kids. You just had them and left them for Franny to try to struggle and raise."

"Oh, and I guess you know everything there is to know about your *precious* ass kids?"

"Indeed, I do. Unlike you, George and I were there to raise Frederick and Bethany and to see to it that they got the proper guidance to make it in the world. Now at least they're going to college studying to make something of themselves, instead of being a drag on society."

"Your damn kids ain't perfect, honey."

"At least they're not a prostitute, a drug dealer, and an accused murderer that's got the whole damn city and nation watching him being escorted to jail."

"Carolyn, now that's enough of that!" Frances shouted. "We don't need this useless bickering."

"No, let her keep going if she wants to," Ernestine said defiantly. "She thinks her kids are so moral and upright, she's going to have a nervous breakdown when Bethany comes home from school pregnant or Frederick gets expelled for smoking weed in the dormitory."

"Coming home from school pregnant. Now don't that sound familiar." Carolyn gibed. "Seems to me you're referring to yourself when you came home from school and Franny discovered that you were pregnant at age fifteen."

"I wasn't fifteen *Miss Thang*—I was sixteen. And Dexter and I were going to get married."

"Yeah, right. And you dropped out of school to follow his sorry butt out to L.A. thinking he was going to be some hot shot actor in Hollywood. The only thing he turned out to be was bad news for you."

"Look, I was in love at the time. All that was in the past."

"Oh, yeah, he really loved you." Carolyn jeered. "He loved you so much that he turned you into one of video's horniest sluts ever."

Ernestine rose from the couch with anger flushed in her face. "Look, bitch, you ain't going to sit here and judge me like that!"

"Who the hell are you calling a bitch?" Carolyn quickly rose.

"You bitch!"

"Now that's enough! I've had enough of you two!" Frances yelled as she stepped between her feuding daughters.

When the rage in the living room was about to explode, there was a knock at the front door. Frances wasn't about to depart and leave these two squabbling sisters at it again.

"Carolyn, go answer the door?" she said exasperated.

When Carolyn opened the front door, she turned and looked cautiously at Frances in the living room. Frances could see the apprehension on her face as she stood there with the door open.

"Who's that at the door?"

"Speak of the devil," Carolyn muttered.

Travis slowly entered the house along with two of his sidekicks as they came into the living room. His two sidekicks, his devoted posse as they were, stood a pace or two behind Travis as he stepped into the room. Travis, all but twenty-one-years old, looked like a thirty-year-old gangbanger who knew his trade well. Dressed in a Du Rag, a Lakers jersey, baggy jeans, Nikes, a Rolex watch, and enough gold chains and ice to virtually light up the room, there was nothing about Travis that didn't suggest that he didn't know the streets. Frances' eyes glared red as she bored straight into him. Her face began to scowl like a bull ready to charge.

"What are you doing in my house?" Frances words came harsh.

"I heard what happened to Terrence over the radio," Travis said calmly. "I just came by to lend my support."

"Support," Frances said indignantly. "And just what kind of *support* can you give?"

"Well, I know how hard you struggled the last time to come up with the money to get me a lawyer when I was in trouble, Franny. I just thought it would be best if I shelled out some Benjamins to ease the burden."

Travis pulled out a roll of hundred-dollar bills that could choke an elephant. He started counting off bills like a busy bank teller who had plenty more at his disposal.

"You just say what you need, Franny," he said arrogantly as he kept counting, "and it's yours."

Frances slowly walked over to Travis as they virtually stood face to face. The anger that pulsated from her face was like a fuse from a bomb, and the bomb was about to explode.

"How dare you come into my house and flaunt your drug money in my face." Frances steamed. "You ain't nothing but a heathen and ain't never going to be nothing more. Now get out of my house!"

Travis looked into Frances' penetrating eyes and there was nothing but utter contempt for his presence. He slowly put away his roll of money as he kept his eyes on Frances.

"Alright, Franny," he said slowly. "It's all good."

Travis took a quick look over at Ernestine. "Mama . . ." he said fleetingly as he signaled his sidekicks as they departed from the house.

When Travis and his posse left, Frances slammed the door and headed straight for her room. Carolyn and Ernestine could only stand in the middle of the living room and stare at one another in silence, like two boxers who no longer had a referee.

------ ⊷ ------

THE LATE-NIGHT NEWS gave Frances a headache as she lay under the covers in her bed watching the continuing coverage of Terrence's arrest. His arrest had turned into a news frenzy on all the local stations, and even the night time talk shows on the cable channels had turned it into a soap box.

During all the coverage from the local news anchormen to the babbling talking heads on the various cable channels, Frances' phone didn't stop ringing once. Everyone from close friends, to long forgotten friends, to downright strangers had called giving their support, advice, criticism, skepticism, to some even being downright callous, rude, and nosy. Everyone wanted to know the finest details from someone closest to the accused, and everyone knew that Frances had raised Terrence since he was a toddler.

Frances was now tired of all the hysteria that the incident had created. She'd already had a long day, and now the night was beginning to go on much too long.

Frances finally turned off the TV and shut off the lights as she prepared to go to sleep. She could still hear Ernestine's TV on down the hall in her room. Ernestine had lived with her since she started her drug rehabilitation treatment over a year ago. With Ernestine going to her drug rehab class every week and working steadily down at the restaurant, she slowly began to turn her life around. It had taken a lot of pain, suffering, and patience to get to this point, but Ernestine was slowly making progress. Frances didn't mind her daughter living with her when she was making an effort to better her life. And Frances knew better than anyone that the life Ernestine led now, was certainly better than the troubled mixed-up life that she'd once lived.

No sooner when Frances' head hit the pillow and she began to relax, the phone rang once again. Frances had enough of her friends calling for one night, even though some of them meant well under the circumstances. But she was tired and it was late, and now it was time for all the interruptions and intrusions to stop.

"Hello!" Frances' cranky voice blared as she answered the phone.

"Yes, may I speak to Mrs. Frances Jackson?" the strange voice said.

"Who is this?"

"This is Skip Hughes from the *Atlanta Sentinel* newspaper. I was wondering could I ask you a few questions about your late husband, William Jackson?"

Frances suddenly cringed. "For what purpose?"

"Well, your husband led quite an insurgency against the Detroit police. I'd just like to get some information on it for the column I'm writing. Will you give me a few minutes of your time?"

Frances' heart beat like a jackhammer as she held the phone limp in her hand. Her anger quickly took control over her. "No, I will not." She screamed. "And don't ever call here again!"

Frances slammed the phone down as she stared at it with a wretched scowl. Her heart still pounded like a jackhammer, and for a second, she wanted to pick the phone back up and curse the arrogant caller back to the hole that he'd crawled out of. Instead, she lay back down as she tried to put the intruding caller out of her mind. But as Frances lay in the darkness trying to go to sleep, the thought of her late husband had suddenly brought back all the terrible misgivings that her family had gone through over the years. It still haunted her to this day the way the family struggled through one misfortune after another. The pain was etched and scarred in her mind forever, like the brutal markings of a whip slashed across a slave's back.

The pain all started when her late husband, William Jackson, returned home from serving over in Vietnam in 1967. William and Frances were living in Detroit and raising three young kids. Detroit, at the time, festered with police brutality—especially in the black community. Harassing, beatings, and killings in the streets of the black community were out of control, and many blacks saw the predominately white police force as the most visible symbol of their oppression. William, disgruntled at having to serve in the fierce jungles of Vietnam only to come back home to even more violence and brutality in his own streets, vowed for a change. He became an outspoken voice against the Detroit Police Department like no one had ever done before.

Determined, passionate, and fierce in his conviction, William began to organize a movement to stop the brutality at the hands of the police. He organized meetings and rallies to discuss the protection of the black community against the racist police force that patrolled their streets. A natural fiery speaker who could capture the heart and soul of a crowd, William soon had a substantial following.

The message he proposed to stop the corruption in the streets was to take up arms and protect their community and ghettos against the endless brutality and killing. Young men, inflamed by his passionate zeal, began to heed to his fiery call. They began to unite in numbers that quickly swelled to over a hundred. This group of young black renegade guardians called themselves the Black Power Front, and signified themselves by wearing green outfits and bandannas in support of their outspoken leader, William, who always wore his green army fatigues from Vietnam whenever he rallied his meetings.

The Black Power Front, armed and ready for conflict, took to the streets of their community to guard against the corrupt police. Clashes with the police soon occurred as the two forces converged in the streets of the black community. Hostility and hatred for both sides quickly grew rampant, and as the weeks passed, even more dangerous and deadly clashes occurred in the streets.

The situation in the streets of Detroit was on the verge of exploding when the July 23rd incident happened that precipitated the riot that followed. Early on that morning of July 23rd, the Detroit police raided an illegal black drinking establishment on popular 12th Street in the black community. The patrons of the club were all handcuffed and forced into police patty wagons waiting outside the club. A crowd of black spectators, which quickly swelled into the hundreds, converged in the street and watched as the patrons were roughly detained by the police.

A loud uproar soon went up through the growing crowd as they watched their brothers and sisters beaten and treated harshly by the brutal white police. A couple members of the Black Power Front, dressed in their green outfits and bandannas who were present at the scene, began to urge the growing crowd on to take action against the white police and defend their brothers and sisters. The situation soon turned volatile as bottles and bricks were thrown, creating chaos through the angry crowd. The outrage on 12th Street quickly escalated to further ruckus, and within hours, it had ignited into an all-out race riot through the streets.

The disorder and uproar continued to build until finally two days later, the disturbance was put to rest. In the end, the upheaval in the streets of Detroit became one of America's worst race riots ever. With many killed, injured, and arrested, and thousands of buildings burned and looted, order had to be restored. More importantly, the police were going to make sure that a disturbance of that magnitude never happened again.

When the riot was over, word quickly filtered among the police rank that the Black Power Front had incited the crowd on 12th Street that early morning of July 23rd and had set in motion the deadly riot that followed. The police wanted desperately to tear apart this fracas outfit, and the best way they knew to do that, was to eliminate its brazen outspoken leader.

Word quickly spread on the streets that William was a marked man. Intimidation, pressure, and threats from the police continued to build until everyone on the street knew that William was a dead man. The Black Power Front vowed to protect their charismatic leader against the racist police that threatened their existence. William, seeing the danger that was coming, sent Frances and the kids to Buffalo to live with her sister and her husband until the tension died down.

The tension in the streets, however, continued to build. A few days later, the police gunned down William viciously in the street. The Black Power Front, in a show of solidarity for their fallen leader, sought revenge against the police.

More gun battles and heated fights took place in the streets, only to cause further strife and tension in the black community. The police, seeing the problem in the streets once again getting out of control, changed directions and began to use other methods to usurp the radical militant group. They soon infiltrated snitches within the organization, used bribes, and other coercive measures to bring down the group from within. The method showed fast results as the group began to quickly wear down. Finally, after weeks of William's death and after weeks of bitter fighting in the streets, the Black Power Front was finally finished.

Frances, now a widow with three kids to raise, wanted justice for the murder of her husband. However, she quickly found out that nothing was going to be done in his defense. There were no charges, review boards, suspensions, terminations; absolutely nothing was done to the violators who murdered her husband in cold blood. Frances, who was furious at the abandonment of due process, sought support from the people in the streets to bring about retribution for the murder of her husband. But as time began to pass, the climate in the streets began to change also.

A new mayor's administration began to put pressure on the police force to clean up its image with the people in the streets—particularly within the black community. The change, though slow and certainly not perfect, did begin to subside some of the burning animosity that the black community had for the police. With the change brought a new attitude, and with a new attitude brought a slight degree of respect for the men in blue.

The days of fighting law and authority in the street were slowly resending, and the days of heeding to the rally cries of radical militants like William Jackson were coming to an end. William's name, once shouted proudly through the streets of Detroit, slowly became unspoken in the black community. A new movement began to take shape, and the movement of integration and association simply didn't mix anymore with the rebel call for arms and blood in the street. For the progress and for the upward mobility of the black race, William's name soon became hated, despised, and loathed for his divisive, antiquated ways. No longer was his methods and actions admired in the streets. William simply became the scapegoat for the problems of yesterday, and Frances, unfortunately, became the beneficiary of his burdens.

Tired of all the contention, strife, and blame that the William Jackson name was circulating throughout the streets of Detroit, Frances had finally had enough. With animosity growing by the day for the Jackson name, Frances had to get away and find a new beginning.

Frances gathered her belongings and kids as she headed south for Atlanta. Broke and a widow with limited education, Frances put her faith in God to make a way for her and her kids to survive as she got by as best as she knew how. She did odd jobs here and there, sometimes working as much as eighteen hours a day to feed her kids and to make ends meet. Finally, after five years of saving, scrimping, and working to the bone at odd jobs, Frances put a down payment on an establishment on Auburn Avenue and started her very own soul food restaurant. With hard work, blind determination, and a supreme faith in God, Frances' soul food establishment began to grow.

Meanwhile, Frances raised her three kids as best as she could. William Jr., Carolyn, and Ernestine were all raised in a good home with a roof over their heads and plenty of food to eat, but each one grew up dealing with situations that were far different than the others.

William Jr., the oldest of the group which everyone referred to as simply Willie Joe, grew up as a troubled young man. He grew up despising his father's image and wanted no part of being even remotely like him. The stories and rumors he heard of his late father shrouded him growing up like a dark cloud that wouldn't go away. He was ashamed when anyone even mentioned his father and was more than proud to claim he had no father at all. The sight of his father's picture that hung along the walls of their home literally repulsed him to his utter soul. It were as if his late father's photo were cursed, and Willie Joe, fearing the deadly curse of his father, never allowed himself to look into those hard, menacing eyes.

Despite his hatred for his father, Willie Joe did well in school. A natural athlete, he excelled in sports and earned a scholarship to play football at Alabama A&M. When he graduated with a degree in Criminal Justice, Willie Joe wanted to shake his father's notorious image against law enforcement once and for all as he enrolled in the police academy to become a police officer. Having the makings of a true cop from the word go, Willie Joe finished at the top of his class and entered the force ready and eager to serve the public. He fought crime with bitter passion and even earned numerous citations on the force for his outstanding work of going above and beyond the duty of a police officer.

For ten years, Willie Joe's record was unblemished until one fateful night he responded to a call. Gunshots were heard in a notorious drug infested neighborhood. Officer William Jackson arrived at the scene in his patrol car as the sound of gunfire still erupted. With the street lights knocked out, Officer Jackson brandished his weapon and began to pursue the sound of the gunfire.

When he suddenly heard someone approaching around a dark corner, he turned and saw an individual running his way who looked as if he had a weapon in his hand. Willie Joe, with his adrenaline pumping, quickly fired his weapon and killed the approaching assailant, which turned out to be an innocent eighteen-year-old black kid carrying an umbrella as he returned home that night from his fast-food job.

The tragic incident languished for days in the news. The police department immediately placed Willie Joe on suspension as a review of the incident took place. A few months later, a police review board found that Officer William Jackson didn't use proper police procedure during the night in question and was fired from the force. The young boy's mother returned that action by suing the police department in court for the wrongful death of her son. Two years later, she won the case and was awarded ten million dollars as William and the Atlanta Police Department were found liable for the wrongful death of her son. Willie Joe hired a lawyer and was able to avoid any further legal action, but the tragic incident left him emotionally scarred.

Constantly haunted by the shooting, Willie Joe resorted to drinking heavily. He hopped from job to job, unable to hold down any kind of employment because of his habitual drinking and emotional instability. His marriage to his wife, Patricia, began to suffer as they bickered and fought constantly with one another. Things plunge to worse a few years later when their only child was killed in a car wreck as Willie Joe drove her home from school. Willie Joe survived the terrible car wreck with only minor bruises, but his ten-year-old daughter, not strapped into her seat-belt, was killed instantly.

The catastrophic event plunged Willie Joe into even further emotional disillusion. He blamed himself for his daughter's death and began to drink even more. With the weight of his problems continuing to bear down on him daily, Willie Joe virtually withdrew from the world.

Carolyn's life, fortunately, was void of all the drama and turmoil that had ripped apart the soul of her older brother. She grew up the perfect daughter who seemed to excel in everything she pursued. A standout student from start to finish, Carolyn stayed away from trouble as she pursued her goal of becoming a teacher.

Valedictorian of her high school class, she went on to Fisk University and majored in education. She quickly met George McMillan, a medical student at Meharry Medical College, and within a year the two were married. They soon had two kids, Frederick and Bethany, as both George and Carolyn continued to pursue their goals and juggle family life at home. Carolyn, with a B.S. Degree and a Masters in Education, went on to get her Ph.D. from Vanderbilt as George began practicing medicine in Nashville. A few years later, the McMillans moved to Atlanta when George was offered a job at one of the top hospitals in the city. Over the years, the affluent life soon followed George and Carolyn as they both excelled in their respected fields. With plenty of money and clout, they were able to send Frederick and Bethany to only the best schools.

The McMillans became the perfect model of success. George, a rich successful doctor, was praised for his work and contributions to the field of medicine, while Carolyn, an acclaimed professor at Georgia Tech, was lauded for her academic achievements in the field of education. Frances knew from the very beginning that Carolyn was the daughter who had the drive and the will to someday become a success. She knew she was the daughter who would excel in life.

Then there was Ernestine.

Ernestine, unlike her older sister, grew up like a cursed tree that produced nothing but poisonous fruit. Her unrestrained promiscuous ways began early in her teenage years. By fourteen, Frances could hardly control her. Ernestine, with her hormones raging full of lust, became hooked on one boy after another until Dexter came along.

Dexter Freeman, a much older smooth talking young man, became Ernestine's one and only. By sixteen she was pregnant with his baby, and at seventeen, she was pregnant once again. Totally in love with Dexter, she quit school and left her two babies with Frances as she followed Dexter out to Los Angeles when he convinced her that he would make it as an actor in Hollywood.

Six months later when his attempt at acting had failed, Dexter quickly tried his hand in video production—mainly that of directing homemade porno films. Trying to get his adult entertainment film business up and running, Dexter persuaded Ernestine to *act* in a few scenes of his initial film with a couple of male actors, promising that it was just a one-time thing. Ernestine, blindly in love with Dexter, went along with his endeavor.

One film, however, quickly turned into another and another, and before long, Ernestine was deep into the porno film business. Two years later, Dexter had moved on to bigger and better things as he left Ernestine behind like a used-up whore who no longer had any value. Sad and depressed, Ernestine soon turned to drugs as she tried to cope with the loss of the only man she ever loved. The drugs quickly began to spin her life totally out of control. With a growing drug habit, no money and with no skills to earn a living, Ernestine's only recourse was to turn to the streets to survive.

Ernestine, however, quickly found that life as a prostitute came at a terrible price. She suffered being robbed, raped, and beaten at the hands of johns as she tried to endure on the mean streets of L.A. Things couldn't get any worse for her until one night she was badly stabbed in an alley. With her life hanging in the balance, Frances rushed out to L.A. and saw Ernestine through her life and death ordeal.

Frances paid all of Ernestine's hospital bills and prayed for her quick recovery. When Ernestine finally did recover, Frances took her back home to Atlanta hoping that she could get her going on the right track. Ernestine, however, was quick to fall back on her wretched ways. The drugs, the late-night clubs, and the men became like a revolving door in her life. Ernestine soon found she was pregnant again, but was unable to take care of yet another child as her fast lifestyle sucked her up like a wild tornado.

As Ernestine succumbed to the lure of the streets, Frances tried diligently to raise her three children. But now much older, Frances quickly discovered that trying to raise three motherless kids and running a successful soul food restaurant were simply more than she could handle.

Terrence, Travis, and Trinika grew up like wild weeds as Frances struggled to raise them. Terrence, the oldest of the three, shot up tall and handsome. He quickly discovered at an early age that he had a special effect over the opposite sex. Girls became his play toys, and by the age of sixteen, he found that they were more than willing to submit to and quench his ever-growing sexual desire.

Terrence's easy way with the opposite sex compromised his judgment one night when he forced himself on an unwilling partner. The girl charged that Terrence violated her and he was arrested for rape. Frances hired a lawyer as the case headed for trial. Right before legal proceedings began, the lawyer Frances hired was able to work out a plea agreement with the prosecution as the case never went to trial and Terrence was spared the potential of being incarcerated. Although he avoided incarceration, he was put on five years' probation and his name was tainted as a sexual violator.

Travis, on the other hand, was no ladies' man. Instead, he had the makings of a true gangbanger from the start. Travis became compulsive to crime like it was a magnet that just wouldn't turn him loose. First it started with shoplifting candy at age six, to taking CD's at age eight, to stealing the latest Air Jordan's at age ten, to stealing cars at age fourteen. Travis went in and out of juvenile like it was no more than a favorite clubhouse that he liked. Frances nearly pulled her hair out trying to stay on top of this wild, wayward child. More than once she went before a judge to convince him not to send Travis off to reform school, hoping that her guidance would somehow turn him around. Nothing, however, ever worked.

By age sixteen, Travis was a dropout and supported himself selling crack. At eighteen, he'd gotten busted and was looking at fifteen to twenty years in prison. Once again Frances hired a lawyer for one of her troubled grand kids, and once again, Frances' lawyer was able to get a plea bargain. Travis was sentenced to seven years in prison, but eventually released in less than three due to overcrowding. By age twenty, Travis was back on the street and he soon got started up again in his chosen trade.

This time he was a veteran in the game and he knew the right connections. Now he pushed strictly powder cocaine and it wasn't long before he became a major player in the business. Frances, tired of driving down a tunnel where there was no light, simply washed her hands of Travis and wanted nothing more to do with him.

Frances became so busy trying to keep Travis under control that she virtually had no time for Trinika. Trinika grew up quiet and shy and virtually became a loner. Feeling neglected and abandoned because of Ernestine's constant absence from the home, she grew up hating her mother as much as Willie Joe despised his father for his militant stand against the police. But just like Ernestine, Trinika fell into the same trap of falling for the wrong man.

Looking for love and attention at the ripe age of sixteen, Trinika soon fell under the influence of a much older gentleman who was more than willing to splurge and pamper this innocent, pretty young girl. The expensive cars, the wads of cash, and the fine clothes were just a pretext for what was to come. Before long, Daddy T., one of Atlanta's most dangerous pimps, had Trinika in the palm of his hand. Now at eighteen, Trinika was just another one of his girls roaming the late-night streets. Frances tried in vain to stop her baby granddaughter from going down that same destructive path as her mother had taken, but once again, the lure of the streets had claimed one of her kin.

The saga of Frances' family had been torturous to say the least. The turmoil and misery that she had to endure over the years with her family was incredible. Each crisis had produced nothing but pain, suffering, and sorrow, only for the very next crisis to produce even more pain, suffering, and sorrow.

Now, when Frances didn't think any more pain or tragedy could be piled onto the heap of misery her family had already endured, a new crisis had suddenly come to the forefront. Only this crisis, with the eyes of the entire city and nation watching, threatened to swallow her family and destroy it once and for all. Frances, fearing the worst, could only lay in bed and pray that God would somehow save her family before it was too late.

Chapter 5

The next morning, Frances and Ernestine got up early and hit the streets as they went searching for a lawyer to defend Terrence. The process quickly turned into an unwanted obstacle course that neither Frances nor Ernestine had expected. After five visits to various attorneys, Frances discovered just how prominent Terrence's arrest had captured and inflamed the city of Atlanta. No lawyer had yet offered to represent Frances' grandson against the accusations standing before him. Despite all the media attention the case was bound to create, no one was willing to put their reputation and record on the line for the defendant accused of murdering the daughter of Mayor Hobskin Anderson. The ramifications were just too great, and no one wanted to take that risk.

Tired and frustrated, Frances and Ernestine finally made it to their downtown noon appointment with Attorney Michael Baldwin. Despite rushing as fast as they could to make the appointment on time, they were already thirty minutes late.

Frances was referred to Attorney Baldwin when the last lawyer declined to take her grandson's case, but recommended Michael Baldwin when he knew she was desperate to retain the service of a good lawyer. She was told that Michael Baldwin was a young black lawyer in his mid-thirties who'd just started his own practice after working in the Public Defenders office for the past ten years. He was determined and motivated, and after spending over ten years defending the poor and the downright dregs of society, he wasn't afraid to accept the difficult challenges that no one else wanted. Frances had her apprehensions of hiring, in her mind, such a young lawyer, but after virtually having the door slammed in her face by everyone else she'd tried, there was simply no time now to be worried over matters she couldn't control.

After waiting patiently in the reception area, Frances and Ernestine were finally ushered into Attorney Baldwin's office by his secretary as she closed the door on her way out. Michael Baldwin, a strong compelling gentleman who had an endearing look about him, greeted Frances and Ernestine warmly as they entered his office. There was an immediate sense of good will and camaraderie that Frances hadn't received all day.

"Thank you for seeing us on such short notice," Frances said when they finished shaking hands.

"My pleasure, Mrs. Jackson." Michael Baldwin smiled. "In fact, I believe we've met once before. I've dined in your restaurant a few times and the food was excellent."

"Thank you."

"Please, have a seat ladies."

Frances and Ernestine sat in the two chairs offered by Attorney Baldwin as he went around his desk and slowly sat down. When everyone was seated, Frances wasted no time taking the lead.

"I guess you know why we're here, Mr. Baldwin," Frances said as she began. "We need a lawyer to represent my grandson on the allegations that's been brought up against him. And as you know, time is of essence."

"Yes, I've been watching the events unfold in the news, and it's quite a situation your grandson is in."

"My son is innocent," Ernestine spoke quickly as if she wanted to be heard.

"He could very well be, ma'am. But the process of the law will have to determine that."

"Terrence *is* innocent," Ernestine's voice rose.

Frances quickly put a hand on Ernestine's arm to recoil her emotions.

"Mr. Baldwin, we know the process of the law will have to determine Terrence's innocence or guilt. That's why my grandson needs a lawyer—*a good* lawyer—I might add," Frances said pointedly. "So, what I'm asking is will you represent him, or if not, we'll just move on?"

Michael Baldwin got up slowly from his chair as he turned to his twelfth-floor window and looked out at the sprawling city of Atlanta. His deep contemplation could've cut a hole straight through the window.

"Mrs. Jackson, I know you were referred to me because I've been a court appointed lawyer previously and have dealt with undesirable cases on a daily basis, and have dealt with poor disadvantaged defendants who were a scourge on society," he said slowly. "But I have deep reservations on taking on your grandson's case."

"Why?" Frances griped. "Because you think he ain't nothing but another thuggish black male who needs to be thrown in prison?"

"No, not at all, Mrs. Jackson," the attorney said as he turned and looked at Frances. "It's just that this murder has cast a very dark shadow over the city. And unfortunately, your grandson has already been painted very negatively in the media. Plus, on top of that, Mayor Anderson has been good for Atlanta and his daughter has been seen as a virtual saint around the city over the last few years. The prejudice against your grandson will be overwhelming. Under the circumstances, it will be very hard to find twelve jurors anywhere in this city who'll believe in his innocence."

"Mr. Baldwin, I didn't come here to get the damn run around thrown in my face," Frances said roughly. "I came here for one purpose, and that's to attain representation for my grandson."

"I'm not trying to give you the run around, Mrs. Jackson. I'm just stating the facts."

Frances rose slowly from her chair as she rested her palms on Michael Baldwin's desk. She peered hard into his eyes as if she were getting ready to lecture a sinner of his wicked ways.

"Well, let me state a couple of facts to you, *Mr. Baldwin*," Frances said in an acid tone. "I've been all over this city all morning trying to find a lawyer for my grandson, and everywhere I've looked, I've been turned away. It's a shame that young woman has been murdered, and it's a damn shame that it so happens to be the mayor's daughter. But despite that, I know my grandson didn't kill that girl. I know the city and the whole world thinks that he did, but I'm his grandmother, and I raised him up to know that he ain't no killer. And if so be it that I'm the only one left in this city who believes his innocence, then I'll go in that courtroom and defend him myself if I have to!"

"Mrs. Jackson, I didn't mean to come across—"

"No, you've said enough, Mr. Baldwin," Frances said quickly. "Ernestine, let's go. I can see this is going nowhere."

When Frances and Ernestine got up to leave, Michael Baldwin rose from his desk and quickly stopped them.

"Please . . . don't leave," he said respectfully. "I can sympathize with the ordeal that you're going through and I know that it's been tough. Please . . ." he said as he held his arm out toward the two chairs that Frances and Ernestine had sat in. "Please . . . have a seat."

Frances and Ernestine slowly returned to their seats as Michael Baldwin sat down likewise. There was a sudden uneasiness that hung over the silence.

"Maybe I was a little too assertive with my personal beliefs of this case," Mr. Baldwin said slowly. "But this case is certainly—"

"Mr. Baldwin, I don't have all day. I have a restaurant to run," Frances said to the point. "Will you, or will you not, represent my grandson?"

Michael Baldwin studied Frances' face carefully. Frances' countenance was of a woman who was steadfast in her determination.

"Yes, Mrs. Jackson," he finally said. "I'll represent your grandson."

"What is your fee?"

"Well, considering the magnitude, all the ramifications, and the workload that this case will entail," he said slowly, "my fee will be fifty thousand. I'll require a five-thousand-dollar deposit to get started. We can work out an installment plan and other essential details later."

Frances looked over at the attorney but didn't hesitate for a second. She pulled out her checkbook from her pocketbook and wrote the check out for the appropriate amount. Michael Baldwin offered a contract and Frances signed at the required places. When all was finished, Frances and Ernestine stood as Michael Baldwin extended his hand.

"I'll do my best for your grandson, Mrs. Jackson," he said as he shook both Frances and Ernestine's hands.

"Terrence didn't kill that girl," Frances said in an unwavering voice. "I just hope you make everyone else see that, too."

Frances and Ernestine turned and left out of Attorney Baldwin's office as they headed on their way.

———⊙———

SKIP HUGHES HAD BEEN with the *Atlanta Sentinel* newspaper for eight years. At age thirty-two, he was part of a growing number of young

African-American journalists beginning to stake their place in the vibrant ever-changing field of journalism.

For eight years, Skip had written a weekly editorial column in the *Atlanta Sentinel* focusing on the plight and evolution of black America. Politics, business, sports, economics, entertainment, and the urban social structure of the African American race in society were essential subjects of his weekly commentary. Skips' column, *Skip Hughes Speaks*, was noted for its strong, aggressive approach. He was often fierce and unrelenting in his criticism of the problems facing black America, and his views often stirred contentious debates in various circles of Atlanta's society. With over a million readers tuning in to his weekly editorial column, Skip had virtually become the ultimate voice in the streets of Atlanta.

By 11 p.m., Skip was exhausted as he sat at his desk in his office trying to collect the final details for his column tomorrow. Most of the other editorial staff at the newspaper had already gone home for the night, leaving Skip alone to himself. Skip, however, was use to the late nights. He was a certified workaholic with a natural pulse for news.

Running on nothing now but the pure adrenaline of caffeine, Skip had been busy all day gathering information on the Jackson family and the many scandals that had followed and rocked that troubled family over the years. He was especially fascinated with the William Jackson story. That intriguing piece had stuck to him like hot glue, and the further he delved into it, the more interesting it continued to get. He'd been burning up the phone lines the last couple of hours calling back and forth to Detroit trying to get all the information on the story that he could. He was going to find out everything there was to know, even if he had to stay at his desk all night.

When the phone on his desk suddenly rang, Skip jolted out of his peaceful meditation and answered the phone.

"Skip Hughes."

"Yes, this is Tony Burrow from the *Detroit Free Press*. I was returning your call from earlier today."

"Oh, yes," Skip said excited. "I had left a message that I was doing an article pertaining to William Jackson and the Black Power Front organization he started in 1967. I was wondering did your department still have any back press releases, material, or anything remotely connected that could be of any use."

"We have plenty. I'll be happy to fax it to you."

"Thank you. I'd appreciate it very much."

When Skip hung up the phone, he went over to his fax machine and immediately began to receive page after page of back press releases of William Jackson and the Black Power Front. Twenty minutes later when he'd received the final page, he poured deep into the contents of the material absorbing every piece of information there was.

With the finest details of William Jackson and the entire Jackson family thoroughly covered and explored, Skip returned to his desk and went straight to his computer. As he stared at the blank screen, he thought long and hard for the appropriate heading for this tormented family and typed out the title—The Jackson Jinx. Skip pondered over the title for a few seconds, then finally smiled with approval. Then without further delay, he plowed headstrong into his article.

Chapter 6

By 2 p.m., the busy lunch rush down at Frances' Soul Food Restaurant had finally died down. Most of the crowd had already departed, leaving the restaurant virtually empty except for a few regulars who remained talking and fraternizing in a languid fashion. Frances came from out of the kitchen when the hectic lunch rush was over as she wiped the perspiration from her face with a rag. She and her ten member staff had been going non-stop since 11 a.m., and now she was finally glad to have a few moments away from the kitchen. She approached Ernestine at the cash register as she finished ringing up a lone customer.

"Ernestine, why don't you go on and take your break now while it's slow," Frances said as she continued wiping her face. "I'll look after the cash register while you're away."

"You mean the boss is actually giving me a break," Ernestine said facetiously. "How long do I get today—*two minutes*?"

"Just don't be gone too long."

While things were slow, Frances went out into the dining area as she normally did when the lunch rush was over as she greeted and socialized with some of her customers. Today she could tell there was a bit of coolness, or a reticent mood in some of her everyday faithful customers that usually wasn't there. She could sense that they were trying to avoid her, or simply trying to avoid talking about a specific topic. Even though Terrence had been apprehended for the murder of Joletta and his name and face were lambasted in the media, everyone was still friendly and responsive in their show of support. Business was still good, and there had been no hostility or no nasty incidents that would cause alarm. Today, however, there was something different circulating in the air, but Frances couldn't quite put her finger on what it was.

When Frances left the dining area, she took over the cash register while Ernestine was still on her break. The few customers who came through the line seemed to avoid eye contact with her as she rang up their meals, and

Frances knew that there was definitely something different about today. When she finished with the last customer who was in line, Curtis and Ronnie slowly approached her as she closed the cash register. She could tell by the look in their eyes that something was amiss.

"You two look like you got heartburn. Was the catfish that greasy?"

"Have you read today's paper?" Ronnie asked cautiously.

"Now, you know I ain't had time to read no paper as busy as this place has been," Frances said suspiciously. "Why do you ask?"

"Well, I think you should," Curtis said as he slowly handed her the *Atlanta Sentinel*.

Frances took the newspaper and looked warily at the folded part of the editorial section. She saw the Skip Hughes' column, *Skip Hughes Speaks*, and at the top was written the title, The Jackson Jinx. Frances looked at Curtis and Ronnie as if they'd just given her a death certificate. Without saying a word, she turned back to the newspaper and slowly began to read:

THE JACKSON JINX by Skip Hughes

Over the years, the Jackson family tree has done nothing but produce one bad apple after another. The recent arrest of Terrence Jackson for the murder of Joletta Anderson is only the latest adversity to have riddled this turbulent family.

The dreadful start to this sad, family legacy began with William Jackson, the late husband of Frances Jackson who owns the very popular Frances' Soul Food Restaurant on Auburn Avenue.

William Jackson, a veteran of the Vietnam War, formed the militant organization the Black Power Front in Detroit during 1967. Under his fanatical leadership, William, a masterful agitator, incited the young black men of his organization to take up arms and defend their community against the racist white cops who patrol their streets.

However, William's belligerent methods and tactics to end the police brutality that was so prevalent in the black community, only produced more anarchy and disorder in the streets of Detroit. Bloodshed and violence became a common occurrence. Black people suffered needlessly as constant unrest and fighting ran rampant in their streets. William organization's unrelenting determination to bring down the police during the hot summer of 1967 continued to rage out of control, until a full-blown race riot erupted in the streets of Detroit.

William and his radical band of cohorts, inflamed their divisive message even louder in the streets during this hostile provocation as their power and numbers continued to grow. But like any revolution that relies on violence and unrest to maintain its power, the Black Power Front was eventually brought down and disintegrated by the own violence that it perpetrated in the streets. In the end, their seditious leader was eclipsed from power as he was shot down dead in the streets by the very establishment that he fought so hard to usurp.

The ill-famed legacy of William Jackson would ordinarily be enough dirty laundry for one family to try to stuff into a closet, but the difficulties and afflictions for the Jackson family were only beginning.

William's son, William Jackson Jr., became embroiled in the killing of an unarmed eighteen-year-old kid late one night when he was on the Atlanta police force that caused a nasty scandal within the police department and around the city of Atlanta. Ernestine Jackson, William's daughter, ran off to Hollywood some years back with a shady character and began making numerous obscene porno films. Terrence Jackson, Ernestine's son and the one who's currently arrested for the murder of Joletta Anderson, was convicted for raping a sixteen-year-old girl a few years back. Travis Jackson, the other delinquent son of Ernestine Jackson, was busted for selling crack to an undercover cop and sentenced to seven years in prison. The third wayward child of Ernestine Jackson, Trinika Jackson, is reported to be a hooker selling her body nightly on the streets.

The numerous troubles that have encompassed the Jackson family over the years have been enough to write a book about. Their magnetism to conflict and trouble has been nothing but astounding. This family simply has bad karma, and there may never be any kind of remedy to turn this disillusioned family around.

William Jackson may have brought upon a hex to this family, as one member after another of this ill-fated group keeps following in the footsteps of his wayward ways. If there was ever a jinx, the Jackson family would have to qualify as bona fide prime suspects of it. There's no way around it, this family is jinxed. And anyone who thinks otherwise, is to the contrary.

Skip Hughes, Columnist for the *Atlanta Sentinel*

WHEN FRANCES FINISHED reading the editorial, she was stunned and silent. The hurt and pain etched on her face shrouded her like a dark cloud. She stood there holding the newspaper limp in her hand as she stared off into space. She was definitely off in her own world.

"That damn Skip Hughes has gone too far." Curtis suddenly snapped. "It's a scandalous shame writing something like that."

"If I were you Frances, I'd sue him for defamation." Ronnie followed.

Ernestine suddenly came back from break as she slowly approached the group. She quickly looked at Frances' dispirited face.

"What's going on here? Y'all look like somebody done died or something," she said with concern. "What's that you reading, Franny?"

Frances looked at Ernestine as if her voice had shaken her from her deep thought. Without saying a word, she shoved the newspaper at Ernestine and headed off toward the kitchen.

WHEN FRANCES ARRIVED at the Peach Street Baptist Church later that evening for choir rehearsal, she was still flustered and irritated over the stinging editorial in the newspaper about her family. She felt as if all the misfortune and trouble her family had gone through over the years was suddenly revamped and thrown to the world for their consumption. She could literally hear the gossip in the restaurants and around the dinner tables tonight as the people of Atlanta vilified and maligned her family. Her family had many skeletons, and now the entire city could pick them apart bone by bone.

When Frances entered the sanctuary, most of the members of the choir were already present and waiting to get started on rehearsal. Frances, the most gifted singer in the church and the choir's lead soloist, usually took over and got things going whenever the choir director was late, which was usually the case. When Frances took the floor to get things started tonight, she could sense that rehearsal was far from the minds of her fellow choir members.

"Okay, folks, it's already seven o'clock and we got several numbers to get to. And who knows when Brother Fitzpatrick will get here," Frances quickly said as she tried to get the rehearsal organized. "So, let's get the ball rolling so we can work on these songs. Remember folks, we got that gospel festival coming up in less than a month. So, we need to be getting ready."

"You sure your mind will be *clear* enough to focus on singing tonight?" Sister Mildred Cox suddenly spoke in a pointed voice. "I'm sure with all the problems your family has been going through this past week, you'd be home trying to straighten them out instead of trying to straighten us out."

Frances looked at Sister Cox sitting on the front pew and she could immediately detect the nasty undertone to her pointed statement. She and Mildred Cox were always getting into minor squabbles, and because of that, they always kept their distance. Frances knew that Sister Cox was somewhat jealous of her position within the choir. Sister Cox could sing, but no way could she ever come close to Frances' strong robust voice. And Frances, more than anyone, knew it ate her to the heart.

"My mind is very clear," Frances responded in kind. "Despite what you may think."

"I don't see how," Sister Cox retorted. "With that murderous grandson of yours all in the news, and your wayward hapless family being scandalize all over the paper, it's a wonder that you even have the nerve to try to come here and give us any kind of direction. Seems to me you need to work on *directing* your own family."

"First of all, my grandson is not a murderer," Frances said sharply. "Second of all, this is a church—*Sister Cox*," her voice rose, "and the Bible does say who is without sin, let them cast the first stone. And I certainly think that implies to you."

"Well, if you would've *raised* your family on the ways of the Bible, your family wouldn't be in the mess that it's in."

"What do you mean if I would've raised my family on the ways of the Bible?" Frances said with anger. "All of my family was raised on the Bible, Miss Lady!"

"It certainly doesn't look like it."

"Please, Sister Jackson and Sister Cox, can we not argue in such a mean, spirited way," one of the members suddenly intervened. "This is the house of the Lord, not some old heathen drunken bar. Let's have some respect for the Lord's house."

"Well, tell that to her." Frances quickly pointed her finger at Sister Cox. "Obviously, she's the only one sitting in here perpetrating to be a Christian."

"Excuse me!"

"Yes, excuse you!"

"Ladies! ladies! ladies!" Brother Fitzpatrick declared as he suddenly entered the sanctuary. "What in the devil is going on in here?"

Frances and Mildred Cox suddenly became silent as the rest of the choir looked on riveted with interest. Brother Fitzpatrick came to the front of the sanctuary and stared at the two squabbling ladies.

"There's nothing going on, fine," he said decisively. "So, I guess that means we can all get down to business. So, shall we."

With an air of dissension hanging over the members of the choir, the rehearsal got off to a slow and uneasy start.

Chapter 7

Monday morning the scene in front of the courthouse was like a circus. Reporters, camera crews, the press, and other media outlets jammed and packed the steps of the courthouse all the way down the sidewalk to the street. Journalist from the *New York Times, Washington Post,* to the *LA Times,* were all locked and cluttered together along with local and national TV crews as they waited for the proceedings that were about to occur. The place sizzled with anticipation as nearly every major news outlet in the business was present and ready for this event.

Late Friday afternoon the grand jury had handed down the indictment against Terrence Jackson for the murder of Joletta Anderson, and now this morning at 9 a.m., his arraignment was about to be held. By eight-thirty, Frances and Ernestine, along with Terrence's attorney, headed together toward the courthouse for the arraignment. The media, seeing the defense attorney and the defendant's relatives approaching, quickly besieged them like a pack of rabid dogs salivating over a couple of juicy steaks. The questions, both bold and forward, came from all directions as the reporters and camera crews followed them every step of the way.

"Will your client plead guilty?" a reporter shouted.

"No, my client will not," Terrence's attorney answered.

"Is it true your client was tried for rape in a previous case?" another one shouted.

"No comment."

"Do you believe your client will receive the death penalty?"

"No comment."

"Mrs. Jackson, was the editorial in the *Atlanta Sentinel* a true portrayal of your family being a scourge on society?"

Frances, insulted by the rude malicious question, suddenly stopped and glared at the reporters. Before she could vent her anger, Terrence's attorney quickly implored her to ignore the media as they headed on toward the courthouse.

BY 9 A.M., THE COURTROOM was solid packed. Frances and Ernestine sat on the front row behind the defense table, along with a couple of members of the press, as they waited for the proceedings to begin.

While everyone waited, Frances took the time to slowly look around the courtroom. She could swear that every eye watched and appraised her every move as she scanned the packed room. When she suddenly saw Travis and a couple of his sidekicks standing in the far back with the others who couldn't get seats, her skin began to get hot. The mere sight of Travis and his thuggish bunch of friends made her stomach churn and boil. The more she thought about that day last week when he came to the house with his sidekicks flashing his ill-gotten money in her face, the more her skin began to burn.

When Frances suddenly heard the courtroom come alive, she quickly turned around and watched as two heavy set deputies escorted Terrence into the courtroom. They took him over to the defense table and placed him down in the seat next to his attorney as the deputies removed his handcuffs and took up their positions along the wall near the defense table.

Almost at the same time, Frances watched as another murmur went up in the courtroom. This time it was Mayor Hobskin Anderson. He suddenly entered the courtroom and strolled down the middle aisle in a suit that a Wall Street lawyer would crave to have. He came to the railing where the prosecution table was as he shook hands with the two prosecuting attorneys, and the district attorney who was also present at the table.

The entire courtroom seemed to watch this greeting of power and position with a slight sense of awe. When Mayor Anderson finished shaking hands with the prosecution team, he turned and looked over at Frances who sat across the aisle. Frances and Mayor Anderson's eyes quickly met as Frances could immediately feel a deep loathing for her in his eyes. He kept his penetrating eyes locked on Frances for a few seconds, then he slowly had a seat on the front row behind the prosecution table.

The courtroom suddenly went silent as the bailiff called everyone to rise as the judge entered the courtroom. When Judge Lewis T. Haskins took the bench and told everyone to be seated, he quickly got the proceedings underway.

"Call the case," the judge said to the bailiff.

"People versus Terrence Jackson," the bailiff announced.

Judge Haskins looked down at the prosecution table. "Are the people ready?"

The lead prosecutor rose. "We are, Your Honor."

The judge looked over at the defense table. "And the defendant?"

Terrence's attorney, Michael Baldwin, quickly stood. "Yes, Your Honor."

The judge then looked at Terrence. "Will the accused rise."

Terrence rose from his seat. Dressed in his orange jail issued suit, at the moment, he looked like another young, black male headed for prison.

"You've been accused of the crime of murder," the judge said as he looked sternly at Terrence. "How do you plead?"

Everyone in the courtroom waited in utter silence. "Not guilty," Terrence said loudly.

The judge reviewed his calendar. "Mr. Jackson, your trial is set for October 27. All pretrial motions and matters must be filed by September 15, and disposed by September 30. You shall remain in the custody of the Fulton County Jail without bail until your trial. Are there any questions?" the judge said as he looked at both the prosecution and the defense. "Very well," he said when no questions came up. "Court is adjourned."

When the judge smashed his gavel and departed from the bench, the deputies quickly handcuffed Terrence and took him away. The packed courtroom suddenly sprang to life as everyone began to depart. Frances and Ernestine were once again joined by Terrence's attorney as he fought off the rush of questions fired and lobbed at him by a group of reporters. They slowly departed with the other spectators as they made it into the rotunda. Mayor Anderson was already there fielding a barrage of questions from another large group of reporters. He was in full control as the cameras and microphones captured his every word.

"Mayor Anderson, you're currently campaigning for a congressional seat in the U.S. House of Representatives in this upcoming November general election. Will the untimely murder of your daughter affect you anyway running for congress?"

"Although I am deeply saddened by the senseless murder of my beautiful daughter," the mayor said mournfully, "I will wholeheartedly continue my campaign for congress."

"Wasn't your daughter, Joletta, involved in your campaign?"

"Yes, she was," Mayor Anderson said proudly. "She was very fundamental in the fund-raising aspects of the campaign. Not only will my staff miss a dedicated key worker, but the entire city of Atlanta will certainly miss one of its most beloved, cherished citizens."

"Mayor Anderson, do you believe that the accused, Terrence Jackson, did in fact murder your daughter?"

Mayor Anderson's face suddenly turned grim. "Yes, I most certainly do," he said with heated passion. "This degenerate scum took advantage of my daughter's good nature and murdered her when he no longer knew he couldn't have her. My daughter gave this no a count bum a break when she hired him as an employee of her club, but that wasn't enough for him."

"So, is it true that Joletta and Terrence were intimately involved?"

"Yes," Mayor Anderson said shamefully. "But certainly not by my approval!"

When Mayor Anderson suddenly saw Frances along with Ernestine and Terrence's attorney, he abruptly halted the questioning from the reporters as he walked over and approached the defendant's family. The reporters and cameras quickly followed suit and waited for the exchange.

"I don't know why that criminal of yours didn't just plead guilty and save the city and taxpayers the anguish of going through a lengthy trial," the mayor said tersely. "It's evident that he murdered my daughter."

"My son did not *murder* your daughter." Ernestine countered with just as much tenacity.

"Then what do you call what your son did, *Ms. Jackson*?"

"Mayor, I would think that you, of all people, would want to see that justice prevail," Frances said calmly, "and not let the strain of emotions sway ones thinking."

"The only way I see justice prevailing is for that hoodlum admit that he killed my daughter."

"Whatever happened to a fair trial, and being innocent until proven guilty, Mayor?" Frances countered.

Mayor Anderson looked at Frances and slowly shook his head in disgust. "Well, I wouldn't expect a family of drug dealers, rapists, murderers, and prostitutes to know the meaning of decency."

Frances glared viciously at the mayor and she suddenly was ready for a fight, but before she could explode in a tirade, Terrence's lawyer cautiously placed a hand on her shoulder, pleading for her not to cause a scene. When Frances felt his restraining hand on her shoulder, she heeded to his request.

"And you have a good day . . . *Mayor Anderson*," she said in a sneering tone as she followed Ernestine and Terrence's lawyer as they headed out of the courthouse.

Chapter 8

When Sunday morning service at Peach Street Baptist Church was over, Reverend Speight stood outside and greeted his members as they filed out of the church. Frances, who was ready to go home and relax, stood patiently in the long line as she waited to speak to the reverend.

Despite the genuine brotherly love that had always existed in the church, Frances felt like an outcast and for good reason. Since she'd been a member at Peach Street Baptist Church, there had never been any animosity or ill feelings between her or any of her fellow church members, other than the occasional chicken fights she had with Sister Cox which Frances had come to accept. But today was the first Sunday in twenty years that she felt a bit unwelcomed in the church. She could detect a coldness beginning to form among some of the members, which in the past, would've never even existed. The whispering, the staring, and the pointing were starting to become quite evident. And Frances had a deep suspicion, that it was only going to get worse.

Reverend Speight said a few final words to the last family in line, and then when they departed, he turned and saw Frances. By now he looked a little tired from greeting the long line of members, but Frances knew that Reverend Speight always had time to greet his favorite singer.

"Sister Jackson, that was a mighty lovely hymn you sung today," Reverend Speight said with sincerity. "You really blessed the congregation with your powerful voice."

"Well, you'll have to excuse me if I didn't feel any love from the church today, Reverend," Frances said somberly. "It just seems that some members are more concerned about the latest gossip that's going around."

"Don't let that drag you down, Sister Jackson," Reverend Speight said with conviction. "I know what a heavy burden you must be going through right now with the situation that's going on with Terrence, but don't think that the church isn't with you, because we are, Sister Jackson."

"I have my doubts, Reverend?" Frances said skeptically. "I detect a different mood than you."

"Everything will work out, Sister Jackson. Have faith in God," Reverend Speight said with assurance. "By the way, Sister Jackson, where's Ernestine? I believe this is the first Sunday she's missed in quite a while."

"Well, Ernestine wasn't feeling too good this morning, Reverend. She decided not to come."

"I hope everything is alright. Ernestine has been making a very good effort over these last couple of months to make a new life for herself. I hope she won't let anything turn her astray."

"She's been trying really hard, Reverend. She's been going to her drug rehab class every week, coming to church, and working pretty steady down at the restaurant. But I believe she was a little shook up over the editorial that was written in the paper. Though she won't admit it, I believe she may be hurting a little more than she's letting on. In fact, Reverend," Frances said slowly, "we've all been a little hurt by that story in the paper."

"That's quite understandable," Reverend Speight said reassuringly. "The world will try to tarnish us and make us run from our problems. But you stay strong, Sister Jackson. Don't let the world tear apart your family."

"The world won't if I can help it, Reverend," Frances said with bold resolve.

"Amen, Sister," he said admiringly. "Amen."

When Frances departed from the reverend and got into her car and left out of the church lot, instead of heading home, she made the short drive over to Decatur to see Willie Joe and Patricia.

Frances hadn't had the time to talk to Willie Joe since the media circus of Terrence's arrest, and she wondered how he took the news of the arrest—and even more importantly—how did he feel about the recent article of their family in the *Atlanta Sentinel* that had so many people talking. If Frances knew Willie Joe, he was coping with it the only way he knew how; and that was with a bottle of whiskey to his lips.

The fatal shooting of that unarmed kid had occurred nearly ten years ago, but the ghost of that night still haunted him as if it were only yesterday. The pain that Willie Joe and Patricia had gone through since the shooting, and since the tragic loss of their only child, had been nothing but torturous.

Willie Joe, through mostly his own fault, had become nothing but a recluse to the world. He was now a shattered bitter man, with little hope for the future. Frances knew that any reminder of his tragic past as the recent editorial had so vividly betrayed, could serve no purpose but to sink him even further down into his bottomless pit of despair.

Frances pulled into Willie Joe and Patricia's driveway as she parked her car next to Patricia's Cutlass. She got out of the car and immediately frowned at the sight of the front yard. The lawn looked as if it hadn't been mowed in weeks, and Frances could see empty liquor bottles strewn all throughout the high grass. Frances shook her head with disgust as she headed on up to the front porch. Before she could ring the doorbell, she could hear Willie Joe and Patricia arguing inside. For a second Frances thought about just turning around and going on home, but then again, she'd driven all the way out here, plus she knew she had to see Willie Joe.

When Frances rang the doorbell, the arguing inside the house suddenly ceased. There was a long silence as Frances stood patiently waiting for someone to answer the door. Then without warning, the front door suddenly swung open.

Patricia stood in the doorway with her face flushed with anger. She had her nurse uniform on and it looked as if she were in a mad rush—or in a mad rage—when she applied her make-up. Patricia's vicious scowl slowly went away when she saw that it was Frances standing outside her door. She almost looked embarrassed at the heated rage that she was in.

"Oh . . . I didn't know it was you, Frances," Patricia said as she apologized. "Why don't you come in."

Frances entered the house as she slowly came into the living room. Willie Joe sat in his sofa chair cradling a bottle of Jim Bean as he stared at the blank screen on the T.V. He was a pure mess. His hair was wild and nappy, and by the look of his overgrown matted beard, one could tell that he hadn't shaved in weeks. Willie Joe was a big man, a man that usually commanded respect by his mere presence. But since he'd let himself go over the years, his presence wasn't nearly as imposing. Frances sat down on the sofa across from his chair and stared at her son.

"Franny . . ." Willie Joe said as he turned up his bottle of Jim Bean and took a hefty swig.

"Willie Joe," Frances said softly. "How you feeling?"

Willie Joe merely shrugged his shoulders as he took another swig from his bottle. Patricia still looked as angry as an alley fighter who wanted a second go around at their heated fight. She stood in the middle of the living room with her arms folded as she glared down at Willie Joe.

"Answer her." Patricia demanded. "You certainly had plenty to say just a few minutes ago."

"Woman, why don't you leave me alone and go to work!" Willie Joe yelled back.

"Work is something you need to be doing." She scolded. "You been sitting around here on your butt doing nothing, while I'm working nearly double shift down at the hospital. You ain't tried to find a job in months. You just sit around here drinking all day."

"Woman, I told you nobody will hire me. There ain't nothing I can do about it."

"I wouldn't hire you the way you look. If you stop drinking so much, maybe somebody *would* hire you."

"What's the use," Willie Joe said pitifully as he took another swig. "I've already tried."

Patricia threw her hands up in exasperation. Fuming mad, she looked as if she desperately wanted to take Willie Joe's bottle of Jim Bean from him and smash it up against his head.

"I don't have time for this, I'm running late," Patricia said hastily. "I'm sorry Frances for rushing off, but I'll have to talk to you later."

"I understand." Frances acknowledged. "Go right on."

Patricia grabbed her pocketbook off the stand in the hallway as she headed for the door. She gave Willie Joe one last glare, then headed on out the door. When Patricia got into her car and drove off, Willie Joe and Frances sat silently in the living room. Neither one, it seemed, was in a hurry to speak to the other.

"How long are you going to keep this up, Willie Joe?" Frances finally said.

"Keep what up, Franny?"

"Feeling sorry for yourself!" she yelled. "Sitting around here drinking yourself to death, not caring about nothing. Just wasting your life away.

You used to have more pride for yourself, Willie Joe. You used to be a dedicated, hard-working man that everyone used to look up to. You had goals, ambitions. You served the community and helped people. You were respected."

"That's when I was a cop!" Willie Joe shot back. "Everyone respected me because I was a good law-abiding cop. No one respects someone who shoots a defenseless kid."

"That's ancient history, Willie Joe. Life goes on, and you must go on with your life. You can't change the past."

"Don't you get it Franny—I was a cop!" Willie Joe exploded. "I was a *damn* good cop! That was all I ever wanted to be was a cop. Now that's all been taken away from me."

"So, you just going to give up because you can't be a cop anymore?"

Willie Joe ignored Frances as he took another swig from his bottle. Frances, however, wasn't about to be ignored.

"Listen, Willie Joe," Frances said in a determined voice. "Things might not always go like we want them to go in life, but we got to continue to fight. We got to meet our problems head on and fight them as best as we can."

"Like my beloved father did," Willie Joe said sarcastically. "You want me to get some guns and round up some buddies of mine so we can go fight society. Is that what you mean, Franny?"

"Don't get flippant with me," Frances said sternly. "Your father may have taken a radical approach to fight the problems that were facing our people, but he fought back the best way he knew how."

"Yeah, and look where it got him." Willie Joe countered. "Hated, scorned, despised, and shot down like a ruthless villain in the streets."

"That was a different time, Willie Joe." Frances bellowed. "Things are different now, and we must fight on."

"I don't see how different they are. Your dear husband's actions have left a stain and a mark on all of us. No matter what any of us does, we can never get out of the shadow that he's cast over us. He's cursed us all. The whole family is screwed up, Franny. Isn't that what the paper said . . . that we're all *jinxed*?"

"This family is not jinxed!" Frances roared as she suddenly rose from the sofa with anger. "I don't care what that paper said. We're not, or never have been, or never will be—*jinxed*!"

"The world certainly thinks we are," Willie Joe said calmly. "And how are we going to dispute that?"

Frances glared down at Willie Joe like he was a thief who'd just stolen from the church collection plate. She suddenly turned and stormed out of the living room. But before she opened the front door, she looked back at Willie Joe one last time.

"I'll never ever let this family think that it's jinxed. Do you hear me?" Frances roared. "As God as my witness—I WILL NOT ALLOW IT!"

Frances went out the door and slammed it as she went out. Before she headed back down the steps to her car to leave, she peered through the outside window to get one last look at Willie Joe. There he still sat in the living room, continuing his blank stare at the T.V. as he slowly nursed his bottle of Jim Bean.

Chapter 9

Travis pulled to the curb on busy Rice Street in his eighty-thousand-dollar Hummer as he parked and got out. He didn't worry about putting any money into the meter as his two sidekicks got out and stood watch over his ride like two valet drivers at a fancy restaurant. He said a few words to his boys, then quickly crossed the street as he headed over to the Fulton County Jail.

When Travis registered as a visitor and was finally allowed into the visitation room, he picked the furthest seat toward the end as he tried to get as far away as he could from the other visitors. He didn't have to wait long for Terrence. A heavy-set guard quickly brought Terrence down to the place across from Travis as he removed his handcuffs and left. Terrence and Travis quickly acknowledged each other as they touched the glass partition with their fists. Terrence then had a seat and picked up the phone on his side, as Travis did likewise. The two brothers remained silent for a few seconds as they stared across the glass and smiled at one another with appreciation.

"What's up, bro.," Travis finally said. "How you holding up over there?"

"You know that sounds strange coming from you, considering the number of times you've been over here on this side?"

Travis laughed. "That's a cheap shot."

"It was meant to be." Terrence smiled. "You still holding them streets down?"

"They don't call me prime time for nothing." Travis bragged. "I got the Midas touch, baby. Business couldn't be better."

"Sounds like you're blinging a little too hard."

"The harder you ball the more dollars that fall," Travis said with confidence. "I'm shipping more stuff than FedEx."

"How much you pushing these days?"

"Enough to have a different chick in my bed every night," Travis said with assurance. "But that's all been petty stuff up until now. I'm about to step to the plate and knock the ball straight out the park."

"What do you mean?"

Travis suddenly looked around at the other visitors who were in the room. He moved as close to the glass partition as he could, trying to preserve as much privacy as possible.

"There's some major stuff that's coming in in about two months. The best these streets has ever seen—straight from Colombia," Travis said slowly. "This stuff is going to bring in top dollar, and is going to make me one of the richest young brothers around. It's a can't miss," he said with enthusiasm. "A can't miss, my brother."

"And what if you miss and your ass ends up in the slam. You'll be a lifer this time, little brother. Won't be no more chances if you slip up."

"Naw, naw, big brother." Travis quickly corrected his incarcerated brother. "This deal is can't miss."

Terrence and Travis suddenly looked at one another as if they knew their conversation had gotten a little too deep. Travis decided to change the subject.

"So, you think you going to get off of this charge they got you pent up on? Hell, the news has virtually proclaimed you guilty and got the buzzards already circling over your ass."

"Man, this ain't nothing but some bull!" Terrence ranted. "I didn't kill that chick. They trying to railroad my ass."

"You got any idea who could've killed her?"

"Man, hell if I know. Me and Joletta were pretty tight some time back, but those last couple of months before she was killed, I hardly saw her. She was staying so busy getting her record company together, and taking care of all the other stuff she was doing, she was never hardly around. That night when we left the club together and went back to my apartment, was the first time in months we'd slept together. Other than working together at the club and trying to get my rap career going on her record label, me and Joletta really wasn't close at all. I didn't keep tabs on her no more."

"Yo, man, I don't know if you know," Travis said in a subtle voice, "but I used to hear some things about that chick."

"Things . . ." Terrence said skeptically. "What kind of things?"

"Things like she was tight with big dope dealers. That she was laundering dope money, and creating legitimate businesses with dope dealers' money."

"Dope dealers . . . like who?"

"Couple dudes name Romeo and Big Bam. They from out in L.A. and been in the game for years. I heard they had big time connections and were trying to establish a base in the south. Particularly here in Atlanta."

"How the hell did Joletta get hooked up with two dope dealers from L.A.?"

"I don't know. But I've seen them together one time a few months back at this big, plush party one night here in Atlanta. It was one of those parties where all the big time music execs, rappers, music scouts, and those fine ass women you see in the videos were at."

"And how you know?"

"What you mean how I know, because I was there!"

"How?"

"Cause I'm a baller," Travis said with bravado. "You come blinging and pushing money around in this city, and you can get into anything, anywhere, at any time."

"So, you think Joletta could have been mixed up with some heavy dudes?"

"You just don't hang around cats like that if you're not involve with them in some way," Travis said seriously. "And that ain't no joke."

When Terrence and Travis went silent, the heavy-set guard suddenly returned and headed down toward Terrence's way. Terrence saw the guard coming his way as he took a last look over at Travis.

"Don't go too fast in them streets, little brother," Terrence said earnestly as he touched the glass partition once again with his fist and hung up.

When he hung up the phone, the guard quickly handcuffed him and led him out of the room.

<hr />

EVERY FRIDAY NIGHT for the past year, Ernestine had borrowed Frances' car and had driven to her weekly drug rehab class. She'd made great strides in keeping herself clean since she started her sessions, and since then, she'd made a concerted effort not to miss any of her weekly sessions. Tonight, however, would be the first.

The stress and pressure of Terrence's arrest, and the media circus that surrounded the entire affair, had finally worn her down. For some reason tonight, she just wasn't in the mood for listening to other people's problems and their daily battles with their addictions. Tonight, she just needed to be somewhere where her mind could relax, and her body could be free from the strain and pressure that had tied it up. It had been a long time since she'd been out on the town, and she needed the stimulation that a funky nightclub could provide. What was the harm anyway? She was totally drug free and now a hard-working woman bringing home a steady check. Altogether, she was a brand-new person. So, what was one night on the town anyway?

Ernestine found her old favorite hangout over in Buckhead as the club started to get hot. The Groove Palace had now become Atlanta's hippest joint since the closing of Seven Flavors due to Joletta's death, and by 10 p.m., the hippest joint in Atlanta was already packed.

Ernestine quickly immersed herself into the free-flowing night life of the club. After a few beers and a couple of dances with some male suitors, Ernestine felt the strain and pressure of the last two weeks lift from her body like a bad flu finally starting to evaporate. The lively sounds and the bright lights of the club were just the therapy Ernestine needed. The media circus of Terrence's arrest and the recent scrutiny of their family name in the newspaper suddenly seemed a thousand miles away. Tonight no one cared about the murder or anything connected with it. Everybody just wanted to party and have a good time, and so did Ernestine.

When Ernestine finished a dance with a handsome, muscular gentleman, she left the dance floor and headed back over to the bar and had a seat. She'd been quite conservative with the men who approached her, only giving them the courtesy of a dance or two, but not giving them the extended personal time that some wanted. She was likewise conservative with the alcohol that she consumed. The few beers that she drank had made her feel loose and free, but by no way was she out of control. She knew the counselors of her drug rehab sessions would probably frown upon her activities tonight, but she was well in control of the situation. With that in mind, Ernestine decided to forgo the beer and ordered herself a shot of bourbon. She was in control, and there was no harm in having a little taste of whiskey.

When the bartender poured her drink, a handsome gentleman suddenly approached her from across the bar. From head to foot, he was dressed in the finest threads that money could buy and he had the looks that could tempt any woman in the place. He smiled at Ernestine, and for the first time tonight, she felt something move down deep in her. She had a funny feeling that she knew the impressive looking man standing in front of her from somewhere, but at the moment, she just couldn't place where. Although she didn't know the gentleman standing before her—*this one*—she knew she wouldn't mind getting to know.

"Well . . . well. Look who we have here," the gentleman said in a smooth voice. "It's been a long time, Ernestine."

"Pardon me?" Ernestine said perplexed. "Have we met?"

"I believe we have sweetheart. I believe we have?"

Ernestine stared at the gentleman standing before her and it suddenly hit her like a nightmare that had just come back to haunt her. Gone were the long Jeheri Curl, the sideburns, and the youthful, boyish look that she was accustomed to. Now this man of his mid-forties had his head shaved and sported the trendy mustache and goatee that made him appear like a man of power and statue. His smile, however, was still cunning and deceptive, like a fast hustler in a hurry to make a quick buck. Dexter still had that voracious smile; that tempting smile of a leery snake.

"What do you want?" Ernestine said rudely.

"Is that anyway to greet the man of your dreams," Dexter said playfully. "The man that took you all the way to Hollywood and made you a star?"

"The only thing you *made* me was a slut." Ernestine hissed. "I should've never trusted your ass and followed you all the way out to L.A. I should've never let you talk me into doing those damn videos. You made my life a living hell."

"You made your own self a slut, sweetheart. I didn't force you to make those films."

"You knew I was in love with you. You knew I'd do just about anything you wanted."

"Love is a bitch, ain't it?" Dexter said with a straight face.

Ernestine's eyes bored hard into him as she did everything in her power to restrain her temper and not cause a heated scene.

"What do you want?" her voice gritted.

"Oh, that maybe you and I can discuss a little business."

"Business?" Ernestine said as her eyes glared. "What the hell you mean *business*?"

"I don't know if you realize, my dear, but that article in the paper about your family has got a lot of people round this town talking. Specifically, that part where it talks about the days you were making porno films."

Ernestine glared even harder. "So, what of it?"

"Well, I just made a deal with a distributing company to re-release two of the videos. *Heat Between the Sheets* and *Cashmere Bitch*, you remember those?" he said with a seductive smile. "They're going to be hitting video counters all around Atlanta real soon. And if things go well here and with a little luck, they'll get distributed all over the country. And in the process, make me a ton of money."

"What the hell you mean you made a deal!" Ernestine's voice rose. "I ain't give you no consent for nothing like that."

"I don't need your consent, sweetheart. I owned the rights to every film we made."

"The hell you do!" Ernestine ranted. "You ain't about to release a damn thing."

"Just watch me, sweetheart," Dexter said coolly.

Ernestine got up quickly from the bar as she prepared to leave. But Dexter stopped her as he grabbed her arm.

"Let go of me!"

"We got business to discuss, sweetheart." Dexter demanded as he squeezed her arm tighter. "I'm offering you five-thousand dollars to shoot two new videos I'm about to make. Your name is hot right now, baby. Every man in this town wants to see you spread them legs and take it like you use to. It'll be just like old times."

"I said let go of me!" Ernestine ranted.

"Not until we talk business."

"LET GO OF ME!" Ernestine shouted as she suddenly jerked away from his strong grasp.

Ernestine ignored the looks and stares from everyone as she made a mad dash out of the club. Enraged, furious, and angry, she stormed over to her car and quickly got in as she took off out of the parking lot like a mad woman on fire. She headed back toward the center of town not really wanting to go home, but wanting so badly to release the pent-up pressure that her ex had suddenly cast over her. Tonight, which had started out so well, had suddenly turned into a literal nightmare. The more she thought of Dexter and his *business* proposition, the more heated she became.

Finally, Ernestine couldn't take it anymore. When she saw the flashing lights of a liquor store, she pulled over and headed into the store. She quickly got a bottle of J&B Bourbon, paid for it, and got back into the car and took off. She drove around not really heading in any particular direction as she sipped freely from her bottle of bourbon. Soon the anger and rage that she felt when she stormed out of the club, began to ease with each sip that she took.

Thirty minutes later, Ernestine felt good and relaxed. She drove round and around on the streets nursing her bottle and listening to the grooves on the radio as she tried to wrench out all of her pent-up emotions. When she suddenly turned down an avenue that was notorious for prostitutes, Ernestine couldn't help but to remember her days on the streets of L.A.

The women, all dressed in their seductive naughty outfits, were just like her. They sold their bodies just like she did to get enough money to feed their hungry stomachs, to feed that ever-growing habit, and to feed that overbearing pimp who would never allow them to rest. Ernestine knew the game all too well, and she knew from hard cold experience, that the game always won.

When Ernestine pulled up to a stoplight at an intersection, she sipped from her bottle and just watched the girls working the cars that cruised by. She turned and looked over at the other side of the street, and there she stood on the corner waiting for a customer to come by. Ernestine peered hard out her window to make sure it was really her, and there was no mistaking it. It was her daughter, Trinika, and despite her tender age of nineteen, she looked every bit of a thirty-year-old hooker with that gaudy outfit on as she stood there on that street corner. Ernestine quickly rolled down her window as her innate motherly instincts took over.

"Trinika!" Ernestine yelled. "Trinika, come over here!"

"Who's that?" Trinika called back.

"It's Ernestine—your mama."

"What do you want?"

"I want you to get over here, right now!"

The light at the intersection suddenly turned green as the car behind Ernestine blew for her to take off. Ernestine, seeing that she held up traffic, turned out of her lane as she pulled over to the corner where Trinika stood. She turned off the car and got out to confront her daughter. Their mother and daughter reunion certainly wasn't going to be a pleasant one.

"What are you doing standing out on this corner, girl?" Ernestine said as she rushed up on her daughter.

"What the hell does it look like I'm doing?" Trinika said roughly.

"Girl, don't you know this is dangerous. Any fool out here can be wandering around. They're murderers and rapists everywhere. Girl, you need to get off these streets and come back home!"

"I already got a home."

"Don't tell me you love living with that no good pimp."

"He takes good care of me. Takes care of everything I need."

"He don't love you!" Ernestine blasted. "He's just using you to keep his money coming. Girl, can't you see that?"

"I don't give a damn what you say," Trinika said belligerently. "He loves me and I'm going to keep on staying right with him. So, you might as well take your ass on and leave."

"I'm not leaving until you get into this car. And I'm taking you home whether you like it or not."

"And just who are you?" Trinika countered.

"I'm your mama," Ernestine said defiantly. "And I've been on these streets to know far more than you think you'll ever know."

"I ain't got no mama and never had no damn mama," Trinika said in a feisty voice. "You were never around to take care of nobody. The only one that took care of any of us was Franny. Your ass was never around. So don't come up here now thinking you my damn *mama*."

"I might not have been around back then. But I've been down that road that you're on, and I'm trying to keep you from making that same mistake."

"So, you think just cause you been going to some drug rehab classes, and done started working in Franny's restaurant that you something special now.

Well, honey, you ain't nothing. You still the same old crackhead skeezer that's going to fall right back down. You look like you already done had a damn relapse."

"How dare you talk to me like that!" Ernestine exploded. "How dare you!"

"I'll say anything I damn well please!"

Ernestine suddenly hauled off and slapped Trinika with such vicious force, that Trinika fell hard to the pavement like a boxer floored with one punch. She slowly got up as she tried to stop the blood dripping from her mouth with her hand. Ernestine suddenly felt horrible and tried to console her daughter.

"Look, baby, I'm sorry." Ernestine pleaded as she reached out and grabbed Trinika's arm. "Just get in the car so we can—"

"Let go of me!" Trinika yelled.

"Look, just get in the car so we can go home and—"

"Let go of my arm!" Trinika shouted as the blood continued to pour from her mouth.

When a car suddenly pulled over to the curb, Trinika jerked away from Ernestine's grip as she walked over to the car. The man inside the car held out fifty dollars as Trinika proceeded to open the door on the passenger side.

"Trinika, don't you get in that car—GIRL DO YOU HEAR ME!" Ernestine hollered as she tried to stop her daughter, but this time Trinika pushed Ernestine away as she fell helplessly to the pavement.

When Ernestine finally got up from the pavement, Trinika had gotten into the car and was long gone. Ernestine, feeling helpless and defeated, walked back over to her car and got in as she leaned back against the headrest. She was totally drained and exhausted. She unscrewed the top from her bottle of bourbon once again, and this time she took a hefty, generous swig. When she felt the calming effects of the bourbon began to take over, she started the car and took off.

WHEN ERNESTINE FINALLY pulled into Frances' driveway, it was well after two o'clock in the morning. By now, she was good and drunk. She put the near empty bottle of bourbon into her pocketbook as she got out of the car and headed toward the house. When she unlocked the door and entered the house, Frances waited for her in the living room. She immediately got up from the couch as she walked over to Ernestine.

"Girl, where have you been?" Frances demanded. "I've been sitting here worried that something has happen to you."

"I've been out," Ernestine said curtly.

"You've been out . . . where at?"

"Do I need your permission to go out these days?" Ernestine said harshly. "I'm forty-years-old, Franny!"

Frances looked into Ernestine's bloodshot eyes and began to smell the aroma from her breath.

"Have you been drinking?" Frances roared.

Ernestine ignored her as she headed to her room.

"Answer me, Ernestine! Have you been drinking?"

"I don't want to talk about it!" Ernestine said as she kept walking.

"You answer me. Where have you been?"

Ernestine went into her room and slammed the door behind her as Frances followed. Frances tried to turn the knob of the door, but found that it was locked.

"Open up this door!" Frances yelled as she banged on the door. "Ernestine, do you hear me? Where have you been? Ernestine! Ernestine! Ernestine!"

Chapter 10

Early Monday morning, Frances got an unexpected call from the Department of Children Services wanting her to come in for a hearing concerning the custody of Trinika's six-month-old child. Since the Department of Children Services had taken custody over Trinika's child, Frances had been taking steps and fighting diligently to be awarded custody of her child. The process up until now had been nothing but uphill. All the red tape, formalities, and bureaucratic hurdles that Frances had been taken through was literally nerve-racking. Frances only hoped that in the end, it would all be worth the trouble and anxiety that she'd endured. The circumstances under which Trinika became pregnant was terrible enough, and Frances only hoped that out of all the mess, an innocent young life could be spared the life of foster care and given a proper decent home.

Frances quickly put on one of her Sunday best dresses and made herself up to perfection as she prepared to leave. She phoned the restaurant and told Earl that she'd be running late, and to go ahead and start preparing the menu for today. She didn't bother asking Ernestine if she were going to work today, because she already knew the answer.

Since Ernestine came into the house drunk early Saturday morning, she'd pretty much stayed locked in her room and hadn't bother to venture out. Ernestine had been doing great since she'd started going to her drug rehab classes, but Frances began to worry that something serious had happened over the weekend to make her slip from her program. Every time she tried to talk to her, Ernestine would refuse to talk or yelled at her to mine her own business.

By Sunday, Frances was tired of trying to talk to her and decided to just let it go, and only hoped that her slip from her rehabilitation program was only a one-time thing. Frances knew that if Ernestine ever got started back up on her dope habit, she knew from past experience, that it would be a mighty struggle to ever get her clean again.

FRANCES ARRIVED AT the Department of Children Services slightly nervous about her meeting. She was never one to get nervous and uptight in tough situations; she was always the steady rock of the family, the one whom everyone relied on and came to when they needed strength and assurance. On certain days like today, however, she needed a little guidance and strength of her own. Whenever she felt like that, her well used little, tattered Bible that she kept down deep in her purse, often gave her that little boost of strength she needed.

A panel of five greeted Frances as she entered a huge conference room on the third floor of the building. The two men and three women sat at a long conference table as Frances sat facing them at a much smaller table a few feet away. Frances carefully studied the faces before her as she tried to gauge the temperament of their personalities. The all-white panel didn't give much indication as they stared rigidly back at her as they waited for the lead associate to begin the hearing.

"I want to thank you for coming in on such short notice, Mrs. Jackson," the lead associate said. "I'm John Fullwitz. To my left are Nancy Wiggins and Jim Eldridge. And to my right are Florence Gilbert and Barbara Banks," he said as he slowly flipped through a thick file before him. After a few silent seconds, he once again looked over at Frances. "Mrs. Jackson, I'd like to start by asking a few questions about the mother of the child, Trinika Jackson. She is your granddaughter, is that correct?"

"Yes, she is."

"What is the condition of the mother as of now? Or do you have any contact with your granddaughter at all?"

"Trinika has been away from under my care for a while," Frances said slowly. "She's been enticed and lured to the streets by the man she's been associated with."

"By that do you mean that she's a prostitute?"

"Yes."

"I see. And the state of the child's father, would it be the man that she's associated with now?"

"Yes . . . it is."

"And by what means does he make a living?"

"He's a pimp," Frances said stoned faced.

"I see," he said slowly as he gazed around at the others. "Now, Mrs. Jackson, Trinika's child was discovered in the back alley of a grocery store. How did you come to learn that it was Trinika's child?"

"Trinika came to my restaurant one evening a few weeks after the birth of her child and informed me of the incident. She was quite torn up about it and she thought that I'd know best of how to handle it."

"Did she come to you because she wanted you to seek custody of her child?"

"Trinika didn't express it in those such words, but she came to me because she felt bad for what she did. I knew when she told me that day, that she still had love for her child. Trinika has just been confused lately and under a lot of stress. She's a good girl," Frances said with empathy. "It's my only hope that I may attain custody of her child, so that when Trinika gets delivered from the abusive situation that she's in, that she won't have her child taken away from her forever."

The lead associate scribbled something down in his file, then he gazed around at the others.

"Mrs. Jackson, as you know it is imperative that a child be raised in a good environment and have a stable home life," Mrs. Florence Gilbert suddenly spoke. "It says here that the child's grandmother, which is a member of your household, has been enrolled at a drug rehabilitation center for drug abuse. Is that correct?"

"Yes . . ." Frances said as she eyed the woman. "That's correct."

"What particular drug is she being rehabilitated for?"

"Cocaine."

"And how long has she been in therapy?"

"For a year now. And my daughter has been doing very well with her program," Frances said firmly.

"That's very good to hear, Mrs. Jackson. But don't you think that a child being raised around a recovering cocaine addict can be very detrimental to the child's upbringing?"

"There'll be no drugs around this child, period!" Frances said with authority.

"Mrs. Jackson," the man next to Mrs. Gilbert quickly jumped in as he spoke. "I'm sure your intentions to raise this child are well. But the question of your age is a serious matter. It says here that you're sixty-seven-years old."

"Yes, I am," Frances said with a stern look. "What does that have to do with it?"

"Well, Mrs. Jackson, a child grows up fast and goes through many changes. How will you be able to handle and help guide this child when it's ten, twelve, or even fifteen? Surely you ought to know that your age and the child's age will be far and between. There'll be a *very* huge gap," he said pointedly. "Surely you don't believe that you'll have the physical, nor emotional stamina that it'll take to raise this child for the long run?"

"I believe God will provide for this child," Frances said in a determined voice. "No matter what my age may be, sir."

"And you believe you'll be there for the child?"

"If that's His will."

"Mrs. Jackson, there's another matter concerning raising this child that hasn't been discussed," the last person finally spoke. The others on the panel listened intently as they peered hard at Frances. "It has to do with the recent arrest of your grandson for the murder of Joletta Anderson."

"Which has not been proven," Frances said adamantly.

"Yes, I understand that," the woman said. "But the egregious circumstances surrounding not only this particular matter, but of past circumstances surrounding your family may not be conducive to raising a child around. The unfavorable attention to your family's past history could be pegged to this child. Other children may use it to taunt, ridicule, or even isolate the child altogether. It could cause harm to a young person's psyche, and very well cast a dark shadow over the child. A shadow that the child may never be able to overcome."

"This child won't have any shadow of no kind over it," Frances said through clenched teeth. "And this child will be a part of my family, and my family will be a part of the child."

"But your family seems to have a predisposition to unfortunate events."

"You mean is my family *jinxed*?" Frances said like a rattle snake ready to strike.

"Well, to put it bluntly, Mrs. Jackson," the woman said in an unabashed voice. "How do we know that this child won't go down the same path as some of your other family members have taken?"

Frances rose slowly from her chair and placed her palms firmly on the table. She glared at every member on the panel as if she stood behind a pulpit getting ready to deliver a fiery message to a group of condemned souls.

"I'm going to tell each and every one of you this only once," she said in a heated voice. "My family may have made some mistakes. We've had our scrapes and bruises, and we're certainly not perfect. But this child's home should be with the one true family that'll love him like no other. And that's with me and my family! And no matter what this panel says or does to try to eradicate this child's memory of my family, that child will *always* be a part of my family!"

Frances grabbed her pocketbook and stormed out of the conference room like a wild bronco on the loose. She kept right on trotting out the building, panting and breathing heavy with anger.

Chapter 11

D r. Carolyn McMillan's eight o'clock sociology class on the campus of
Georgia Tech had just gotten underway. Her eight o'clock class was her
first class of the day, and it was also her largest. Seventy students filled her
room to capacity and there wasn't a single seat empty. Many students had
chosen her class only as an elective, as nearly three-fourth of her students had
far different ranging majors. But Dr. McMillan was known as an excellent
instructor, and her reputation as a lively lecturer and debater drew many to
her class.

The subject that Dr. McMillan focused on today was on the concept of
behavioral learning. Her packed class listened with undivided attention as
she spoke on stage from her lectern.

"As we all know, learning plays an important role in socialization,"
Carolyn spoke. "A person must acquire a wide range of information and skills
to participate in the day-to-day social structure of society. Who can answer
where a person first learns his social skills to adequately function in society?"

"From the family," a student said.

"That's correct. The family plays a key role in the socialization of a child.
From the family, a child first learns how to interact within a group and how
to perform according to his or her expected role within the social structure of
a group. From the family, a child first learns many basic attitudes and values
by observing their parents or older brothers and sisters. Then that child in
turn brings those attitudes and values that he or she has learned from the
family, to the social structure of society as a whole."

"But Dr. McMillan, not all attitudes and values a child learns from his
family that they bring to society are not all good," another student quickly
added.

"Absolutely not," Carolyn responded.

"I mean as we all know there have been some real nut cases from some
families that have inflicted nothing but total havoc on society."

The class erupted into light laughter. The student seemed suddenly spurred on by the flattery.

"I mean take the Menendez Brothers, the Charles Manson's, or the Timothy McVeigh's, those individuals definitely didn't bring anything productive to society."

"There are certainly some deviant behaviors in some families." Carolyn added.

"And no disrespect, Dr. McMillan," the student said as he charged on, "but maybe your own family may have brought some deviant values and behaviors to society. Your own family may be somewhat of a case study if I may say so."

"Excuse me," Carolyn said shocked.

"I'm just saying that some of the stuff we've been hearing in the news and reading in the paper about the trials your family has gone through could rank right up there with some of those families I just mentioned," the student said boldly. "It seems as if y'all have had plenty of social disorder and chaos stirring around in your family."

Complete silence reigned over the entire class. Carolyn, flushed with embarrassment, stood staring out at her packed class. Her dignity was suddenly crushed, and with it came a rage of anger.

"Get out of my class!" Carolyn yelled in the direction of the student. "Get out, *right now*!"

The student picked up his books and rose slowly from his seat as he headed out of the class. He gave Carolyn a quick smirk as if he enjoyed badgering her, then he turned and headed on out the door. When the student was gone, Carolyn looked over her silent class as she tried to regain her composure. She cleared her throat and once again asserted her authority.

"Now . . ." she said slowly, "shall we continue . . . ."

LATER THAT EVENING Carolyn met her husband, George, for dinner and drinks at the City Grill restaurant in downtown Atlanta. They were celebrating the splendid article *Ebony* magazine currently ran in their magazine recognizing George as being one of the most successful heart surgeons in America. They were joined by a few of George's colleagues and their wives as they all sat together at a round table drinking, laughing, and discussing the article. The outing was lively and festive as George sat at the table, thoroughly enjoying all of the attention.

"That was a very good picture they had of you, George." One of his colleagues gushed. "You looked like a candidate running for office."

"You could've fooled me. I thought it was a mug shot of some sleazy politician that just got arrested." Another colleague joked as everyone laughed.

"Oh, that's very funny, Larry." George replied. "You know how you like to drink before going into the office. You better watch yourself. One of these days you're going to have one too many drinks and one of your patients is going to sue you for trying to stitch up their private. You'll be the first gynecologist ever sent to death row."

The laughter exploded around the table.

"But seriously, George, you must be feeling mighty good." Another colleague spoke. "That was a glowing article about your career."

"I do feel good, Bob. It's taken a lot of years and a lot of hard work to get here, but I'm certainly proud of where I'm at."

Suddenly a gentleman from another table came up and approached George and Carolyn as they sat at their table. Everyone at George's table instantly grew silent as they stared at the man.

"Aren't you related to that filthy, no-good family?" the man said in a drunken slur.

"What . . . uh . . . family are you speaking of, sir?" George said rather cautiously.

"You know who I'm talking about!" the man said in a drunken rage as everyone in the restaurant suddenly looked on. "That Jackson family—both you and her!" He slurred again as he pointed at both George and Carolyn. "Well, I say they ought to lock all of y'all up. 'Cause ain't none of you worth a damn!"

The man took off and stormed out of the restaurant in a drunken rage. Everyone in the restaurant continued staring over at George and Carolyn's table as the gossip and whispers began to circulate. George quickly tried to defuse the situation as he ignored the stares and went on with the conversation with his colleagues at his table. After a few moments, everyone went back to their own affairs as the restaurant returned to normal. But the jovial atmosphere that was once at George's table, was now replaced with conversation that was forced and strained.

———◦———

WHEN GEORGE AND CAROLYN arrived back at their upscale home on the outskirts of Atlanta after returning from their dinner outing, they went straight to their bedroom as they quickly got undressed and prepared for bed. The silence between them was like a massive brick wall. Neither George nor Carolyn didn't dare to look at one another as the strain and tension between them grew unbearable. After a while, Carolyn finally grew tired of the silence.

"You just going to walk around here sulking all night, George," Carolyn said exasperated. "No one knew that man was going to approach our table acting the way he did."

"It was embarrassing!" George shouted. "Here we are supposed to be having a dinner celebration, and some nut comes over and starts ranting about your crazy family. You should've seen the look on the faces of Bob, Larry, Ted and their wives. They were looking at us like we were nothing but some damn plum fools. And the whole damn entire restaurant for that matter!"

"George, will you calm down and stop all that crazy shouting."

"Don't tell me to calm down, woman!" George said in a rage. "I'm sick of every time one of your family members does something to make the news, that my name somehow gets tied up in it. How long has this been going on?" He glared at Carolyn. "I tell you how long—*too damn long*!" He shouted. "People everywhere have been coming up to me asking all kind of weird questions about this murder and looking at me like I'm one of the members of your twisted family. People at the hospital, the guys on the golf course, at church—everywhere! Well, I'm sick of it, Carolyn! I've had it with your damn family!"

"You think you're the only one who's getting harassed and badgered over this murder," Carolyn said as she followed George into the bathroom as he began brushing his teeth. "Why just today some smart mouth kid confronts me in front of my own class saying that my family is a case study, and compared us to notorious families like the Menendez brothers and the Mansons. Now just how do you think that makes me feel?"

"The damn kid was probably right."

"George, how can you say that!" Carolyn said in a riled voice. "How can you possibly believe that my family is as bad as those notorious families?"

"Look, Carolyn," George said as he returned to the bedroom and put on his pajamas as Carolyn followed his every step. "Maybe if your family was brought up better than it was, maybe you and your family wouldn't be going through all of these headaches that you're constantly going through now. It all starts in the home, Carolyn."

"Are you trying to say that my mother didn't raise us right?" Carolyn said with offense.

"That's exactly what I'm saying!"

"How dare you insult my mother!" Carolyn shouted back. "Franny did all she could to raise us, feed us, and keep clothes on our back, while the same time trying to run a hectic restaurant seven days a week. She did more than any two parents could've ever done."

"Well, obviously she didn't do enough or you all wouldn't have turned out the way you did."

"You better take that back George or you're not sleeping in here tonight!" Carolyn steamed.

"Fine with me," he said as he grabbed his pillow from the bed and stormed out of the bedroom.

"George, you better get back here this second and take back what you said about my mother!" Carolyn yelled.

He wasn't listening.

"Did you hear me, George?" Carolyn ranted as she followed him out into the hallway. "George, I'm talking to you! George, do you hear me—GEORGE! GEORGE!"

When Carolyn heard the guess room door slam shut, she went to the door and banged on it until her fist began to ache. When she finally realized that George wasn't about to answer her, she had no choice but to give up her futile effort.

Reluctantly, Carolyn returned to her bedroom as she got into bed and turned off the light. As she lay alone under the sheets, she tried to blot out the heated argument that they'd just had as she tried to get some well needed sleep. It had been a long day, and tomorrow promised to be even longer. But her boiling temper, wasn't about to let her rest.

Chapter 12

The dinner rush at Frances' Soul Food Restaurant had finally slowed down. Ernestine, tired from the long steady line of hungry customers, was more than ready for her much needed break. Since her minor relapse when she returned home drunk after her night on the town, Ernestine had virtually stayed at home locked away in her room. Today was her first day back to work in over a week, and Ernestine definitely wasn't ready for all the hustle and bustle that often accompanied Frances' successful restaurant.

All day she worked the cash register in a reserved, quiet manner, which was totally unlike her talkative, bossy way in which she normally engaged with the customers. Frances kept a close eye on her all day making sure she was alright, but despite Ernestine's refusal to talk about whatever that bothered her, Frances seemed to sense that she was worried about something.

When another staff member took over the cash register, Ernestine finally went on her break. She desperately needed a smoke and some fresh air as she went out into the dining area and headed for the front door. Most of the dinner crowd had already cleared out as only a few customers remained scattered throughout the dining area. Two men sitting at a table in the dining room saw Ernestine heading for the door and suddenly called her over to their table. Ernestine was a little befuddled why these two strange men had called her name, but she went over to their table anyway.

"Yes . . ." Ernestine said politely, "may I help you?"

"You sure can, sweetheart," one of the men said in a lascivious voice. "What's a fine woman with a body like yours doing working behind a cash register? It seems a woman like you would be doing more of a *sexual* type job to bring home the money," the man said as his partner laughed.

"Excuse me?"

"I mean that body of yours was really hot in that video. I had to watch it three or four times until I finally got enough."

"What?" Ernestine said with a baffled look.

"This DVD, sweetheart," the man said as he laid a DVD of *Cashmere Bitch* onto the table. "Two whole hours of some of the best screwing I've ever seen."

Ernestine's heart dropped when she suddenly saw her nude, lustful body displayed on the cover of the DVD. It had been some years since she'd last seen that tape around, and now there it was, lying on the table as if it were just fresh from the stores. She slowly picked up the DVD as her hand slightly shook as she stared at the wanton woman on the cover.

"Where . . ." her voice shook, "where did you get this?"

"Down at Jimmy's Video Store, baby. They got a whole stock of them just fresh in from the truck."

Ernestine slung the DVD onto the table as she began to head out the door, but the man quickly grabbed her arm.

"Hold on, sweetheart. Where you going?" the man stood up as he held Ernestine with a tight grip. "My friend and I wanted to get a little taste of the action that was on that DVD. I know you can handle the two of us just like you did the two guys on the tape. So come on, sweetheart, we'll throw a little money your way for your time."

"Let go of me!" Ernestine snapped.

"Come on, sweetheart. I know you like it good and rough."

"Let go of me!" Ernestine yelled.

"Come on, baby, and stop fighting it!"

"LET GO OF ME!" Ernestine roared.

When the ruckus in the dining area exploded, Frances, along with Earl and the rest of the staff, rushed out into the dining area. Frances was quick to approach the man holding Ernestine.

"What in the hell is going on out here!" Frances yelled.

The man slowly released Ernestine's arm when he saw the look on Frances' face. "We . . . uh . . . we're just discussing a little business, ma'am," the man said as he tried to smile. "There ain't no problem here."

"Get the hell out of my place—both of you!" Frances roared. "And don't ever come back in here again!"

The two men slowly heeded to Frances' demand as they turned and left out of the restaurant. When they left out, Frances saw the DVD on the table. She slowly picked it up and saw Ernestine's nude, lustful body on the cover.

"Ernestine . . ." she said perplexed as she stared at the DVD. "What in the world is this?"

Ernestine felt a rush of embarrassment suddenly siege hold of her body. She couldn't dare to look into Frances' face, let alone the faces of Earl and the rest of the staff who'd gathered around. The sight of her past sins had suddenly resurfaced for everyone to see. Now Ernestine, ashamed and hurt, wanted to crawl under the table and hide from the world.

When the silent stares of everyone became too much, Ernestine tore out of the dining room as she rushed to the kitchen and quickly grabbed Frances' car keys. She charged back through the dining area and tore out of the restaurant like a mad gust of wind. Frances followed on her heels as she tried to stop her.

"Ernestine! Stop—where are you going?" Frances pleaded. "Ernestine! Ernestine! *Ernestine!*"

Frances frantic calls were useless. Ernestine quickly jumped into Frances' car and skidded out of the parking lot like a mentally deranged woman.

———

FRANCES LOOKED UP AT the clock up on the wall for the fifteenth time as she sat at her kitchen table drinking coffee. It was almost eleven p.m. and Ernestine was nowhere to be found. Frances had been worried to death since Ernestine tore out of the restaurant parking lot in her car nearly four hours ago. She'd called virtually everyone she knew and over twenty different bars and hangouts hoping to find the whereabouts of Ernestine, but no one had seen her description or heard from her. Frances hoped for the best, but somehow, she feared the worst. There was nothing that she could do for now, but just wait and hope that Ernestine would come home soon.

While Frances sat at the kitchen table waiting for Ernestine to walk through the front door, she began to listen to a late-night local radio talk show discuss the murder of Joletta Anderson and the upcoming trial that was still many weeks away. As all the information about the murder was rehashed and the different strategies that both the prosecution and the defense would more and likely use to conduct the trial were thoroughly discussed, the subject quickly turned to Frances' family.

Frances listened as one caller after another began to vilify and lambaste the members of her family. Everything from her late husband's armed conflict with the Detroit police, to Willie Joe's unfortunate shooting incident, to Ernestine's notorious porn films, Travis' drug arrest, and Terrence's former rape case to his current murder charge were raked over and scandalize by the overzealous callers. Frances became crushed when she began to recognize a few of the callers; callers who'd been to her soul food restaurant many times and she'd gotten to know on a personal basis over the years. The measure of a true friend was how loyal that person was during times of trouble and crises, and Frances found to her consternation, that she had very few indeed.

Finally having enough of all the mud and dirt thrown at her family, Frances turned off the radio. She finished the last of her coffee as she got up from the kitchen table and prepared to go to bed. When she suddenly heard a knock at the door, she quickly went to answer it hoping that somehow it was Ernestine who'd finally come home. But when she opened the door, she was stunned to see Carolyn standing on the porch. As far away as Carolyn and George lived, Frances knew that it had to be something mighty important for Carolyn to be at her doorstep so late.

"Carolyn, what in the world are you doing here at this hour?" Frances said startled. "I was hoping that you were Ernestine."

"I was just out riding around," Carolyn said in a depressed voice. "I just had to get out of the house."

"Out riding around," Frances said as she looked at Carolyn suspiciously. "Well . . . come on in."

Carolyn came into the house as she went straight to the living room and had a seat on the sofa. Frances followed her to the sofa and sat down as she stared over at Carolyn and saw the deep troubled look on her face. She didn't have to ask Carolyn what troubled her, because Carolyn quickly opened up like a flood gate that had too much water to dispose.

"George and I have been fighting!" Carolyn quickly said as if the words literally burned her tongue and she had to spew them out. "The last couple of nights, we've been arguing and bickering at each other so much that my throat is literally raw. And I'm just sick and tired of it—sick of it!" Carolyn ranted.

"Sick of what?" Frances said as she looked at Carolyn confused. "Fighting about what?"

"All this mess that's going on with Terrence and the rest of the family. George is getting a lot of heat from his colleagues at the hospital and from other people around the city and he's blaming me for it."

"Why's he blaming you?"

"Because he feels our family is dragging him down and embarrassing him. He thinks his accomplishments as a doctor are being tarnished by our family name."

"Is that so?" Frances said in a leery voice.

"All this pressure surrounding this murder, and this recent scrutiny of our family is affecting our marriage." Carolyn declared. "I don't know how many more nights of this arguing, bickering, and fighting our marriage can take. It can't take much more."

"So, George blames you for our family," Frances said pointedly. "But now you've come here at this hour of the night to blame me."

"To blame you," Carolyn said defensively. "I'm not blaming you. Whatever gave you that crazy idea?"

"Because I can hear it in your voice and see it in your face, Carolyn," Frances said with authority. "Ever since you and George have *moved* up in society, you've been ashamed of this family. Every time something has happened in this family, you and George seem to get into one of your drag down fights. Then you come here and want to blame me because our family is ruining your marriage."

"That's not true, Franny."

"It is true!" Frances berated. "You just too damn proud to admit it."

"Maybe I do," Carolyn said flustered. "But I'm just so sick and tired of our family always causing so much controversy and embarrassment. This latest thing with Terrence has just made life a living nightmare. George is chided by his peers at the hospital, I hear little nasty remarks at school, Frederick is getting pressured at Morehouse, and Bethany is constantly getting ridicule over at Spellman. George and I can't even go out with friends to a restaurant without someone criticizing our family. When is it ever going to stop?"

"People may say some mean and spiteful things about us," Frances said with determination, "but you never turn your back on your family, Carolyn. Never!"

"Our family is already too far gone, Franny. There's no hope for saving us."

"Don't you dare say that," Frances said as she eyed Carolyn. "This family must stick together and pull one another along no matter what the world says about us. We're a family, and we all must help each other whether it's Terrence, Willie Joe, Ernestine—"

"Where is Ernestine?" Carolyn suddenly said.

Frances quickly remembered the incident that occurred today in the restaurant. She closed her eyes as she slowly massaged her temples.

"I don't know," Frances said as she sighed deeply. "She took off in the car earlier and she hasn't come home."

"Where did she run off to?" Carolyn snipped. "To some crack house to try to get a fix?"

"Now you stop that right this minute." Frances demanded as she pointed a finger over at Carolyn. "I don't want to hear another word from you bad mouthing Ernestine. She's had a very rough day."

"What happened?"

"Two guys came into the restaurant today with one of Ernestine's old, nasty sex tapes. They started coming on to her really hard out in the dining area, making obscene advances and causing a scene in the restaurant. When me and the rest of the staff came out to the dining area to see what the commotion was about, this guy had Ernestine by the arm. When I finally threw them out, everyone suddenly started staring at the DVD that was left lying on the dining table. Ernestine was so embarrassed, she just stormed out of the restaurant with my keys and took off in the car. And I ain't heard from her since."

"How in the world did they get one of Ernestine's old porno tapes?"

"Ermma called me about an hour ago," Frances said slowly. "She said that someone told her that a new shipment of that DVD is being sold in video stores all over Atlanta. And they're selling like hot cakes."

"What?" Carolyn said in disbelief.

"I'm afraid so," Frances said softly.

"See, that's what I'm talking about. This family has too much damn baggage!" Carolyn raged. "If is not Terrence getting arrested for murder, then it's Travis getting busted for drugs. If it's not daddy's old heyday in the streets of Detroit coming back to haunt us, then it's Willie Joe's shooting or Ernestine's wild sex days being thrown back in our face. Something is always going on in this family and I'm sick and tired of it. Just sick and tired of it!"

"I'm not thrilled about it either, but you don't give up on your family, Carolyn."

"This damn family is like a magnet for trouble." Carolyn threw up her hands as she complained. "Maybe that paper was right about us all along. Maybe we are jinxed."

"We are not *jinxed*!" Frances yelled. "And I don't want to hear any more about us being jinxed again—do you hear me!"

The phone suddenly rang as Frances quickly went over to answer it, hoping that it was Ernestine calling from someplace. But when she hung up, Carolyn sensed by the disappointment on Frances' face that it wasn't her.

"Who was that?" she asked fearfully.

"That was Patricia." Frances sighed. "She said Willie Joe has been arrested for fighting in a bar and disturbing the peace. She said he took off in the car and she has no way to get down to the jail."

"And she wants us to go get him out?"

"Yeah, and Ernestine is off who knows where in my car . . . Do you mind?"

Carolyn shook her head in disgust as she and Frances headed out the door.

Chapter 13

Frances and Carolyn arrived down at the jail as they quickly sought Willie Joe's release. After posting his bail, Willie Joe was soon released as Frances and Carolyn took him from the jail as they headed out to the car. Bloodied, bruised, and still reeking from his intoxication, Willie Joe slumped into the back seat of Carolyn's car as Frances and Carolyn got in up front. Carolyn started the ignition and took off as they headed on their way to take Willie Joe home. There was a tense, strained silence in the car as neither Frances nor Carolyn seemed to want to bring up the fight. Willie Joe, however, soon shattered the tense silence once he saw the approaching sign of a liquor store.

"Hey, pull over there." Willie Joe grumbled. "I need me a fifth of Jim Bean."

"I'm not pulling over to no liquor store!" Carolyn ranted. "You're already drunk and stinking as it is now."

"Hell, that's just like you. Too damn stuck up to do somebody a little favor."

"I just paid your damn bail!" Carolyn yelled as she glared at Willie Joe through her rear-view mirror. "If it weren't for me, your butt would still be sitting in that damn jail."

"I didn't tell you to come get me." Willie Joe shot back. "So, you can just keep all that high-minded bullcrap to yourself."

"Well, someone had to come get your drunk behind out of jail. The last thing this family needs right now is another scandalize story in the paper. I tell you, between you and Ernestine, I don't know which one of you is more pitiful."

"Who you calling pitiful?" Willie Joe roared.

"You!"

"Will you two stop it!" Frances yelled. "It's too late for all this damn yelling and bickering. Carolyn, let's just get Willie Joe home so he can sleep off that drunk."

A speechless quiet quickly returned in the car as Carolyn drove in silence. She fumed madder than a hornet's nest and now wished she'd just stayed home and gone into the study and prepared for tomorrow's lecture, or just gone to bed after she and George had their paint splitting argument. Anything, right now, was better than dealing with her trifling, irritating family.

By the time Carolyn pulled into Willie Joe and Patricia's driveway, Willie Joe had passed out in the back seat. Carolyn and Frances did all they could to wrestle Willie Joe's two-hundred-and-seventy-pound frame out of the car. Patricia came out of the house when she saw the car in the drive and gave Frances and Carolyn a hand as they all pushed and guided Willie Joe's lumbering, heavy body toward the house. Willie Joe, through the haze of his drunken stupor, still demanded that they take him to get a fifth of Jim Bean. If it weren't for the pitiful, drunken state that he was in, the entire scene would be comical as Frances, Carolyn, and Patricia wrestled, pulled, and fought with Willie Joe's heavy, lumbering body.

When the three women finally got Willie Joe into the house and stretched out onto the bed in his bedroom, they were all tired, exhausted, and panting for air. Willie Joe weighed a ton, and Frances, Carolyn, and Patricia felt every bit of his dead weight. They stared down at him lying on the bed as he began to snore like a loud train speeding through a tunnel. It seemed that none of them could've care less about his ear-piercing snoring. The only thing that mattered was that he was finally off of their aching shoulders.

"Thanks for doing this," Patricia said to Carolyn and Frances. "I don't know how I would've gotten down to that jail. Willie Joe took the car when he went down to the bar, and the police just said that they impounded it when Willie Joe left it in a no parking zone."

"Well . . . do you need a ride to go get it?" Carolyn asked hesitantly. "I'll take you down to the impound station."

"No, don't worry about that. I'll have one of the girls from the hospital to come pick me up in the morning and take me over there. You've done enough already. How much was Willie Joe's bail?"

"I took care of it," Carolyn said respectfully. "You have enough on your hands to worry about."

"Patricia, have you tried getting Willie Joe into any kind of counseling?" Frances said as she stared down at her snoring son. "This can't keep going on like this."

"I've tried many countless times." Patricia sighed. "But every time I try, Willie Joe balks and argues that he don't need no counseling. We'll just end up in a big, old argument about his drinking, and he'll just storm out of the house and end up at some old bar just like tonight."

"He's still not trying to look for any kind of work?"

Patricia shook her head sadly. "Lately he hasn't. And when he does try to search for something meaningful, he always says he gets rejected because of the shooting incident."

"What's he been doing lately?"

"Nothing but drinking and gambling," Patricia said pitifully. "And it's only getting worse."

Frances stared at Willie Joe solemnly for the longest as she listened to his snoring grow ever louder. She finally looked over at Patricia's worried, pained face.

"Don't give up on Willie Joe," Frances said as she laid a hand on Patricia's arm. "We're going to get Willie Joe some help. I know Willie Joe, and he's still hurting down deep inside about what happened. We're going to get him through this if it's the last thing I do, and I mean that," she said reassuringly as she looked rigidly into Patricia's eyes.

Frances gave Patricia a firm hug. After the hug, she and Carolyn left the house as they got back into the car and headed on.

Carolyn and Frances rode in silence as they drove through the light late-night traffic. Carolyn tried to ease the tense silence as she turned on the radio to listen to some quiet, soothing music, but when she heard the late-night DJ make a joke about their family before he began to play his next song, Carolyn quickly turned off the radio. She'd heard enough of her family criticized and stigmatized from students at school, from strangers at the grocery store, and even from George at home and she definitely didn't want to hear any side cracking jokes at this late hour. She looked over at Frances to see her reaction, but Frances simply stared out the window as if she were deep in another world.

When they pulled up at a stoplight, Carolyn yawned deeply as the long, tiring day of lecturing students and fighting with George had finally caught up with her. Frances, however, liked to scared her right out of her skin when she heard her yell. She quickly looked over at Frances to see what was the matter, but Frances was too hysterical to answer any questions.

"Oh, my God." Frances screamed. "Pull over there! Pull over there!"

"What . . .?" Carolyn said confused.

"Just pull over there, right now!"

Carolyn whipped her car over to the corner where a man repeatedly slapped a scantily dressed woman. The young woman was Trinika, and the man slapping her was Daddy T., her pimp. Frances quickly jumped out of the car when Carolyn stopped. She rushed up on Trinika's pimp like a linebacker getting ready to make a killer hit.

"What the hell are you doing to my granddaughter?" Frances yelled as she hit Daddy T. upside the head with all the force that her sixty-seven-year-old body could muster. "Get away from her this instant!"

Daddy T., who stood nearly a foot above Frances, merely took a step back from the hysterical woman. Her lick was good, but it only seemed to make his heated temper rage even more.

"Look, old lady, you better get the hell out of my business before you get yourself hurt!" He exploded.

"This is my granddaughter and she is my business!"

"Lady, this is my bitch and I'll do whatever I feel like!"

Frances looked over at Trinika and saw her bloody, bruised lip and the swelling forming around her eye. She had tears coming down her face as she looked back at Frances.

"Trinika, get in the car!" Frances yelled. "I'm taking you home right now."

"I'll be alright, Franny," she said with a whimper. "Really . . . I'm alright."

"Girl, get in this car right now!"

"Lady, you better get the stepping before you wish you had." Daddy T. demanded as he glared down at Frances.

"Carolyn, call the cops!" Frances yelled as Carolyn grabbed her cell phone out of the car and began dialing 911. But Daddy T. quickly whipped out his gun and pointed it dead at Carolyn.

"You better hang that phone up, bitch," he said as he held his finger on the trigger, "or I'm going to put a bullet right dead in your head."

Carolyn slowly hung up her phone as her knees began to shake. Frances appeared determined to save her granddaughter no matter what it took as she immediately plowed straight forward and grabbed Trinika's hand. Daddy T. quickly swung the gun on Frances, but Trinika was quick to halt her pimp's itchy trigger finger.

"No, no, please . . . it's alright," she said as she pleaded with her pimp. "You don't have to do that. Everything is alright. Please . . . I'll be right there. Just give me a second . . . please . . . ."

Daddy T. slowly put away his gun as he glared at Frances. By his arrogant, conceited look, he gave off the impression that he knew his woman better than the days of the week and knew she'd obey him and be by his side no matter what. He slowly began to relax as he scowled at Frances.

"Alright . . . you got twenty seconds," he said as he strolled over and got into his sparkling cream-colored Cadillac parked on the corner.

When they were finally alone, Frances reached out and touched Trinika's cheek as a tear rolled down her face. All of a sudden, it seemed that Trinika was once again that young, precious little girl that Frances had once raised.

"Trinika . . . baby . . . let me take you home," Frances said sincerely. "You don't need to take this crap on this street. You got a home, a place where you're needed and loved."

"Daddy . . . he loves me," Trinika said as she tried to be brave for Frances. "He just got a little angry at something I did . . . that's all. It's nothing really."

"That animal don't love you, Trinika!" Frances sneered. "Look at your face. That animal needs to be locked up!"

"No, it's alright, Franny." Trinika pleaded. "He's not like that all the time. He just got upset tonight."

"Trinika—get in this damn car!" Daddy T. shouted from his Cadillac.

"I'll be alright, Franny." Trinika pleaded again. "It's alright . . . I got to go now."

"No, Trinika, don't you get in that car with him." Frances demanded as she tried to hold onto Trinika's hand. "Let me take you home Trinika—please!"

"Trinika, I'm not going to tell your ass again!" Daddy T. roared. "Get in this car!"

"I'm sorry, Franny," Trinika said as she pulled away from Frances' grip. "I got to go . . . I'll be alright."

"Trinika, don't you get in that car!" Frances yelled as she watched Trinika head toward his car. "Trinika! Don't you get in that car! Trinika!"

Frances watched as the sparkling cream-colored Cadillac drove away with her granddaughter in it. She stood on the corner long after the Cadillac was gone, like a bag woman with nowhere in the world to go. Finally, Carolyn came around and touched her gently on the shoulder and helped her back into the car. She closed her door and got in on the driver's side as she pulled from the corner and took off down the road.

———◦———

WHEN THEY ARRIVED BACK at Frances' house, Frances slowly got out of the car and headed for her front door. Carolyn wanted to see her into the house, but Frances ignored her daughter's requests as she unlocked her door and closed it back without saying a word to Carolyn.

Frances, tired and emotionally drained, went straight to her bedroom and changed into her nightclothes as she prepared for bed. Before she pulled back her sheets, she knelt down beside her bed and began to pray like never before.

Everything in the world seemed to be going wrong at the same time, and there seemed to be little hope on the horizon. Her family was in shambles and Frances didn't have a clue of what to do. Trinika was being controlled by a manacle, overbearing pimp; Willie Joe was lost in a sea of alcoholism; Ernestine was on the verge of going back to her destructive ways; Terrence was hanging on a thread for his life, and Travis, who she'd long ago given up on, was headed fast for a violent collision with death.

The confusion that surrounded Frances constantly grew wider and deeper by the day. She was quickly sinking; sinking fast with the rest of her family down to that pit of destruction. She needed energy, she needed power, and she needed guidance if she were going to stay afloat and survive. And now, more than ever, Frances needed that energy, power, and guidance that only the Lord could provide.

Chapter 14

Ernestine was on a verge of a breakdown. She'd checked into a sleazy motel on the outskirts of Atlanta and had virtually barricaded herself inside her room. Two days had now passed since she'd skidded out of the restaurant parking lot like a bat out of hell with Frances' car, and Ernestine had no plans of leaving the motel anytime soon. She knew Frances was probably worried sick about her whereabouts, but right now, she couldn't worry about that. With everything all in an upheaval, the sanctuary of her motel room felt like the safest place for her. The world outside simply seemed like a wild ferocious jungle, and Ernestine felt like an animal constantly hunted and tracked.

Before checking into the Sunnyview Motel around 10 p.m. two nights ago, Ernestine had stopped by an all-night adult video store near the motel. Wearing dark shades to try to conceal her appearance, Ernestine immediately began to scan the enormous list of titles available along the walls. When she suddenly spotted her naked lewd body once again on the cover of *Cashmere Bitch*, she felt a nauseating tremor ripple over her stomach.

As if out of fear of someone recognizing her, Ernestine quickly looked around to see if anyone else watched as she picked up the DVD and took it to the counter. The attendant behind the counter, it appeared, could've cared less who the woman behind the dark shades was as he rang up the price of the DVD. Ernestine, with nervous trembling hands, quickly paid for her purchase and departed the store.

For the last forty-eight hours, Ernestine had watched herself on tape performing some of the lewdest acts of sex ever filmed. Over and over, she watched herself on tape until she was literally repulsed at what she saw. A number of years had passed by since she'd last made the DVD, but even watching herself now made her realize how much she was used and abused for the sake of a lover who didn't love her.

The pain of watching herself on screen in the most unpleasant light horrified her more than it embarrassed her. She felt angry, hurt, and misused in such a vile contemptible way, that the pain she felt made her ache all over. Ernestine had once thought that her treacherous past was buried and would never come back to haunt her ever again. Now with the re-release of her notorious porn film, her wayward past was suddenly publicized like a flashy new billboard for everyone to see.

Ernestine simply couldn't take the torture on the screen any longer. She finally ejected the DVD from the machine and slung it on the floor as she yelled and cursed at it, as if it were a misbehaving pet that had gotten on her last nerve. Frustrated and totally fed up with the way things were going, Ernestine plopped down on the edge of the bed and buried her head deep within her palms. Her whole head pounded from all the stress and turmoil that she'd been up under for the last two days. She tried to massage her temples to try to relieve some of the stress and pain, but nothing—absolutely nothing—worked.

Finally, Ernestine got up from the bed and went over to her purse sitting on the dresser. She rummaged frantically inside her purse until she found her little black book. When she found the telephone number she was looking for, she went over to the phone on the small table by the bed and quickly dialed the number. Ernestine's heart galloped faster than a race horse as she waited for the person on the other end to pick up.

"Yeah?" a calm, collected voice answered.

"Hey . . ." Ernestine said nervously. "Do you . . . uh . . . you have anything?"

"Who's this?"

"You know who this is!" Ernestine blasted. "I need something right now. Something just to clear my head with."

"I thought you were all dried out. What are you doing calling me looking to cop?"

"Look, I don't want no lecture from you!" Ernestine shouted. "I just need a little something to clear my head with . . . something just to calm down my nerves."

"I . . . I don't know if I really should—"

"Just do you have anything or not?" Ernestine sneered through the phone. "I need something and I need it now!"

The voice on the other end became silent for a few seconds, but Ernestine could definitely hear him debating within his heavy breathing. "Yeah . . ." he finally said reluctantly. "I got some stuff."

"Well, I'm at the Sunnyview Motel. It's about twenty miles north outside of Atlanta, right off of I-75. I'm in the back in room 149. Alright . . . ?"

The voice sighed deeply as if he regretted what he was about to do. "Yeah, alright." He finally consented. "I'll be there in forty minutes."

When Ernestine hung up the phone, she immediately began pacing anxiously back and forth in the room waiting for her contact to arrive. When she grew tired of pacing, she plopped down on the edge of the bed, only to get right back up seconds later and began pacing all over again. The agony of waiting only fueled her desperate desire for a hit. She needed a hit so badly that she could almost taste it; and that taste for a hit was driving her crazy.

Nearly three hours later when Ernestine finally heard a knock at the door, her legs and feet were completely worn out. But Ernestine quickly went to the door and flung it open like she was running from a burning building. The look in her eye was that of a desperate junkie searching for a fix.

"Where the hell you been?" Ernestine scolded. "I've been in here waiting all night for you to show up!"

"I had to take care of some business," Travis said as he entered the room. "It took a little longer than I expected."

"Was that *business* more important than your own mama?"

"I made it, didn't I?" Travis said quickly. "And what are you doing way out here anyway? What the hell are you doing in this crummy motel?"

"Look, I had to get away," Ernestine said before Travis went any further. "I just had to find a place where I could be alone for a while."

"You came all the way out to this damn dump just to be *alone*?" Travis said sarcastically.

"Never mind why I'm here!" Ernestine stormed. "Just where's the stuff?"

"I thought you were cleaned out for good," Travis said as he frowned. "What's up with this stuff all of a sudden?"

"Look, I told you I just need a little something to clear my head. It's nothing really . . . I just need a hit is all."

Travis sighed as he shook his head. "You know Franny ain't going to like this," he said with reservation as he looked Ernestine in the eye. "She finds out I'm giving you the stuff, she's liable to—"

"Never mind that!" Ernestine exploded. "Just give it to me!"

Travis finally relinquished as he handed Ernestine a small bag of crack cocaine and a pipe. He turned and headed for the door, but stopped suddenly before he left out.

"Just don't tell Franny about our . . . transaction," Travis said with a deadpan look as he finally turned and headed out the door.

Ernestine was too busy filling her pipe to even notice Travis leave. When she finally lit the pipe and began to inhale the smoke, she quickly began to feel all of her pent-up stress, anxiety, and pain melt away.

Chapter 15

The lunch hour rush at Frances' Soul Food Restaurant was in high gear as the line trailed outside the door. Jalina, one of Frances' employees working the cash register in Ernestine's absent, had her hands full ringing up the customers as they steadily poured through the line paying for their meals. The steady stream of customers soon became just one face after another as Jalina rang up prices and took money in a rapid, swift fashion. One gentleman, however, who approached her to pay for his meal, suddenly provoked her interest more than the others. She could've sworn she'd seen him before, but somehow, she just couldn't picture where she'd seen his face. The curiosity quickly began to eat away at her as she continued to stare at him.

"Eleven-ninety-five," she quoted the price for the lunch special. When the gentleman handed her a twenty and Jalina handed back his change, she gave him a long, critical look. "Excuse me, sir, have you been in here before?"

"No, I haven't," the man said as he smiled.

"I could've sworn I've seen you somewhere before. Your face really looks familiar."

"Is that a fact." The man chuckled as he seemed to enjoy this young girl's curiosity.

"May I ask what is your name?"

"Skip Hughes." He laughed. "You've probably seen my picture at the top of my editorial. I get that all the time."

Skip Hughes departed for the dining area as Jalina continued ringing up the other customers coming through the line. Jalina, now flushed with the news that she'd just heard, could hardly keep her mind focused on the task of running the cash register. She was like a tea pot on a hot stove ready to explode. The juicy gossip burning on her lips was too much for her to take, and she desperately wanted to tell the other workers who'd just wandered into the restaurant. The lunch hour rush couldn't die down fast enough for her. She was ready to tell someone—*anyone*—what burned on her lips.

When Jalina finally rang up her last customer in line, she quickly darted back to the kitchen. The other workers were busy cleaning pots and pans, and laying out more food for the next wave of customers who were about to invade and besiege the restaurant in the next hour or so. Jalina, with the hot news burning on her lips, quickly looked around the kitchen for Frances.

"Where's Frances?" she asked hurriedly.

"She's out back talking to the delivery man," Earl said as he eyed Jalina. "Why?"

"Y'all will never guess who just came into the restaurant," she said as the other workers began to gather around.

"Who?"

"That Skip Hughes guy. The one who wrote the article about Frances."

"What?" came the stunned responses from the workers. "You're lying?"

Jalina shook her head fiercely. "I ain't lying. He's sitting right out there in the dining area now."

Frances suddenly came back into the kitchen. She looked suspiciously at her workers as they started staring at her.

"Why y'all looking at me like that for?" she said cautiously. "What's going on?"

"Frances . . . uh . . . I think you might want to go out into the dining area," Earl said as he eyed Frances. "Jalina said that Skip Hughes fellow from the *Atlanta Sentinel* just came into the restaurant."

Frances' eyes suddenly bored hard into Earl's face. The other workers stared at Frances and waited silently for some kind of response. Without saying a word, she slowly took off her apron and exited the kitchen. She headed straight for the dining area as Jalina and the rest of the staff followed.

The dining room was packed with the usual customers and faces that normally besieged Frances' restaurant during lunch-time, and Frances quickly got the usual hellos, greetings, and questions heaped upon her from her everyday faithful customers. Frances, however, appeared in no mood for fraternizing. With a stone rigid face, she scanned over the entire dining area like a cop looking for a fugitive on the loose. When she finally spotted Skip Hughes sitting alone eating at a table in the far back, she plowed straight for his table. Everyone in the dining room suddenly looked on as Frances approached her intended target.

"You got some nerve showing your damn face in my restaurant!" Frances exploded.

"Pardon me," Skip Hughes said as he looked up.

"You're not going to just say any filthy thing you want about my family and then come flaunting your pompous behind in my restaurant like nothing has happened." Frances fumed. "You've already caused my family enough grief and pain."

"I only wrote the truth," Skip said in an arrogant voice as he looked up at Frances. "Perhaps you're just in denial of the pain that your *own* family has caused upon itself."

"My family may have made some mistakes and we may have our problems," Frances said heatedly. "But we're no different than any other family—and we're certainly not *jinxed*!"

"Over a million readers seem to think so," Skip said in a calm, self-assured voice.

Frances suddenly glared down at Skip Hughes with all the passion of an angry bull.

"You listen and you listen good," Frances said as she breathed heavily. "You may have the power to scandalize and slander my family in your paper. But you will never—*ever*—destroy the heart and the will of my family. Because we have survived many obstacles, and together we're going to keep right on surviving and striving," she said proudly. "Now get the hell out of my restaurant!"

Skip Hughes looked up at Frances' defiant face and he seemed to know that it was time to leave. He looked around the packed dining area and saw the same defiant looks from the other customers as they stared back at him. As if the negative vibe around the room became too hot for him, Skip wiped his mouth with his napkin as he slowly rose from the table. He gave Frances one last look as she stood only inches from him.

"Well . . . at least I know the Jackson family can cook," Skip said facetiously.

"GET OUT!" Frances roared.

Skip Hughes quickly exited the restaurant as everyone watched in utter silence. When he was finally gone, Frances suddenly looked around at the customers in the dining area as if she just realized that they were there. After a few awkward silent seconds, she finally turned and headed for the kitchen.

———◉———

WHEN FRANCES ARRIVED home that night, she was tired and exhausted from the long, hectic day she'd endured down at the restaurant. She was still somewhat fuming over the incident with Skip Hughes as she flicked on the lights in her kitchen as she headed over to the coffee maker and started up a fresh batch of coffee.

The thought of Skip Hughes blatantly coming into her restaurant after all the scandalous mess he'd created for her family over the last couple of weeks, still burned her to the core of her stomach. She wished she'd just wrapped her hands around his throat right there in the restaurant and strangled the living daylights out of him until he stopped breathing. Even then, Frances wasn't so sure that justice would've been served; somehow, she knew deep down, that his treacherous deeds would still end up haunting her family.

As Frances poured herself a cup of fresh brewed coffee and had a seat at the table, the thought of Ernestine once again began to deeply worry her. It had now been three days since she'd torn out of the parking lot of the restaurant with her car, and still Frances hadn't heard a word from her. She knew that Ernestine was in trouble, but she still held out hope and prayed that Ernestine would just make it back home so they could talk about her problems. However, now Frances began to seriously worry about her health and safety.

Up until now, Francis had avoided contacting the police, knowing that Ernestine probably just needed to get away for a while so she could clear her mind. Now Frances began to feel a nagging, eerie feeling in the pit of her stomach that something was wrong. For the last day or so, she'd felt that eerie feeling steadily growing in her stomach, and for the last day or so, she'd tried to ignore it. But no longer could she ignore it. It had now twisted her stomach into so many lumps and knots, that Frances had to take some kind of action just to relieve the pain.

Without delaying any further, Frances got up to call the police. As soon as she picked up the phone, however, she heard the sound of her car pulling into the driveway.

Frances, stunned and relieved, quickly hung the phone back up as she raced to the door. When she opened the door, she saw Ernestine getting out of the car with the same work clothes she had on the day she tore out of the restaurant parking lot. Frances could immediately tell that Ernestine had fallen prey to her old, destructive habit as Ernestine approached the door. Her hair was wild and uncombed, her clothes were a disheveled mess, and her eyes were bloodshot red. Frances' initial reaction of relief quickly turned to anger when she saw Ernestine's condition.

"Where have you been?" Frances yelled as Ernestine walked past her and went into the house. "I've been worried sick about you. You ain't tried to call or nothing. You hear me talking to you? Ernestine . . . Ernestine!"

Ernestine ignored Frances as she went straight into her room and slammed the door. Frances, boiling with rage, wanted to bust down her door and have a drag down fight. Seeing the situation was all but useless, Frances simply threw up her hands in a defeated gesture and headed for bed.

Chapter 16

Frances arrived at church Thursday night for the weekly seven o'clock choir rehearsal. Tonight was the last tune-up the choir had for the big gospel festival coming up Saturday night at the downtown Civic Center.

For over a month, the choir had worked diligently over the songs that they were going to sing and they'd never sounded better. Frances, who had several important solo parts, had fine-tuned her boisterous voice over the last few days and now sounded better than ever. She'd been looking forward to the gospel festival for a long time and was finally glad that something would take her mind off the problems and woes that had submerged her lately into a pit of misery. Trying to run a hectic restaurant and dealing with the issues of her family all at the same time, was like trying to put out a fire with gasoline. If Frances were going to stay above ground and make it during these troubled, turbulent times, then she needed some kind of escape and release from all of her constant tension and stress. Singing in the choir was the one true joy that gave her the freedom that she so much needed and cherished.

When Frances got out of her car and headed for the church, she noticed that the church parking lot was already filled. Frances checked her watch and knew that she wasn't running late. It was only ten minutes till seven, and more often than not, some of the members of the choir wouldn't arrive until nearly seven-thirty. Frances wasn't about to fret over the early arrival of her fellow choir members. She was only glad that everyone had arrived on time so they wouldn't have to sit around as usual and wait for everyone to slowly trickle in.

The sound of the bellowing voices from the choir startled Frances as she entered the doors of the church. She didn't know if some of the members were merely getting an early start as they ran through a few songs before the full choir began rehearsal.

When Frances entered the sanctuary, however, she was stunned to see the entire choir already deep into rehearsal. As she walked slowly up the aisle, one by one, the members of the choir instinctively stopped singing as if they'd just been caught doing some dastardly deed. Brother Fitzpatrick, the choir director, immediately turned around when the singing began to wane. He almost looked as guilty as the rest of the members of the choir as he watched Frances approaching up the aisle.

"What's going on here?" Frances asked in a confused manner. "I thought rehearsal started at seven."

"Well . . . uh . . . we moved it up to six," Brother Fitzpatrick said rather nervously. "Didn't Reverend Speight talk to you earlier today?"

"Talk to me about what?" Frances said as she glared at Brother Fitzpatrick.

The entire choir stood stock silent as everyone stared down at Frances. Brother Fitzpatrick, as if fearing that the situation was about to get out of hand, quickly turned to his piano player.

"Sister Fellman . . . uh . . . could you take over and start from the very top," the choir director said to the piano player as he stepped down from his post and headed toward Frances.

Frances followed Brother Fitzpatrick as they left out of the sanctuary and headed into Reverend Speight's office. Reverend Speight sat behind his desk preparing his Sunday morning sermon text as they walked in. Brother Fitzpatrick had a seat in one of the empty chairs facing Reverend Speight's desk, as he extended his hand for Frances to sit in the other empty chair. Frances, however, simply folded her arms in a defiant motion as she remained standing. Brother Fitzpatrick seemed to sense that this wasn't going to go easy by the way he began to fidget nervously.

"Reverend Speight . . ." he said with a slight tinge of tenseness in his voice. "Did you contact Sister Frances about the . . . uh . . . arrangements concerning Saturday night."

Reverend Speight sighed as he put away his text. "No, I didn't," he said with deep trepidation. "I thought that since it was your idea, Brother Fitzpatrick, that you should be the one who told Sister Jackson."

"Tell me what—*Brother Fitzpatrick?*" Frances said harshly as she glared down at the choir director who sat nervously in his chair.

Brother Fitzpatrick took off his glasses and began to wipe them clean with a handkerchief that he'd pulled out from his shirt pocket. He seemed in no hurry to speak as he slowly put his glasses back on and looked up at Frances.

"Well, Sister Jackson, it's no secret that you've been under tremendous stress these last few weeks," Brother Fitzpatrick said with a tone of sympathy. "With everything that's been going on lately, I thought it would be best if you didn't push yourself so hard and just relax Saturday night and don't worry about singing with us at the gospel festival. I just thought it would be best with the strain you've been up under and all."

"Oh, you thought it would be *best* for me, huh?" Frances said with a tone of contempt.

"Yes . . . I did, Sister Jackson."

"No, you just don't want my face around to cast a bad shadow over the choir," Frances said with force. "You ain't fooling me one bit!"

"That's not true, Sister Jackson. I just thought it would—"

"It is true!" Frances stormed. "I've been singing in this gospel festival every year for the past fifteen years, and I'll be damn—excuse my language Reverend—if I'm going to let a few bad incidents that's happened with my family over the past few weeks keep me from singing to God."

"Look, I just think it's best if . . . if you didn't."

"I'm singing in that festival, Brother Fitzpatrick," Frances said in a determined voice. "And I ain't going to let you nor the devil stop me."

"I'm sorry, Frances," Brother Fitzpatrick finally said with complete authority in his voice. "The decision has already been made."

Frances felt the finality of his statement hit home like a powerhouse blow straight to her stomach. She looked over at Reverend Speight, and for the first time, she saw the face of a pastor whom she'd always relied on and trusted, suddenly turn away from her. At that moment, she felt a sense of betrayal like she'd never felt before.

"Well, who, may I ask, will be singing the solo parts?" Frances asked in a defeated voice. Brother Fitzpatrick looked over at Reverend Speight, and then he slowly looked back at Frances.

"Sister Mildred Cox will be filling in," he said hesitantly. "Though I know Sister Cox cannot measure up to your powerful, rich voice, I'm sure she'll do quite well."

"Yes . . . I'm *sure* she will," Frances said in a biting tone as she turned to leave. Before she could get out the door, Brother Fitzpatrick quickly stopped her.

"Sister Jackson, you're still a valuable member of this choir," Brother Fitzpatrick said in an encouraging voice. "I just hope you can understand the reason behind my decision."

"Oh, I understand perfectly well," Frances said in a rigid voice. "I just hope you understand that God remembers all ugly things done unto his children."

Frances left out of Reverend Speight's office and stormed out of the church as she headed for the parking lot. When she unlocked her car and got in behind the steering wheel, the tears started falling down her face as she could no longer contain the pain of her emotions. Her body began to shudder as she heaved and cried like never before. The pain and the anguish that she felt attacking her, felt like a million knives cutting into her body; and Frances, for the first time in her life, simply wanted to roll over and die.

When the tears finally subsided, Frances started her car and took off out of the church parking lot. Instead of going straight home, Frances decided to head over and see her best friend, Ermma, the only true friend she still had left in the whole world. With everything going on in her life, Frances needed someone whom *she* could talk to, and a shoulder that *she* could lean on. For the first time since William's death over four decades ago, she no longer felt the invincible role of super woman. Now, feeling deflated and rejected, she felt like plain ordinary Frances in desperate need of a friend.

When Frances parked her car in Ermma's driveway, got out and headed for the house, Ermma had already opened her front door.

"Well, at least I have the common courtesy to call before I just show up." Ermma chided her best friend as she laughed. "But I guess you think you just too good for that."

"I'm sorry, Ermma," Frances said in a dejected voice as she climbed Ermma's porch. "I was feeling so bad . . . I just had to talk to someone."

When Ermma looked into Frances' dispirited, saddened face, she seemed to sense that her best friend of thirty years was in no mood for jokes.

"Sure thing," Ermma said in a consoling voice. "Come on in."

Frances followed Ermma into her kitchen as she had a seat at the table. Ermma poured up two glasses of ice tea before placing one in front of Frances. She then had a seat across from her longtime friend as she stared into her troubled eyes.

"I can tell you're really paining on the inside," Ermma said slowly. "What's bothering you?"

"Everything," Frances said as she ignored her glass of ice tea. "Terrence's situation, Willie Joe and his problems, Trinika caught up out there on the streets, Ernestine falling back to her old ways, Carolyn and her husband constantly fighting, and let's not mention Travis," Frances said as she shook her head with disgust.

"When did Ernestine make it back?"

"Two nights ago. She pulled into the driveway and came barging into the house all stoned out of her head. Since then, she's been in and out of the house like some junkie scrounging around for some dope. Every time I try to talk to her, we just end up fighting and arguing. I'm afraid to put her out because no telling what will happen to her then." Frances complained. "I just don't know what I'm going to do with her, Ermma . . . I just don't know."

"Maybe you should get Reverend Speight to try to talk to her again."

"He's too busy worrying about the precious image of the church!" Frances bellowed. "He and Brother Fitzpatrick don't want me singing in the Gospel Festival this Saturday. They claimed I've been under too much stress lately, but we all know the real reason behind it. I'm too much of an embarrassment for the church these days."

"Reverend Speight actually said that?"

"He didn't have to," Frances said in a steamed voice. "I could see it plain as day in his face. He just had Brother Fitzpatrick to do the talking for him."

Ermma seemed to feel the overwhelming grief Frances was going through as she reached out and gently touched Frances' hand as if to give her best friend the support that she needed.

"All of this is going to blow over," Ermma said in a reassuring voice. "You just continue on being strong for your family. Because when things get hard and it seems like everyone is against you, all you got in this world is your family. Don't let nobody tear apart what you have, Frances," she said in a determined voice. "Keep your family together no matter what it takes. You hear me?"

"But, Ermma, how in the world am I going to keep my family together?" Frances said hopelessly. "My whole family is in total shambles."

"Well . . . you've always said God will make a way," Ermma said as she peered deeply into Frances' eyes. "Then I suggest you keep right on believing that."

Frances stared into her best friend's eyes for what seemed like minutes. It slowly dawned on her that through all the turmoil and tragedy that she'd watched her family go through over the last couple of weeks, she realized she'd lost the one true thing that mattered the most; and that was her unwavering, unmitigated faith in God that He would always make matters right. She stared at Ermma and slowly nodded.

"You're right," Frances said slowly. "God *will* make a way."

Frances suddenly began to feel a renewed strength in Ermma's powerful words as if God Himself had laid those uplifting words on Ermma's heart to say. They seemed to brush clear all the clutter that had clogged up her mind over the last few days and brought her back to where she knew she needed to be: and that was with her faith that God would make a way to save her family.

Ermma and Frances didn't have much to say after that as they sipped ice tea and talked about old times, but when Frances left and headed home for the night, she wasn't worried anymore about the gospel festival, nor her restaurant, or not even the gossip or rumors constantly swirling around her and her family like dirty, stagnant water. Her one and only mission was to save her beleaguered, lost family from utter destruction, and that God would show her the way.

Chapter 17

I t was six weeks away from Terrence's murder trial and the media frenzy was about to blow through the roof. The scrutiny surrounding the murder, and even more, the scrutiny surrounding the Jackson family seemed to intensify with each passing day. Every night the national talk shows seemed to add a new twist to the facts of the murder as they hyped the upcoming trial like it was a major heavyweight bout about to square off. The constant questions, the probing, and the never-ending inquisitions into the troubling history of the Jackson family, continued to heighten as it soon turned into a national soap opera on the television screens all over America.

The key component driving this massive interrogation of this trouble ridden family and stirring so much talk was none other than the Skip Hughes' editorial. His editorial had now reached national attention and had inflamed widespread intrigue all across the country. Every late-night show scrambled to get this journalist's insight of this family that was wallowing in so much quagmire, and Skip Hughes was more than willing to express his views before the cameras. With so much insight and information spewed forth nightly over the tube, the murder of Joletta Anderson and the woes of the Jackson family quickly became America's obsession.

Frances sat back and watched the nightly crucifixion of her family in muted horror. Since that evening at Ermma's house, she'd vowed to ignore the constant gossip and rumors swirling around her family, and instead, focus her time and energy on bringing her family back from the rift that had separated them and shattered their lives. However, the longer Frances endured watching her family's past problems and misdeeds scandalized and victimized for the world to see, she became more heated and determined to come to the defense of her beleaguered family.

She was determined to give her family a voice—a positive voice—and set the record straight once and for all about the troubled history of her family. Frances, with the power of God behind her, was determined to bring some justice to the Jackson family name. No matter what it took, she was ready to go through the fire for the sake of her family.

With her heart and soul totally committed to this daunting challenge, Frances didn't waste any time pulling any punches. With a generous portion of her money already going out to pay Terrence's lawyer, Frances went out on the limb once again. She hired a publicist to help put a positive spin and image on the face of her family, and to get her out there in the mainstream to defend her family. With so much attention surrounding the upcoming trial, it didn't take long for the networks to start calling.

Frances hit the talk show circuit and went on one show after another as she defended her family against the vicious attacks swirling around her family. *Anderson Cooper 360, The Rachel Maddow Show, Hannity, Tucker Carlson Tonight,* and the morning shows *Good Morning America, Today,* and *CBS Mornings* became stops in an all-out effort to redeem the Jackson family name to the world. Frances, poised but yet undaunted, stood before the cameras and the studio microphones as she professed the diligence, the honor, and the moral integrity of her family.

On numerous occasions she was pitted head-to-head with journalist Skip Hughes as their discussions and debates over the history of her family became heated, fierce battles over the tube. But Frances, with the power of God behind her, wouldn't deter easily. Despite the attacks, the accusations, and charges that kept raining down on her like a fierce hail storm, Frances stood firm in the face of the world's unrelenting criticism. She was undaunted, fearless, and defiant all for the sake of her cause.

THE NIGHT BEFORE FRANCES was to fly to Washington to take part in a panel discussion on the state of the African-American family on the network, BET, God laid it on her heart to call an emergency meeting of her family to meet at her house to discuss their problems. Frances knew no matter how much she defended her family to the world on one talk show after another, that if they as a group didn't iron out their problems and come together as a true family, no amount of preaching to the outside world would make any difference.

They, the Jackson family, would have to fix their own problems and come together before they could stand together against the world. Frances knew that it was downright essential that they try to work out the strife, the conflict, and the division tearing apart her family. They had to try to heal that gaping wound that continued to grow deeper by the day. It was imperative that they come together before the trial began, before the media scrutiny would be even more tenacious than it already was. Things were about to get very heated over the next couple of weeks, and they as a family, needed to stand together as one.

By 7 p.m., Frances' family had scantily filled her living room. Ernestine sat by herself in an armchair looking bored and half stoned; Willie Joe and Patricia sat next to one another on the couch, with Willie Joe looking uncomfortable and in desperate need of a drink; Carolyn and George sat on the other end of the couch, and both looked as if they'd rather be in two separate places. Terrence, Trinika, and Travis were the only other family members who weren't present. Terrence, it was obvious, had a legitimate reason for his absence. Trinika and Travis, on the other hand, were simply nowhere to be found.

The rift and the tension that hovered over Frances' living room were as thick as fog on an early dank morning. No one said a word as everyone ignored one another like strangers at a crowded bus station. Only Frances, who stood in the middle of the room like a street cop keeping the peace, looked as if she cared about what was going on. Everyone knew that she'd called this strange, unexpected meeting, and everyone waited for *her* to start the ball rolling.

"I'm glad that y'all could make it over here on such short notice." Frances began as she looked at everyone. "I called this meeting so we could discuss our problems, so that we may once and for all put aside our grievances and come together as a family. We've been a fractured family for too long, and I believe it's time that we bond together and try to help one another through our personal difficulties. If we pull together and help one another, the process toward healing our deep, inflicted wounds would go a lot smoother."

Frances looked at everyone with a cautious eye. The living room remained silent as if everyone waited for the next person to confess their sins.

The seconds ticking from the huge grandfather clock in the corner of the room sounded louder by the second.

"How long is this going to last?" Willie Joe suddenly blurted out impatiently.

"As long as it takes!" Frances snapped as she glared at Willie Joe.

"How the hell are we going to come together as a family?" Willie Joe pouted.

"God will make a way," Frances said boldly.

"This ain't nothing but a waste of time." Ernestine griped as she folded her arms and pouted. "We just sitting around here looking at each other like a bunch of fools."

"Well, it certainly takes one to know one." Carolyn inserted as she eyed Ernestine.

"I didn't call this meeting for none of that!" Frances blasted as she glared around the room. "There are enough rocks and stones already being thrown at this family by outsiders. We certainly don't need to be throwing any stones among ourselves. We *must* come together and save this family!"

"This family has been lost ever since our wonderful father plunged us into darkness," Willie Joe said bitterly. "And ever since, we ain't been able to do nothing right."

"Will you stop it!" Patricia snapped. "Just stop it."

"Stop what?" Willie Joe griped. "Everyone knows it's the truth. Hell, the whole world knows it's the truth."

"Willie Joe, you've been using your father as an excuse for every problem that you've ever had in your life." Frances scolded. "It's time to let that go. It's time to move on from that."

"We can't move forward, Franny," Willie Joe said with the straightest face. "Daddy has jinxed us all."

"This family is not jinxed!" Frances said with a vicious huff. "And I'm sick and tired of hearing that. WE ARE NOT JINXED!" she roared loud enough to scare an elephant.

A pager went off as everyone suddenly looked over at George. George checked his pager as he quickly rose from the couch. His look was all business, and by his expression, he was more than ready to leave this farce of a meeting.

"Don't tell me you've got to leave?" Carolyn looked up at her husband with concern.

"It's the office, Carolyn," he said hastily as he pulled out his cellphone. "I've got to check in."

"It's Sunday. What can possibly be going on at the office?"

"Will you excuse me, Mrs. Jackson, I have to make an important call?" George said as he ignored Carolyn.

Frances slowly nodded as George quickly headed out of the room to make his phone call. Everyone was suddenly drawn to silence by the interruption.

"Afraid your man stepping out on you?" Ernestine chided as she looked over at Carolyn. Carolyn looked back at Ernestine with contempt.

"No, I'm not."

"You look mighty worried to me."

"You need to be worried about straightening out your own crazy life instead of worrying about my business." Carolyn simmered. "I'm not the one everyone is talking about spreading her legs in the hottest selling horny slut video!"

"I'm not going to stand for this nasty talking!" Frances flared. "I didn't call us together for all this needling and fighting one another!"

"I'm sorry, Mrs. Jackson, but I've got to make an emergency run," George said as he stepped back into the living room. "My presence is required for some important business."

"What business?" Carolyn rose from the couch as she approached George.

"I want you to know that you're very much a part of this family, George." Frances implored. "We're going to need your support to pull this family together just like everyone else."

George reluctantly nodded as he quickly headed for the door. Carolyn was right on his heel.

"What kind of important business you got to tend to, George?" Carolyn persisted as she followed him out the door. "Do you hear me talking to you . . . George . . . George . . . *George?*"

When George got into his car and sped away, Carolyn came back into the living room and had a seat once again on the couch. She was steaming mad and everyone knew it.

"I guess he's headed over to that hot date after all." Ernestine smirked.

"At least I got a husband and a *home*." Carolyn exploded. "What have you got? You still scrounging around here living off of Franny."

"I don't need no husband, Miss Thang!"

"Who would want your ass after you done screwed every Joe Blow west of the Mississippi."

"Carolyn, Ernestine, stop it!" Frances yelled. "Just stop it right now!"

"You need to kick your forty-year-old drug addict, whore of a daughter out of your house," Carolyn yelled as she stood up and pointed over at Ernestine. "She ain't nothing but trash and ain't going to be nothing more."

"Oh, that sounds real educated coming from someone that's got a Ph.D." Ernestine shot back as she rose up and confronted Carolyn.

"At least I got an education. The only thing you learned was how to be a whore on the street!"

"Carolyn, Ernestine, that's enough!" Frances roared.

"It's no use, Franny, we're all jinxed anyway." Willie Joe piped in. "I saw this once on the animal channel. When the head male neglects his family, all of his critters turn out bad. There's nothing you can do about it."

"Shut up, Willie Joe!" Frances sneered as she literally got between her two squabbling daughters who were about to come to blows. "Will you two stop it! I've had enough of this bickering! *Ernestine! Carolyn! Ernestine!*"

When her two squabbling daughters continued arguing at a heated pace, Frances finally threw up her arms and headed for her bedroom. She slammed her door and set on the edge of her bed as she tried to massage away her massive headache. However, the more she tried, the louder it continued to get out in the living room.

Chapter 18

The next morning when Frances' flight arrived at the Washington's Dulles International Airport, Frances departed from the plane and was treated to curbside limousine service compliments of BET. She was taken to the Hilton Garden Inn Hotel where she checked in and received her complimentary room overlooking the prime of Washington D.C.'s famous landmarks and buildings.

Frances, after her long flight from Atlanta, was simply too tired to stare and peer out her hotel window at the extravagance of Washington. After a long, tedious night dealing with her quarrelsome family, she was bushed and exhausted. She'd hardly gotten any sleep after listening to Carolyn and Ernestine fussing and fighting in her living room till virtually midnight. The ruckus in her living room last night could've awakened the dead, and after enduring the long flight to Washington with a massive headache, Frances thought she was dead or virtually near it. The only thing she wanted more than anything to quell her shattered nerves was some good sound sleep. And after a long night listening to arguing, fussing, cursing, and fighting, a nice peaceful room was just what the doctor ordered.

By 5 p.m., Frances was finally rested and refreshed. She put on her most conservative Sunday blue dress, and her most refined, but not gaudy, jewelry on as she checked her make-up in the mirror for the last time.

Frances was ready for this nationally televised panel on the state of the African-American family. After three weeks of appearing on one talk show after another, Frances was used to appearing before the cameras. She was calm and composed under the bright lights, but also tenacious and persistent at answering the tough questions and standing firm for her family's name and reputation. The talk show producers loved her uncompromising tenacity, which made for fierce debates and good ratings.

Tonight's format, however, wouldn't be in the confines of a studio, but aired in front of a live auditorium audience with a panel of experts in esteemed professional fields from all around the country. Frances was the only scheduled panelist without the highly regarded credentials and the educational background that her fellow panelist would have. But as she looked into her hotel bathroom mirror for the last time before heading down to the limousine that waited for her in front of the hotel, Frances knew that with the power of God behind her, she could stand up to any test that came her way. She was a warrior, a fearless warrior, and she was ready to put on the shield of armor to protect her family.

<hr />

FRANCES ARRIVED BACKSTAGE of the Washington Convention Center at 6 p.m., a full hour before the live airing of the nationally televised panel discussion. She was welcomed and greeted by the producers, the behind-the-scenes people, and other guest panelists as everyone chatted and got to know one another. Frances began to relax and feel at ease around her more noteworthy co-panelists until she saw Skip Hughes suddenly enter the backstage door.

Skip Hughes, dressed in a fine dark blue Armani suit, had the swagger of an important politician as he entered the room. Frances' blood immediately began to boil as she glared at this unwanted shyster who'd given her family such a disdainful reputation. She'd gone head-to-head over the last couple of weeks with Skip Hughes on various talk shows since she started this media blitz, and the contempt for this man continued to grow by the day.

Frances wanted no part of this pompous rude scoundrel, but she was afraid she had no choice. She watched him carefully as he made his way around the room shaking hands and greeting other panelists, like a cautious farmer watching a fox getting too close to his barn. Frances almost wished she had a rifle so she could pick off this villainous wolf dressed in sheep's clothing, but Frances knew better than that. She knew the only way to put Skip Hughes in his place was to stand her ground and not budge an inch.

"Why, hello, Mrs. Jackson," Skip Hughes said with a frivolous smile as he approached Frances. He extended his hand for Frances to shake, but Frances just looked at him as if he were one of the devil's angels who'd come to offer her a deadly apple. Skip quickly retrieved his hand when he saw that Frances wasn't about to engage in any small talk, but his frivolous smile remained.

"Why am I not surprised to see a low-down scamp like you here tonight," Frances said with a face deadly enough to scare a rattle snake.

"Wherever you go, Mrs. Jackson, I too must go also," Skip said like a professor lecturing an ignorant student. "Our battles have been good for the networks. Every show we've been on, the ratings have been great, or didn't you know that?"

"I don't give a damn about no ratings," Frances said in a controlled but terse voice. "You think this is some game, but I don't. I'm not here seeking no kind of thrill or some perverted fame as you seem to be, Mr. Hughes. I'm only here to see that justice is served by my family's name and reputation."

"Well, that *justice* you're seeking has brought you all the way to Washington to appear before a panel discussion on BET. Your face has been on television sets all over America because of me. Face it, Mrs. Jackson," he said with a tone of arrogance. "If it weren't for my article, you wouldn't be as well-known as you are today. And I know for a fact that all this publicity has been a tremendous boost to your restaurant. So, instead of saying disparaging things about me and calling me names, I think you owe me a bit of gratitude, Mrs. Jackson."

"I don't owe you a damn pot to piss in." Frances seethed as she glared at Skip Hughes. "I'd go to the moon to defend the honor of my family, which you so viciously tried to destroy. There are some things in life that you hold sacred to and never let go like dignity, decency, honesty, and loyalty to your family. Something I'm sure you were never taught, young man!"

Frances stormed off as she went out onto the stage and took her place at the panel discussion table. She was too early to be seated, but the producers had no luck trying to dissuade this fierce, determined lady otherwise. They could tell right off the bat that Frances was going to be a whirlwind of a guest.

THE PANEL DISCUSSION on the state of the African-American family got off to an energetic start before the packed Washington Convention Center. The live airing before the BET cameras gave the format a special feel to it as this momentous occasion played out before millions of viewers around the country.

The distinguished panel of noted black psychologists, sociologists, counselors, historians, clergymen, and of course the most contentious duo, Skip Hughes and Frances Jackson, spouted off their vast knowledge and expertise as the bright lights shone down on them and the spectators in the convention center hung on to every word they said. The atmosphere of this much anticipated debate was cordial as the participants of the discussion were respectful of their fellow colleague's views. There was no animosity between any of the panelists, even Frances and Skip Hughes seemed to outwardly respect each other's opinions before the cameras.

About an hour into the discussion, though, things became heated. Sensitive topics and issues in the realm of the black family were touched upon, and without surprise, Frances and the dilemma that her family was currently entangled in became the subject of serious debate. The fiery debate created a storm of controversy as Frances stood in the middle of it all. She defended her family as if she were a gallant warrior who had a bloody sword wrenched in her hand.

"There's absolutely no documented proof or any kind of research to my knowledge that supports the philosophy that the black woman is incapable of raising a family and instilling wholesome values within her family absent the black father," the noted psychologist, Dr. Laura Benjamin, said in a steamed voice. "That philosophy is totally inaccurate and a fabrication of a Caucasian male dominated influence within the media."

"But surely you don't contend that without the black father, the mother is still capable of raising a family to the full extent as that family should be raised," the highly regarded sociologist, Dr. Peter Winn countered. "That's a slap in the face of every black man in America."

"No, I do not support such notions, but the black woman has clearly proven throughout countless decades that she can raise her family and instill the necessary values that's needed in society in the unfortunate absence of the father."

A spatter of applause rippled through the convention center. The crowd quickly became just as heated and agitated as the participants on stage.

"Mrs. Jackson, you stated a couple of moments ago that the media has been unduly bias toward you for not instilling the proper values within your family," the moderator said as he injected. "Do you believe that the media promotes that negative view in general for the majority of single black mothers in America?"

"Unfortunately, I do," Frances quickly responded. "I cannot speak for every single black mother in this country, but from the very beginning, I instilled good wholesome virtues in every one of my children right down to my grandchildren. As single black mothers, we're under tremendous strain and pressure to raise our families. Whenever problems do arise within our families, the media is quick to point to a breakdown in the whole structure of the black family."

"Mr. Hughes, as a member of the media, do you attest to the notion that the single black mother is viewed negatively by the media?"

"Well, in my opinion, the black father is the one that has been unfairly tarnished and hasn't been very well respected by the white mainstream media," Skip said as he looked down at the panelists. "But as far as Mrs. Jackson's family, they've given the mainstream media an open door to categorize all black families as being unprincipled, lawless, and rebellious. They've created this negative image in America that all black families are dysfunctional, and that's totally an aberration of what the black family is today."

"I beg your pardon, Mr. Hughes," Frances said heatedly, "but I believe you've created all this hysteria lately in the media about the black family, by martyring my family and making us scapegoats just to advance your personal goals."

"I've done no such thing, Mrs. Jackson," Skip said with just as much passion. "And you're only fooling yourself if you think your family is a victim of some journalistic conspiracy to undermine and shame your family. If anything, your family has done nothing but shame the black race and provided us with a clear example of how the black family *should not be*."

"Every black family, or any family for that matter, has had their share of problems, Mr. Hughes," Frances said vehemently. "Yes, we've had our problems. But we are not monsters, or freaks, or some bunch of crazed fiends running around on the streets—and we're certainly not *jinxed*. You seem to be so much of an authority on my family, but I've never heard nigh a word about your family Mr. Hughes. Let's see what's hidden in *your* family closet, Mr. Skip Hughes."

A round of applause suddenly thundered around the convention hall. Skip Hughes, though, was not about to be deterred.

"I can tell you no one in my family has never incited a rebellion and caused major riots, killings, and widespread destruction to an entire city," Skip said in a fiery voice as his anger began to rise. "No one in my family has never peddle drugs or stood accused for rape. No one in my family has ever shot an innocent harmless kid returning home late one night from work. No one in my family has ever been a prostitute on the street, and no one—absolutely no one in my family—has ever been charged with murdering the daughter of a highly esteemed mayor, Mrs. Jackson!"

"Well just because your mama didn't tell you she was a whore, don't mean that she wasn't!" Frances snapped.

A thunderous sound erupted through the convention hall as the mixture of laughter and applause went off like a bomb. The shocked panelists looked at one another as their stunned reactions were clearly evident on every one of their faces. A commercial was desperately needed to hose down the hysteria that Frances had ignited by her comment, but on this special evening when the panel discussion on the state of the African-American family was aired live around the country uninterrupted, there were no commercials.

The moderator, appearing stunned and shocked himself, grappled for words to say as he tried to get the discussion back on track. But even if he had a gavel and a loud speaker, he couldn't squash the ruckus that Frances had ignited around the packed convention center.

Chapter 19

Frances arrived back in Atlanta the following afternoon as she took a cab from the airport and made her final journey for home. She was truly exhausted and tired from her long extraordinary night, and she wanted nothing better than to crawl into her own bed and take a long, restful nap. Frances thought about going down to the restaurant first to check how things were going there, but she knew Earl and the rest of the crew probably had things under control. Besides, she needed some time alone to herself. After a long night of appearing before a convention center full of folk, she wasn't quite ready for a restaurant full of people and all of their inquiring questions.

When the cab pulled into the driveway of her home, Frances saw Travis' Hummer parked at the curb of her house. Her blood immediately began to boil, but she kept her temper and emotions in check. She quickly paid the cab driver and grabbed her luggage as she headed for her house. She couldn't find her door keys quickly enough as she stood on her porch rambling around inside her purse. When she finally found her keys, she unlocked her door and slowly entered her house.

There was no sign of anyone as Frances came into the living room. The house seemed a little too quiet for her, and for a moment, she wondered was anyone there at all. But when she ventured into the kitchen, she liked to had a heart attack. Ernestine and Travis were sitting at the table snorting lines of cocaine. Totally unaware of Frances' presence, they immediately jumped when they heard her voice.

"What in God's name is going on in here?" Frances boomed.

Travis quickly tried to clear away the cocaine, but it was too late. With white powder smeared all around his nose, he looked up at Frances with petrified eyes.

"Uh . . . it's not what you think, Franny," Travis stammered as he put away the rest of the cocaine. "We were just . . . uh—"

"Get out!" Frances yelled. "Get out of my house, right now!"

"Hey, look, Franny...uh...it ain't my fault." Travis laughed nervously as he suddenly tried to make light of the situation. "She was the one who called me." He quickly pointed over at Ernestine. "*She* was the one who wanted to have a little fun."

Frances' eyes suddenly turned as red as a bull. With one quick motion, she went over to the kitchen drawer and yanked out the biggest butcher knife ever seen. With the knife firmly in her hand, she charged at Travis like a cold bloodied killer in a dark alley.

"GET OUT OF MY HOUSE—RIGHT NOW!" Frances roared as she wielded the knife within inches of Travis' face.

Travis quickly got up from the table and dashed out of the house faster than a bolt of lightning. The sound of his tires burning rubber on the street as he sped away sounded like a race car on the Indy 500 speedway. After Travis left, Frances then turned and glared down at Ernestine. Francis had a fiery, diabolical look in her eyes that would make even the hardest gangster run for cover. Ernestine merely looked up at Frances in a nonchalant manner as if just awakening from a dream. By the look of her dazed eyes, she was on cloud nine and could feel no pain.

"So...you going to kill me now?" Ernestine said calmly.

The words suddenly shook Frances out of her diabolical trance. She heard her daughter's words loud and clear, and they were words of defeat and despair. She looked into Ernestine's eyes and saw a person who didn't care if she lived or died, or cared if she made it to another day. Frances saw the utter hopelessness of the situation as she let the knife slip from her hand as it dropped to the floor. When she could no longer look at Ernestine any longer, she simply turned and headed slowly out of the kitchen.

LATER THAT EVENING, Frances decided to get out of the house. She was so infuriated and outraged with Ernestine, that she was afraid if she stayed a second longer in that house, she'd do something that she'd surely regret later.

With that in mind, Frances headed on down to the restaurant to work awhile as she tried to relieve some of her anger and tension. However, being back at the restaurant didn't help at all. It only made her more irritated and more edgy. She was cranky and in no mood for bantering and socializing with her staff and customers, which was totally unlike her warm-hearted robust character.

Everyone wanted to talk about and fuss over her appearance last night on BET and congratulate her on finally putting Skip Hughes in his place, but Frances didn't care a thing about that. The only thing she could think about at the moment was Travis and Ernestine defiling her house with their filthy drugs, and the more she thought about it, the more it burned her to the core of her soul.

Around eight-thirty when it drew near the time to close up for the night, a young woman came in from off the street and asked to see Frances. The place had virtually emptied of all customers as the staff was busy in the back washing mounds of dishes, putting away food, taking out the trash, and preparing for tomorrow's opening.

The new cashier, who'd been working no more than a few days at the restaurant, headed reluctantly to the back to find Frances. Everyone had pretty much avoided Frances and didn't want any of her wrath after they saw the foul mood she was in. All night she'd constantly snapped and berated her staff, and no one wanted to cross her path.

When the young, new cashier came into Frances' office and said that someone out front desperately needed to see her, Frances shot off a round of obscenities as she stormed toward the front. She was ready to tell whomever it was to get out of her restaurant and keep right on walking, but when she saw Trinika standing next to the cash register in her skimpy little dress with her face all bruised and bloodied, her heart nearly dropped. She could hardly contain her emotions as she looked at the pitiful sight that her baby granddaughter was in.

"Trinika . . . baby . . . are you alright?" Frances said as she slowly approached her and touched her gently on her bruised face. Trinika suddenly began to shake and tremble all over as she let out a shower of tears. A whole minute passed before she was finally able to speak.

"I . . . I just can't take it anymore, Franny." She sobbed. "I got to get away from him . . . I got to get away."

"Who did this to you, child?" Frances demanded as she stared at her face. "Was it that monster?"

Trinika slowly nodded. "He won't stop beating me. It's only gotten worse the last few weeks."

"Why's that fool beating on you?" Frances yelled.

"He said . . . I ain't bringing in enough money," Trinika said through painful sobs. "I just can't take the beatings no more, Franny . . . I can't take it no more."

Trinika finally collapsed into Frances' arms as she let out all the pain and suffering that she'd gone through over the last two years. Frances held her granddaughter tightly to her chest as she comforted and eased her pain. The rest of Frances' staff eventually came out and surrounded them as they watched what took place, but Frances and Trinika were in their own little world.

"It's alright, child," Frances said softly as she continued to hold Trinika. "You're coming home with me."

Frances and Trinika held each other for what seemed like hours; it seemed that neither one of them could've cared less if it were days.

Chapter 20

Frances arrived down at the jail at ten on the dot for her regular Saturday morning visit with Terrence. Since Terrence's high-profile arrest, Frances had made it a habit to visit him at least once a week. She'd stayed faithful pretty much to her routine, missing her regular visits lately only because of her busy whirlwind tour of late-night talk shows and her recent appearance in Washington for the State of the African-American Family Summit. Frances, however, was determined to get back to her routine. She knew Terrence needed all the support that he could get during this trying time, and Frances was going to make sure that she was there to give it to him.

When Frances entered the visitation room and had a seat at the phone station as she waited for Terrence to be brought in, she noticed that every eye in the room was dead on her. By now, Frances was used to all of the attention.

Since she'd been coming to the jail to see her grandson, she'd received all sorts of curious looks and stares. The media saturation of Terrence's arrest, the upcoming trial, and the scandals about her family in the press had created a storm of attention. Frances could tell since the last time she was at the jail, that the looks, the stares, and whispers seemed more intense. She knew that her appearances on the late-night talk shows and being on that panel in Washington a few days ago, had created more of a stir around the city then she could imagine. She realized that despite going in front of the world for the sole purpose of defending her family, that lately, she'd become somewhat of a celebrity. Frances simply didn't want any fifteen minutes of fame. She only wanted a lifetime of respect and justice for her family.

Terrence entered the side of the visitation room where the inmates came in as he went straight to the seat facing directly across from Frances. He wasn't escorted by a guard or wearing any handcuffs as he had on his first initial visitations; he just sauntered in as if this were his home, his place of residence.

Frances picked up the phone on her side as he did likewise. She looked at him with concern as she stared across the glass partition. Every time she came to visit, he looked more disheveled than before. His cornrows were not as neat as before, and his once immaculate goatee had now grown wild and shabby. Frances couldn't stand that orange issued jumpsuit that he wore every time she saw him. She couldn't wait for the day when he'd finally be free from this monstrosity of a jail, and that orange issued jumpsuit that made her eyes burn.

"What's shaking, Franny?" came Terrence's upbeat greeting.

"How you making it, child?" Frances said with deep concern. "You still holding up over there?"

"I'm still holding up, Franny. You don't have to worry about me so much."

"But I do," Frances said with conviction. "As long as you're locked up in this place, I worry."

"I'm staying strong for you, Franny," Terrence said for her reassurance. "I hear you been a busy lady lately," he said with a cocky smile. "I heard you been all over the tube fighting that Skip Hughes guy. I hear you been laying down the law. The way I hear it, Franny, you been working it better than Oprah ever could."

"I just did what I had to do to protect this family, child," Frances said without pretentiousness. "This family has been stomped on and treaded on long enough. It's time for the world to know that we deserve respect."

"Naw, you deserve respect, Franny," Terrence said adamantly as he pointed his finger at the glass as he stared across at Frances. "You the only one this family can truly look up to."

"I want everyone in this family to be looked up to and respected, and not just looked down on and scandalized in some old newspaper."

"Well, I think people are going to have a hard time ever respecting that trifling ass so called mama of mine. If there's anyone who's dragging the family down, it's her," Terrence said with bitterness. "I heard about that porno film being re-released. I got guys in this joint constantly talking about all the stuff that they'd love to do to my mama if they had the chance. Word about that damn DVD is all over this jail. Guys can't stop talking about it. Now how do you think that makes me feel."

Frances closed her eyes as she sighed. She didn't want Terrence to know about the DVD, but she knew she couldn't hide it from him forever. She knew that he wasn't exaggerating about the stories circulating inside the jail. The stories already spreading through the streets were probably more sordid than the ones circulating inside here.

"Look, despite what people may say or think about Ernestine, she's still your mother," Frances said earnestly. "And you must always remember that—*she is your mother*."

"My *mother*!" Terrence said bitterly through the phone. "And just where the hell has my *mother* been since I been in here. That old trifling junkie ain't came to see me since that first day that I was arrested."

"Terrence, you watch what you say!" Frances said loudly. "I'll not allow you to talk that way about Ernestine!"

Frances suddenly realized that she'd gotten too loud as a couple other visitors sitting close to her peered a hard gaze in her direction. Frances ignored the looks and stares as she stared hard across the glass at Terrence.

"Look, I know none of y'all have never really been close to Ernestine, and I know that Ernestine hasn't really never made herself available for y'all over the years," Frances said in a more restrained voice. "But Ernestine has been going through some very difficult times lately, and she . . . she just needs our support. And if this family is ever going to come together, then we're going to have to learn to support one another."

"You really think that our family is actually going to come together," Terrence said in an almost facetious tone. "We've never been together at nothing, Franny, and I don't think that we ever will."

"You're wrong, child!" Frances said heatedly as if she wanted to come through the glass and straighten her grandson out. "This family is going to come together and I'm going to do whatever it takes to bring us together if it's the last thing I ever do."

"And just how are we going to come together, Franny?" he said derisively. "Us come together—you *got* to be kidding me."

"God will make a way," Frances said in a fiery tone. "We're going to be a united family. You, me, Carolyn, Ernestine, Willie Joe, Trinika—we're all going to come together and be one whole family."

"And what about Travis?" Terrence said slowly.

There was a long silence as Terrence stared over at Frances, and as Frances stared back at him.

"There's nothing I can do for him," Frances finally said in a sharp, curt voice as she eyed Terrence.

"Look, Franny, I know Travis put you through the ringer the last time you stood by him. But don't give up on him," Terrence said like a big brother who still wanted to look out for his little brother. "He still respects you . . . you know."

"*Respects* me," Frances said in a mocking voice. "The only thing that child has ever respected was living fast in them streets. That child has *never* respected me. He's a hoodlum, and he ain't nothing but trouble."

"Yeah, I know, Franny," Terrence said reluctantly. "But I'm starting to become really concerned that Travis is moving a little too fast in them streets. I've been hearing some stories from a couple of inmates about my little brother. And the word is that Travis is getting ready to move some heavy stuff on the street. Hell, Franny, he's even told me himself one time when he came here to visit me. Travis is moving too fast, and I think he needs to be stopped before he gets in too deep."

Frances looked across at Terrence with deep set eyes. The venomous look in her eyes was deadly.

"I've done all I could do for Travis," Frances said solemnly. "There's nothing more that I can do for him."

Frances hung up the phone as she rose from her chair and headed out of the room. It was clear by the way she moved quickly, that she didn't want to hear Travis' name ever again.

———◉———

FRANCES WAS SUDDENLY awakened by the sound of knocking at her front door. She rolled over as she tried to strain and see the alarm clock on her dresser through the pitch darkness in her bedroom. The alarm clock said 3 a.m. and Frances didn't have a clue who could be knocking at her door at this hour of the night. She wondered if Ernestine, or maybe even Trinika whom she'd brought home from the restaurant the other night to stay with her, had left the house and was trying to get back in. Somehow, though, her intuition told her that it wasn't. Something just wasn't right, and Frances could feel it in her bones.

When the knocking continued to persist, Frances got up quickly from her bed as she threw on her robe. She flicked on the lamp on her dresser as she reached into her night stand and retrieved her revolver. In the twenty years since Frances had owned the gun, she'd probably held it maybe two or three times. Tonight, however, she gripped it firmly like a seasoned cop as she headed out of the bedroom.

The knocking only grew louder as she proceeded through the pitch-dark living room as she made her way slowly to the door. Her heart raced like mad and her mind rattled with fear, but Frances was ready to protect her home.

When the knocking continued to grow ever louder, Frances inched up against the door as she tried to look out the peep hole. The darkness outside only concealed who stood on the porch.

"Who's out there?" Frances demanded as she continued to strain through the peep hole.

A long, ominous silence hovered in the air.

"Open up this damn door," came a calm, but forceful voice.

"Who the hell are you?" Frances blasted.

"I want Trinika and I want her now," came the forceful voice. "Now open up this damn door before I tear it down."

Frances finally switched on the porch light and saw Daddy T., Trinika's pimp, standing on her porch. Her fear quickly turned to absolute rage when she saw the villain who stood on her porch.

"What are you doing on my porch?" Frances seethed. "How did you get this address?"

"Open up the door, lady!" Daddy T. roared.

"If you don't get your ass off my porch, I'm calling the police." Frances steamed. "Now get off my porch!"

"I ain't going nowhere till I see Trinika." Daddy T. roared. "Now open up this damn door!"

Frances slowly opened the door as she leveled the revolver dead at Daddy T. as she stood behind the locked storm door. Daddy T. seemed unfazed as he stared at Frances with all the vengeance of a street thug willing to do what it took to reclaim what was his. His six-foot-five frame looked imposing as he stood on the porch, but Frances wasn't about to retreat one inch.

"If you don't get the hell off of my porch, you going to be frying in hell a whole lot quicker than you think. Now get off of my porch!" Frances yelled.

"I ain't going a damn place till I see Trinika," he said stubbornly. "Now get her ass out here, because I don't feel like waiting."

Frances cocked her pistol. She was ready to fire. "You got three seconds, mister."

Daddy T. looked at Frances and saw her finger steadily pulling back on the trigger. He was hard and definitely bold, but it appeared he wasn't quite ready to take a bullet.

"You ain't seen the last of me, old woman," he finally said. "I promise you that."

Frances watched Daddy T. as he left from her porch, climbed back into his Cadillac and sped away. She watched as his car disappeared down the street, then she finally closed her door and locked it back. When she turned around, she saw both Trinika and Ernestine staring at her in their nightgowns. Frances could see that Trinika was shaken and nervous, and she could see how much she feared Daddy T.

"It's alright, child," Frances said supportively as she tried to soothe Trinika's worries. "Try to go back to bed and get some sleep."

"How in the hell can we sleep when that fool could be coming back here anytime?" Ernestine griped. "You need to do something before he comes back. Franny, are you listening . . . *Franny?*"

Frances ignored Ernestine as she went into her bedroom and closed the door. She put her revolver away as she picked up the phone and called the police.

Chapter 21

Willie Joe dreaded what he was about to do. He had debated, deliberated, disputed, and questioned over and over in his mind what he was about to do for many days, but now the time had finally come. Deep down he was petrified and scared to death, but he knew he simply had no choice. He had to do it; there was no other way around it.

With his mind made up, Willie Joe stormed out of the house and sped away in Patricia's car. He ignored Patricia as she ran out the door and demanded to know where he was going as he sped off down the street. Willie Joe, determined in his mission, wasn't about to let his wife interfere with his plan; in fact, no one was about to stop him from doing what he needed to do. He was a man possessed, a man bent on doing it his way. He had to do this, if it were the last thing he ever did.

Trying to delay the inevitable as long as he could, or maybe just trying to calm his shaken weary nerves, Willie Joe pulled over to a liquor store as he went in and bought a fifth of Jim Beam. When he got back into the car, he quickly unscrewed the top and took a couple of hefty vicious gulps from his bottle. The whiskey hit like lightning in his stomach as it burned and satisfied his soul all at the same time. He didn't care how drunk he got, just so long as he didn't feel that trembling fear anymore and could face what he was about to do. After a couple more hefty, generous swigs, Willie Joe finally screwed the top back on as he started the car and took off out of the parking lot.

When Willie Joe reached the Westview Cemetery, he pulled over to a parking space and shut off his motor as he stared out at the vast number of tombstones that populated the immense field. He quickly unscrewed the top of his Jim Bean as he took another huge gulp to quell his queasy nerves. Willie Joe knew that this was going to be hard, but now as he sat in his car staring out at the rows of tombstones, he felt weaker than he'd ever felt in his life. He was captured inside of his car like an inmate in a prison cell looking out at a world that he couldn't touch. Every time he tried to break free from his cell, the door handle would only burn his hand back and kept him captured within his tight, little cramped cell.

After nearly an entire hour of trying to compose his nerves, Willie Joe finally felt brave enough to break free from his car. He slowly opened his door and stepped out of the car. The bottle of Jim Beam laying on the car seat looked like a good comforter, but Willie Joe decided to go without it; he was going to be strong and face this like a man. He slammed his car door and headed slowly toward the vast field of tombstones. The evening sun slowly began to fade from the sky, but Willie Joe didn't care one bit. He would stay out here all night if he needed to finally cleanse his soul.

When Willie Joe found Jarques Lewis' headstone among the other thousands that cluttered the vast cemetery, his emotions immediately came forth like a violent, tenacious storm. Ten years ago today, on that fateful night, Willie Joe discharged his weapon and fatally wounded the eighteen-year-old kid who now rested in the plot that Willie Joe stood over.

Since that tragic night ten years ago, Willie Joe could never muster up the nerve to come and visit his plot. Now finally standing here like a guilty man whose conscience had finally dragged him back to face his accuser, Willie Joe quickly found that no amount of whiskey could prepare him for this eventful day. The tears from his eyes, and the sobs and moans from his gut, only echoed a portion of the pain that he felt. The memory of him firing his weapon and killing that kid on that dark night, kept lashing at him like a ghost seeking retribution for his sins.

When the pain became too much, Willie Joe just wanted to run and get away from this place of death as far away as he could, but the boy's soul wouldn't let him escape. He had to stand there and face the victim whose life he tragically ended for as long as it took. Willie Joe had to stand there, before God and the entire world, and receive his punishment.

Chapter 22

By Sunday morning, Frances had finally had enough of Trinika's pimp. Since that heated confrontation on her porch nearly a week ago, Daddy T. had returned several times and had besieged Frances' house with constant phone calls demanding to speak to Trinika and threatening violence if he weren't allowed to see her. Frances remained firm as a rock as she protected her grandchild and her household from the constant demands and threats of a brazen street thug who wouldn't take no for an answer.

Frances, however, quickly found that her efforts to keep Trinika's pimp away were all but futile. The restraining order she had issued out on him proved ineffective as the police were unable to stop him, and as Daddy T. seemed all too willing to continue to encroach upon her property. Other than putting a bullet into his head, Frances saw that her only other alternative for the sake of her granddaughter, was to get Trinika as far away from Atlanta as she possibly could.

With time becoming of sheer essence and Daddy T.'s demands and intrusions becoming more frequent, Frances quickly made arrangements with her sister in Buffalo for Trinika to go there and stay with her for a while.

By eight o'clock that Sunday morning, Trinika was packed and ready to go as her Greyhound bus to Buffalo was set to depart at 9 a.m. sharp. With everything in order, Frances, Ernestine, and Trinika began to head out the door when the phone suddenly started ringing. Frances decided not to answer it, fearing that it was only Trinika's pimp calling to harass and threaten her. At the last second, though, as they began to head out the door, she changed her mind as she slowly ventured into the living room to answer the phone. After the eighth ring, she slowly picked up the receiver hoping desperately she wouldn't hear Daddy T.'s belligerent voice on the other end.

"Hello?" Frances said with caution.

"Frances, this is Patricia. Have you seen Willie Joe?" came her nervous voice across the phone.

"No . . . I haven't."

"Well, he left the house yesterday afternoon in the car and I ain't heard nothing from him since," Patricia said in a trembling voice. "And I'm starting to get really worried."

"Maybe he just went over to one of his buddy's house, Patricia," Frances said in a curt tone as she tried to hurry and get off the phone. "I wouldn't worry too much about it."

"But I'm really worried, Frances." Patricia persisted. "He was acting real funny before he left here yesterday, and I just discovered a few moments ago that his gun is missing from his drawer."

"What!"

"It's gone and no telling what Willie Joe is thinking. He's been acting very strange these last few days."

"Have you called the police?"

"No, I haven't . . . at least not yet."

"Well, call the police and I'll get back with you as quick as I can."

Frances hung up the phone as she, Ernestine, and Trinika headed out the door. They got into the car as Frances took off for the bus station in silence. With so much going on, Frances had a hard enough time just focusing on one problem at a time.

When Frances reached the Greyhound bus station and parked, the three of them got out of the car and entered the bus terminal as Frances went to the ticket counter and purchased Trinika's ticket. With thirty minutes still left until the departure of her bus, Frances, Ernestine, and Trinika had a seat and waited silently in the half-filled bus station for the announcement of Trinika's bus. Between the three of them, the same fearful thought seemed to nag at them as they sat silently and waited; the same fearful thought that Daddy T. would somehow find them and try to prevent Trinika from leaving.

Twenty minutes later, Trinika's bus was finally called over the speaker. Trinika, with her lone suitcase of bare essentials and a few clothing items that Frances purchased for her, rose from her seat to take her place in line. Frances and Ernestine rose also as they gathered around her to wish her farewell.

"You take care of yourself, child," Frances said with teary eyes. "My sister Odella is going to take real good care of you. I'll try to send some money up there in a few days. But if you need anything—*anything at all*—don't you dare hesitate to call me. Day or night," she said with the conviction of a grandmother who'd raised her grandchild on nothing but strong love. "And don't you get yourself tangled up in them streets again, because you got too much going for you for that. You hear me child?"

Trinika suddenly fell into Frances' arms as the two hugged like long lost relatives.

"Thank you, Franny, thank you for everything," she said softly as she cried into Frances' chest. "And I'm so sorry." She sobbed. "I'm so sorry."

"It's alright, child. Everything is going to be alright."

When Trinika finally let go of Frances, she slowly looked over at Ernestine. Neither one seemed to know what to say as they stared at one another in an awkward silence. The years of not having a bond with one another was as clear as a puddle of mud after a heavy rainstorm. The bitterness, the animosity, and the pain that had built up between them over the years hovered over them like a dark, ominous cloud; and on this day, that dark cloud would by no way disintegrate and fade away.

Finally, as if two boxers met in the middle of the ring to touch gloves before a fight, Trinika and Ernestine gave each other a brisk hug, then quickly pulled away. With their brief encounter finished, Trinika quickly picked up her lone suitcase and headed out the gate to board her bus bound for Buffalo.

———⚬———

FRANCES MADE IT TO church just in time for service to start. However, she quickly discovered that she wasn't in the spirit for worshipping. Too many problems and issues clogged her mind this morning and weighed down her soul. Today she was just going through the motions of attending church and being a faithful choir member. Even her rich, resounding voice that would usually bless and enrapture the congregation every Sunday, seemed to fail her today. Today the ways of the world simply had the best of her. With only a week to go before Terrence's media frenzy trial, when the eyes of literally the entire nation would be watching, Frances, more than ever, needed to be in the spirit.

After leaving the bus station and dropping Ernestine off back home, Frances called Patricia back to see if Willie Joe had returned. By the first sound of her voice, Frances already knew the answer. Patricia sounded even

130

more shaken and disturbed over the phone than before that Willie Joe hadn't returned. Frances tried to subdue and calm her fears, but deep down, she felt just as rattled and scared as Patricia.

Frances had feared and dreaded something like this for a long time. Since Willie Joe had slipped into his self-pity assertion that life was against him after his unfortunate shooting incident, Frances knew that one day he could succumb to the temptation that life wasn't worth living. The habitual drinking up until now had been only a slow poison administered to his body; but now it was a gun, and a gun was one of the deadliest poisons around. Frances only hoped and prayed that Willie Joe wouldn't succumb to the evil continuously drawing him in. However, the way things had been going for Willie Joe, Frances knew that it wouldn't take much to pull him into that eternal abyss.

By midway through Reverend Speight's sermon, Frances couldn't take it anymore. Her nerves were flustered and on edge. She'd hoped that she could make it through the remaining of service without leaving out of church, but worrying about Willie Joe dominated her mind and made her ill at ease. The thought of him taking a gun to his head, kept haunting her and making her more and more nervous. Frances didn't have a clue of where he could be or even which direction to look, but she had to do something to help her son. Her only hope was that it wasn't too late.

When Frances gathered her stuff and began to leave down from the choir stand, the doors to the sanctuary suddenly flew open as if a wild gale of wind had ripped them apart. Reverend Speight stopped in mid-sermon as everyone in the congregation turned around to see what the disturbance was about.

Willie Joe, with his clothes all torn and disheveled, came stumbling down the aisle of the church. In one hand he had an empty bottle of Jim Bean, and in the other hand, he had his pistol hanging loosely between his fingers. The gasp from the congregation was of both fear and shock as everyone watched this dangerous intruder interrupt their service. Willie Joe continued down the aisle as he stumbled toward the pulpit and stared up at Reverend Speight with glazed eyes. Reverend Speight—appearing frightened, speechless, and confused—stared back down at Willie Joe and waited nervously. The entire congregation sat petrified and rigid to their seats as they also waited; waited for something to happen.

Finally, as if Willie Joe had come before the altar to confess his sins, he slumped to the floor as he let out a vicious wail. His cries, sobs, and moans lasted a full five minutes before he could finally utter his first word.

"FORGIVE ME!" he screamed toward the ceiling. "FORGIVE ME GOD! FORGIVE ME!"

Everyone sat rigid to their seats and absolutely no one uttered a word. Only Willie Joe's constant shrieks and wails, overshadowed the tense silence.

Finally Reverend Speight slowly moved from his position behind the pulpit as he came down to where Willie Joe knelt and wailed before the altar. He softly laid a hand on his shoulder and waited for his sobs to subside.

"It's alright, son," he said softly. "God has forgiven you . . . He's already wiped away your sins."

Frances came down from the choir and knelt before Reverend Speight and Willie Joe. She slowly took the gun from his trembling hand and hugged her son.

Chapter 23

Ernestine was glad to have the house finally to herself once again. With Trinika gone to Buffalo and Frances at work, she had the whole place to herself to do as she pleased. The one thing Ernestine wanted to do more than anything on this bright early Monday morning: get as high as she possibly could.

When Ernestine heard the knock at the door, she knew Travis had finally arrived. Despite the last encounter when Frances walked in on them, Ernestine still needed her dope, and Travis was the only dealer who'd oblige her with the free stuff she needed.

Concerned that Ernestine was going way too fast, Travis, ironically, wanted to end their little arrangement before she got too deep. He had many junkies as customers and he could tell that his dear mother was fast becoming one once again. Ernestine, however, wouldn't dare hear any of it. After begging and pleading with him for nearly twenty minutes over the phone—*and reminding him in harsh terms that she'd brought him into the world*—Travis, reluctantly, submitted to his mama's will. Ernestine knew she could get to Travis, she always could. However, when she heard the knock at the door and rushed to answer it, she was a little jolted to see who stood there when she opened the door.

"Willie Joe . . . what you doing here?" Ernestine said as her mouth flew open.

Willie Joe, for the first time in years, looked rested and relaxed. He looked like he'd had a good night's sleep, without the residue of a hangover still cluttered in his eyes. To add to that, it was the first time Ernestine could remember, that there wasn't a bottle of Jim Bean in his hand.

"I just stopped by to talk," Willie Joe said easily as he stood on the porch. "You and I haven't really talked in a long time."

Ernestine quickly looked up and down the street. She expected Travis to arrive at any moment.

"Well . . . uh . . . couldn't we talk some other time. I'm really—"

"Look, Ernestine, we need to talk," Willie Joe said adamantly. "There are some things we need to discuss."

Ernestine saw that Willie Joe wasn't about to leave. She knew from their days of growing up that he could be persistent and as stubborn as a bull when he wanted something; after all, he had the raw attributes to police some of the most dangerous neighborhoods and streets in Atlanta. She knew she couldn't stop him from coming in, but she hoped whatever he wanted to talk about that he would hurry up, say it, and leave.

"What do you want, Willie Joe?" Ernestine said in a rough tone as she turned from the door and headed into the living room. Willie Joe entered the house as he closed the door behind him and followed Ernestine into the living room. Ernestine could tell that he was about to lay something heavy on her by the way he looked into her eyes.

"God has transformed me," Willie Joe said in a pious voice as if he'd just come from the altar. "I'm a changed man now, Ernestine. God has taken my burden away. He's forgiven me. I no longer have a taste for whiskey."

"Yeah, I know," Ernestine said offhandedly as she plopped down onto the sofa. "Franny told me yesterday when she came home from church."

"Well . . . God can do the same for you, Ernestine," Willie Joe said as he slowly sat down beside her. "He can take away your burdens, too."

"Willie Joe, I ain't got time for all this church talk!" She yelled. "I don't feel like hearing it!"

"You need to hear it. I've been hearing how you've fallen back to your old ways. That you're hitting the stuff again."

"Who told you to come over here?" Ernestine snapped. "Did Franny tell you to come over here, because I don't want to hear it!"

"Franny don't know nothing about this," Willie Joe said quickly. "I came here to talk to you as brother to sister. So, maybe, we could help each other overcome the hurdles that's been blocking our path."

"You don't know a damn about my situation, and I wish you would just leave."

"I know that you're hurting just like I was. You're upset and embarrassed that your past has come back to haunt you. You think the entire city is laughing and pointing fingers at you because that porn film you made years ago has resurfaced. You think the entire world is calling you a slut."

"You don't know what the hell you're talking about!" Ernestine said in frustration as she jerked away from Willie Joe and stood up. "And I don't need you coming over here throwing your new found religion in my face. Now get out of here!" She screamed.

"Quit lying to yourself, Ernestine, because it's true," Willie Joe said as he slowly stood up and confronted his embittered sister. "Because I've been lying to myself all these years after that night I shot that kid. I've blamed myself, the city, the police department, the courts, the review board, the world, the curse of our family—anything and everybody—because the stigma of the pain hurt so much.

"I thought the entire city was criticizing me and making me out of a scapegoat for every problem that ever occurred in this city," Willie Joe said as he continued. "And for a while, a whole lot of people were and I just couldn't take it. But what I found out when I went to visit that boy's grave the other day was that I can't change the past. I can't stop people from going into the past and remembering that night. No matter how much whiskey I drank, it was never going to erase that night. I just have to learn to live with it and go on. So, what I'm trying to say is that no amount of dope is going to erase that film you made, Ernestine. And it's not going to stop people from talking about you and ridiculing you. You just have to learn to live with it and move on . . . ."

Ernestine stared at Willie Joe lost in a deep trance. Finally, after a long silence, her eyes began to slowly cast down toward the floor. Willie Joe sensed that he'd hit a spot within her, a deep wound inside her lonely shattered heart. He moved slowly toward his lost, distraught sister to give her a loving embrace that she so much needed, but when Ernestine suddenly heard a knock at the front door, her composure quickly changed. Travis was here and her dope had finally arrived. She went quickly to answer the door, leaving Willie Joe standing alone in the living room.

When Travis came into the house and saw Willie Joe standing in the living room, he froze in his tracks. Travis and Willie Joe simply stared at one another like total strangers. There was no recognition that they were even related.

"Willie Joe . . ." Travis finally said. Willie Joe merely nodded as if it were clear that he knew the purpose of Travis' visit.

Ernestine finally yanked Travis by the arm when he began to dally too long. He obeyed his dear mother as he followed her to her bedroom as Ernestine closed the door shut when they went in. In twenty seconds, Travis popped back out as he headed for the door. This time he didn't turn to look at Willie Joe in the living room. He just kept going straight out the door.

When Willie Joe sensed that Ernestine wasn't coming back out, he left out of the living room as he approached Ernestine's door. He tried to turn the doorknob, but he found that it was locked.

"Ernestine, open up." Willie Joe demanded as he banged on the door. "Ernestine, you hear me in there? Open up!"

"Quit beating on my damn door and leave me the hell alone Willie Joe!" Ernestine yelled. "Just leave me alone!"

"What the hell did Travis just bring to you? I know it was some dope."

"A bottle of some *damn* Jim Bean!" Ernestine yelled. "Now get out of here and leave me the hell alone!"

"Ernestine, I ain't leaving till you open this door!" Willie Joe roared. "You hear me in there, girl? Open up! Ernestine, open up this door! Ernestine! *Ernestine!*"

The cop in Willie Joe seemed to suddenly rage within him as he stepped back and crashed into Ernestine's door with all the force that his six-foot-three, two-hundred-and-seventy-pound frame could muster. The door crashed opened with one mighty blow as Willie Joe stormed into the room as if making a bust on a notorious crack house. The cocaine rocks lying on Ernestine's dresser quickly caught Willie Joe's eye. He shoved Ernestine out of the way as he went straight over to the dresser and scooped up the rocks.

"What the hell you think you're doing?" Ernestine blasted when she saw Willie Joe take her rocks. "Give it back, damnit. Where the hell are you going?"

Willie Joe ignored Ernestine as he headed straight for the bathroom. He went to the commode, pulled up the seat, and dropped the rocks in as he flushed them down the toilet.

Ernestine, seeing her high going down the toilet, suddenly went into a rage as she charged at Willie Joe like a wild, ferocious cat. She slapped and scratched at Willie Joe's face and neck until her fingers literally dripped with blood. Willie Joe, with his face all scratched up and bloodied, eventually grabbed Ernestine's wrists. He then pulled out his gun that he had tucked down in the front of his pants as he slowly handed it to his enraged sister. Ernestine, still breathing hard from her heated rage, was all of a sudden dumbfounded. She looked into Willie Joe's eyes and saw a man who wasn't afraid to die.

"If you want to kill me," he said softly, "then do it the right way."

Ernestine peered right into Willie Joe's eyes as she held the gun firmly in her hands. Willie Joe peered right back into her eyes and seemed ready for whatever she was about to do. His eyes were steady and set like a soldier who was about to die for a worthy cause. He had no final words to say, he was just ready and willing to die.

When Ernestine heard the explosion of the gun, her heart fell to her feet. She opened her eyes and saw a gaping hole in the bathroom wall only three inches above Willie Joe's head. Ernestine, shocked and stunned that she'd actually pulled the trigger, began to shake with uncontrollable fear. She dropped the gun to the floor and began to sob like never before. The weight of her actions suddenly hit home as she slowly realized just how far she'd sunken to.

Ernestine, wailing from the sin of her guilt, slowly slumped to the floor and curled around Willie Joe's feet as she moaned and cried in utter pain. Willie Joe slowly knelt down beside Ernestine and softly caressed her back. It seemed that he could feel the pain and the rejection flowing out of her, just as that same pain and rejection, had flowed out of him.

FRANCES WAS IN HER office tallying up the day's receipts and profits as the rest of her staff worked busily to close up the restaurant after a long, enduring night. The restaurant did better business than it ever had in its thirty something year history. Frances knew that it simply wasn't her great soul food that brought this unexpected upturn in business, but it was all the attention that the upcoming trial created around the city that brought people in by the droves.

The supporters, the non-supporters, and the curious alike all flooded into her soul food establishment both day and night. With her recent media blitz of the late-night talk shows still the hot topic around town, Frances had suddenly become the center of attention around Atlanta, and her restaurant benefited greatly from it. Each night as the trial kept looming closer and closer, Frances' restaurant would out do the previous night's tally sometimes by as much as twenty to thirty percent. With Terrence lawyer's hefty bill still to pay, Frances didn't so much mind all of the hoopla surrounding her business.

When Frances had nearly finished counting up today's tally of receipts, Jalina came into her office and informed her that someone out front wanted to see her. In just the last week, Frances had a steady stream of folk wanting to see her for one reason or another. If it weren't a reporter wanting an on-the-spot interview concerning the upcoming trial, then it was some nosy stranger coming in off the street trying to extract some information about her family. Frances was getting fed up with all the intrusions she had to deal with as Terrence's trial loomed closer, but one intrusion she didn't mind, and even encouraged to continue, were the girls from the street coming to her looking for help.

Since Trinika had come to her seeking shelter and aid nearly two weeks ago, one girl after another began to follow her lead as they came to Frances looking to get away from Daddy T.'s overbearing control and abuse. Frances was more than willing to help these young, abused women get away from Daddy T.'s lecherous tentacles and help them find safety from the rigors and dangers of the street.

One girl after another she led to shelters for abused women, to churches that sought refuge for the needy and homeless, and to friends who knew friends willing to house a lost soul. Frances, despite the tension swirling around the approaching trial and trying to deal with the problems that existed within her *own* family, was willing to take the time to do whatever it took to get these battered, young women off the street and away from that overbearing monster who had complete control over their lives. It became more than just a duty to her, it became downright personal. She was going to see to it that every young girl who came to her looking for refuge would find the aid and help they needed, and would once and for all, be free from Daddy T.'s destructive abuse.

Frances dropped everything she worked on as she headed to the front to see who'd come into the restaurant. She had a feeling that it was another girl who'd come in fresh off the street looking for aid and help, but when she saw who it was, her blood immediately began to boil. Daddy T., dressed in the finest clothes that a pimp could wear, stood next to the cash register, and by the scowl on his face, he didn't come for a social visit. By the look on his face, he was ready to kill, but so was Frances.

"What the hell are you doing in my restaurant? Get out!" Frances shouted loud enough to be heard a mile away.

"That's exactly what I came to tell you," Daddy T. said like a viper ready to strike. "I'm warning you to stay the hell out of my business, old woman, before you get yourself hurt. I take my business very serious, and I don't like when someone is interfering with my merchandise."

"*Merchandise*!" Frances sneered. "That *merchandise* you so loosely call are young girls who are being exploited and abused by an overdressed, perverted monster who don't know how to make an honest living, but would rather twist the minds of poor, dejected women and subject them to a life of prostitution just to keep his pockets full. Well, I won't stand by and let that happen not as long as those girls are coming to me looking for help. You've caused enough pain and misery to my granddaughter, and I'll be damn, if I can help it, if you're going to harm any more girls."

"You mess with me, old woman, and you'll be sorry," Daddy T. said viciously. "And I'm not one to make idle threats, old woman."

"And I'm certainly not one to run from a threat." Frances countered. "Now get out of my restaurant!"

Daddy T. suddenly reached into his suit as if he were about to pull out a gun, but just as he was about to, Earl and a couple other members of Frances' staff came to the front when they heard the commotion. Daddy T., appearing to have second thoughts, slowly retrieved his hand from his suit as he calmed his rage. He then looked at Frances with the ferocity of an angry bear ready to kill its prey.

"You'll be sorry you ever got mixed up in my business, old woman," Daddy T. said in an eerie voice. "I promise you . . . you'll be sorry."

Daddy T. then turned and stormed out of the restaurant.

Chapter 24

The months, weeks, and days had finally passed and now the time had finally approached. The night before the trial, Frances lay propped up in her bed watching all of the pre-trial hype on the late-night cable news channels. No matter which channel she flipped to on her remote, there was some coverage of tomorrow's opening day trial discussed.

For the first time since Terrence was arrested on that hot June day more than four months ago, Frances was nervous and fearful of what was to come. The prosecution had already pronounced to the world that they would seek the death penalty if Terrence were convicted, and Frances feared and dreaded that more than anything. Not only did she fear for Terrence's life, but she feared what another tragedy, what another blight on the Jackson name would do to her family that had already been through so much turmoil and tribulation.

Another tragedy, especially one of this magnitude, would surely rot away what little unity they had left together as a family. In her mind, it would be as if the curse that so many people had associated with their family's name over the last couple of months were actually true; that it actually had some validity and merit after all. Frances, more than ever, knew that their family's name and reputation were at a crossroads. If their family were going to survive this major scandal, then Terrence had to be cleared of these vicious charges.

Frances, however, had reason to believe in hope for her family. She was overwhelmed and overjoyed when she came home last night from the restaurant and discovered that Ernestine was ready to recommit her life to the church and to once again pursue her rehabilitation treatment for her drug addiction. The words that came out of Ernestine's mouth came as a shock to Frances, but so did Willie Joe's own transformation before the entire congregation during Sunday's morning service.

This unexpected turnaround from Ernestine, and especially Willie Joe, was what Frances had hoped and prayed for so long. She knew that there was hope, a ray of light after all for her turmoil, ridden family. Just when things looked there bleakest and darkest for their family, an unexpected reversal of hope had suddenly begun to blossom. If only this good fortune could somehow continue right through the trial, then Frances knew her entire family could have a true chance at reconciliation. Frances was merely going to continue to believe in the power of God that He would make matters right.

When Frances had heard enough from the late-night talk shows, she reached for the remote to turn off the TV. However, when the phone suddenly rang, she switched courses to answer the phone. She hoped it wasn't another reporter demanding an interview or another crank caller hoping that Terrence would fry in the electric chair, because Frances had heard enough of them for one night and she wasn't in the mood for any more.

"Hello?"

"I finally caught his ass."

"What?"

"George!" Carolyn's angry voice shrieked. "I caught him coming out of a hotel tonight with one of those sleazy ass nurses who work at his hospital."

Frances sighed when she heard Carolyn's angry voice. She almost wished it was just another crank caller, rather than listen to Carolyn rattle on about her marital problems.

"Carolyn . . . you sure it was him," Frances said in a lethargic voice. "Once before you thought you saw him out at a bar with his secretary and it wasn't even him."

"Yes, it was him!" Carolyn blasted. "Don't you think I know my own husband!"

"Well . . . what did you do?"

"When he got home, I confronted him. I told him I saw him coming out of the hotel with that sleazy whore, and he tried to deny it. He said he was just returning from Chicago from the convention that he was *supposed* to be coming back from. But I told him I just saw him no more than forty minutes ago coming out of that hotel with that woman. He tried to say I was seeing things and that I was crazy. Then we got into this big fight, and he ended up taking all of his clothes and stormed out of the house."

"Well, Carolyn, don't worry yourself into a frenzy," Frances said quickly. "Just let things settle down for a while. Maybe he'll be back in a couple of days, then y'all can go from there."

"Don't worry!" Carolyn blasted. "For all I know, George could be headed right back over to that sleazy wench and they can be shacking up right now. I'll be a fool not to worry—*Don't worry*!" She said in an exasperated tone as if she wanted to come through the receiver and strangle Frances. After a couple seconds of silence, she finally calmed down as her normal breathing returned. "I don't know what to do Franny . . ." She now said in a humbling voice. "I just don't know where my marriage is headed . . . I just don't know."

"And I don't know either, Carolyn," Frances said in a fed-up voice. "My mind is all tied up with this trial tomorrow to be focusing on your marriage and giving you advice. So much is going to be happening tomorrow morning and I'm trying to keep my mind clear and my nerves calm. I don't need no extra burden weighing down on my mind right now."

"But I *need* your advice, Franny." Carolyn pleaded. "I need some direction. That's why I called you!"

"Well, then try getting on your knees and praying!"

Frances hung up the phone as she shut off the TV and turned off the light. She fluffed her pillow and prepared herself for sleep. Terrence's trial would begin at nine sharp in the morning, and Frances knew that if she were going to be ready for the media circus that awaited this trial, then she needed all the rest that she could possibly get.

Chapter 25

When the phone rang at 4 a.m., Frances thought she was in the middle of a dream. She merely rolled over and tried to drown out the ringing in her dream as she stuffed her pillow over her head. When the ringing didn't stop, Frances realized that she wasn't dreaming. She woke out of her sleep and strained to look at her clock on her dresser, and indeed it was 4 a.m. Frances, for the world of her, couldn't figure out who could be calling her at this hour of the morning. She knew if it were Carolyn calling her to rant some more about George and their marital problems, Carolyn was going to get a cursing that she never dreamed her God-fearing mother could ever dish out.

"Hello?" Frances answered with sleep still in her throat.

"Is this Mrs. Frances Jackson?"

"Yes . . . it is," Frances answered as she heard the wail of sirens and other clamorous noises over the phone.

"This is Sergeant Eddie Daily of the Atlanta Police. I'm calling to inform you that a fire has broken out at your restaurant establishment on Auburn Avenue. Fire crews are currently here at the site fighting the blaze."

Frances heard the sergeant's words, but it took a couple of seconds for them to sink in.

"A fire . . ."

"Yes ma'am."

"Well . . . how bad is it?"

"It's pretty bad ma'am. I think you need to come down as soon as possible."

Frances' heart began to beat so hard that her chest began to hurt. "Alright," she said nervously. "I'll be down there as fast as I can."

Frances hung up the phone as she quickly got out of bed and flipped on the light. She went to her closet and threw on a pair of pants, a blouse, and a sweater as she quickly grabbed her keys and headed out of the bedroom.

Ernestine met Frances at the door and wanted to know what was going on, but Frances didn't say a word as she got into her car and sped away.

———◉———

WHEN FRANCES ARRIVED at the site of her restaurant, her eyes couldn't believe what she saw. She got out of her car slowly and watched in utter disbelief as fire raged uncontrollably throughout the entire building of her restaurant. The blaze roared and glowed magnificently from the roof top of the building as the flames leapt high into the night. The fire crews on hand battled the ferocious blaze with all the tenacity that they could muster, but the searing inferno continued to build and grow. It was a monster growing second by second, and minute by minute. And by the way it continued to grow, it wasn't about to be defeated.

By dawn, the raging, roaring blaze that had engulfed Frances' restaurant had been extinguished, but the building was utterly demolished. What was once the best soul food restaurant east or west of the Mississippi was now no more. It was now a smoldering heap of ruins with smoke drifting slowly into the brightening, morning sky. There was no false sense of illusion that the building could've been saved. One look at the massive, burned charred planks and rubble was evidence of the fire's strength and devastation.

Frances, for the past hour and a half, stood by and watched the fire crews fight the devastating blaze in absolute silence. She was shocked, stunned, and astonished to watch her beloved restaurant consumed before her eyes. The very thing that she loved and was well known for across the city of Atlanta and beyond, had burned to the ground in less than a few hours. The restaurant had been a part of her life for so long that it had become her, the essence of who she was. Over the years she'd built, nurtured, and made it into the overwhelming success that it had become. It was her pride and joy, her soul; and now it was all gone.

When the fire crews finally finished putting out the last remaining smoldering flames, the head fireman and the police sergeant came over to where Frances stood. Still staring gravely at the heap of rubble of her demolished restaurant, Frances didn't realize that two others had suddenly approached her.

"Mrs. Jackson, I'm Butch Lewis, the chief fireman of this unit," the head fireman said. "I'm sorry but our crew did the best we could, but the blaze was just too much. I'm sure you have enough insurance to cover the damage to your business."

"Yes . . . I do," Frances said slowly without taking her eyes away from the burned, demolished site of her once restaurant. "What . . . what caused the fire?"

"Arson," the fireman quickly said. "The entire building was virtually doused with gasoline. Whoever started the blaze knew exactly what they were doing."

"I've been on the radio trying to see had anyone reported someone lurking around here about the time the fire started," the police sergeant said. "So far nothing has been reported. But if you know of anyone who may be a suspect, it would help us greatly with the investigation."

Frances' eyes slowly closed as the pain of what had happened finally sunk in. "Yes, officer . . . I certainly do."

Chapter 26

With hardly any sleep and still in an emotional shock over the destruction of her restaurant, Frances, along with Ernestine, arrived at the jail at 7 a.m. to meet with Terrence and his lawyer. She'd brought along the new suits she'd promised for Terrence to wear during the trial as she hauled them over her shoulder on hangers.

As Frances and Ernestine approached the doors of the jail, a couple of reporters eager to get an early jump on today's trial had already gotten word of the fire to Frances' restaurant and were there to greet Frances with a barrage of questions. Frances had nothing to say as she and Ernestine excused themselves and entered the building. They went straight to the visitation desk as a guard came and escorted them to a special wing of the jail on the second floor where Terrence and his lawyer were already waiting.

After walking down a long isolated hall on the second floor, the guard suddenly stopped at a door and knocked. Another guard on the inside peered through a square glass window as he unlocked the door and opened it. Frances and Ernestine were allowed to enter the room as the heavy-set guard closed and locked the door back as he resumed his position by the door.

Terrence and his lawyer, Michael Baldwin, immediately rose from the table that they sat at when Frances and Ernestine entered the room. An uneasiness quickly filled the small cramped room as everyone first laid eyes on one another. The pre-arranged meeting would ordinarily bring about nervous feelings as Terrence was about to stand trial for the guilt or innocence of his life, but the knowledge of what had just happened to Frances' restaurant brought on an air of mixed tension.

"Mrs. Jackson, I'm so sorry to hear about what happened to your restaurant," Terrence's lawyer said as he came and laid a comforting hand on her shoulder. "I heard what happened on the radio when I was driving over here. They said the fire was an act of arson. This is just awful."

"Yes, it came as a shock when I received the call at 4 a.m.," Frances said with pain etched on her face. "It was painful to watch everything that you worked so hard for and put your heart and soul into just burn completely to the ground," she said as her voice trailed off. "Just so painful . . . ."

"Are you going to be alright, Franny?" Terrence said with as much pain stricken on his face as Frances felt at the moment.

Frances turned and looked at Terrence. She'd last visited him only two weeks ago, but even within those mere two weeks, it looked as if the rigors of confinement had aged him. She noticed that he still had on his jail issued jumpsuit, and suddenly realized the suits she'd brought for him to wear.

"Yeah, child, I'll be just fine," she said with a heavy voice. "But right now, we need to be focusing on your trial and getting you out of here. Now is not the time to be worrying about me."

"But your whole entire restaurant, Franny!" Terrence said with agony in his voice. "I know you're upset and hurt. You don't need to be here watching over my ass. You've already done enough as it is. You've got enough trouble as it is, and you certainly don't need to add to it by being in court today."

"Now stop all that nonsense talk. I'll be fine," Frances said with finality. She laid the suits on the conference table and spread them out so Terrence could get a good look at them. "I hope you like them . . . I hope they'll make a good impression in court."

Terrence's lawyer quickly went through the suits. They were *Hugo Boss, Ralph Lauren, and CK*—the top of the line.

"These are perfect," Mr. Baldwin said with admiration.

"I . . . uh . . . helped picked them out when we went yesterday," Ernestine said slowly as she looked at Terrence. "I thought . . . uh . . . you would like them."

Terrence looked over at Ernestine as coldness set in his eyes.

"Is that right," Terrence said in a harsh tone.

"Uh . . . why don't we have a seat so we can discuss a few things," Terrence's lawyer said when the mood in the room became tense.

Everyone sat down around the conference table and waited for the attorney to speak.

"Mrs. Jackson, I just want to fill you in on today's proceedings. The prosecution and I will be selecting a jury. The jury selection will probably go on for a few days, then once we have a jury, the judge will open up the case for opening statements. The jury selection will undoubtedly be long and tedious, and I'd understand if you'd rather not be there, especially considering the terrible ordeal you've already been through."

"No, Mr. Baldwin." Frances quickly shook her head. "I'm going to be there every day for however long it takes. For however long it takes for my grandson to be set free."

Terrence's lawyer slowly nodded. "Alright," he said with admiration. "That's probably better for Terrence. It'll make a good impression."

"We're a family, Mr. Baldwin," Frances said in a determined voice. "And we're going to show the world that we're a strong, united black family."

"I take it that the rest of your family members will be there in court during the course of the trial?"

"If I have anything to say about it, Mr. Baldwin," Frances said with a deadpan serious look. "My family *will* be in that courtroom."

"I'm sure you and your family are fully prepared for all of the media and reporters. I'm sure you're fully aware of the media circus this trial is going to produce?"

"Yes, Mr. Baldwin," Frances said with conviction in her voice. "I'm fully aware of it and ready for it."

Terrence's lawyer nodded once again. When everyone became silent, he looked at his watch.

"Well . . . Terrence we better be moving."

Frances and Ernestine rose slowly from the table as they both looked over at Terrence. Frances walked slowly around to Terrence as he rose from the table and stood.

"You stay strong, you hear me," Frances said as she looked up at her grandson who'd been incarcerated for the last couple of months. "We're going to get through this, you hear me? Together as a family, we're going to get through this. And remember . . . God will make a way," she said with conviction. "So, you stay strong."

"I hear you, Franny." Terrence smiled. "I'll be strong."

Terrence looked over at Ernestine as his smile quickly vanished. Ernestine, as if sensing the animosity that he had for her becoming hotter, quickly evaded his hot look as she lowered her eyes. Frances also noticed the deep growing animosity between her daughter and her grandson, but she let it go. The healing between mother and son would simply come another day.

Right now, there were more important issues to deal with at hand. She went over to Terrence's lawyer and gripped his hand as if he were an old friend.

"I want you to do right by my grandson, Mr. Baldwin," Frances said with deep feeling. "Our family is in your hands."

"I'll do my best, Mrs. Jackson," Michael Baldwin said with a huge smile. "I'll certainly do my best."

When Frances let go of Michael Baldwin's hand, she and Ernestine made their way for the door. The heavy-set guard who'd been standing like a mountain in front of the door, turned and opened the door as Frances and Ernestine headed out.

Chapter 27

A week later, twelve jurors were finally sworn in and seated as the trial of the *People vs. Terrence Jackson* had officially commenced. Monday morning at 9 a.m. sharp, Judge Bernard P. Foster, a no-nonsense judge with many years of experience, opened the proceedings as the attorneys on both sides began giving their opening statements.

The courtroom was packed. Reporters filled up nearly two-thirds of the seats, as the other few remaining seats went to family and friends of the victim and the accused, and a sparse few allotted to a couple of members of the general public.

The Jackson family sat behind the defense table on the front row. Frances, Ernestine, Carolyn, Willie Joe, and Patricia all sat close together dressed in their best attire and looking as dignified as they could. The press, hungry for any morsel of information that they could attain, jumped on them like a pack of crazed wolves as they entered the courthouse. Frances, however, protected her flock with a steady hand up in the air to ward off the press as they shouted one question after another. She was determined that the voracious, biased press wasn't going to acquire any information from their mouths to further slander their family's name in the media. The trial would be hotly debated and controversial enough as it was, and the press certainly didn't need any more ammunition to make it any more contentious.

Frances knew that she needed to be as strong as a rock for her family during the duration of this trial. Despite the emotional setback she had to deal with over the past week with the burning of her restaurant, she knew she couldn't be weak during this most critical time. The eyes of the entire nation were watching, and Frances was determined that with the power of God behind her, she was going to guide her family through this violent, turbulent storm that her family had found itself sucked into.

When the two sides had finished giving their opening statements, and after a short recess, Judge Foster ordered the prosecution to call its first witness. The prosecution called Mayor Hobskin Anderson to the stand.

Mayor Anderson, who sat directly across from Frances' family, stood up from his seat and made his way to the gate at the railing. He stole a quick glance over at Frances, as Frances likewise returned his stare. These two strong willed combatants both stared at one another with heated intensity as the packed courtroom watched with intense silence. When their heated stares began to linger a little too long, Mayor Anderson finally turned and headed through the gate as he made his way to the witness stand.

The bailiff quickly swore in the mayor as the mayor slowly had a seat in the witness chair. Mayor Anderson, dressed impeccably like a politician headed to a fund-raiser, had a sense of power and authority that pervaded over the entire courtroom. Everyone sensed his power and statue as he gazed over the packed room. He was Mayor Hobskin Anderson, the most prominent figure of Atlanta, and it seemed as if everyone could feel the power of his presence.

"State your entire name for the record," the prosecutor spoke.

"Hobskin Langford Anderson."

"And what is your occupation?"

"I'm currently the mayor of the great city of Atlanta," he said with brimming pride.

"And how long have you been the mayor of our great city?"

"For eight years."

The prosecutor, a well-polished black woman in her early forties by the name of Josephine Brown, stood behind the podium and paused for a moment as if to let the effect of the mayor's presence on the witness stand dominate over the courtroom. Mayor Anderson, himself in his mid-fifties, sat with an air of dignified importance as he looked out over the packed courtroom and waited patiently for the prosecutor to continue.

"Now, Mayor Anderson," the prosecutor said after a long pause, "Joletta Anderson was your daughter, correct?"

"That's correct."

"What kind of relationship did you have with your daughter?"

"We've always had a tight, close relationship. Joletta was always very loving and caring toward me as I was to her. She was always the apple of my eye. She was always daddy's little girl."

"And Joletta was your only child?"

"Yes . . . she was," Mayor Anderson said with sadness. "She was the only child that my wife could conceive. Then when Joletta was barely four years old, her mother died in a car accident. It really hurt Joletta growing up without her mother. She really missed having a steady mother figure in her life."

"Now, your daughter, Joletta, was twenty-eight years old when she was murdered?"

"Yes . . . that's correct."

"Describe to us the character of your daughter. The person you knew to be Joletta Anderson."

"Joletta was a very loving, kind, and considerate young woman," Mayor Anderson said with empathy as he looked over at the jury. "She was very outgoing, bright, and ambitious. Her passion was to make other people's lives around her better. Every day she used every ounce of her energy and talent to advance and spread good will among people. There wasn't a person she didn't care about or didn't strife to help. She was truly one to be commended."

"Tell us some things about Joletta's accomplishments and achievements?"

Mayor Anderson slowly leaned back in his chair as he gazed up at the ceiling.

"Joletta was someone who I would refer to as a pioneer. Someone who was very much ahead of her time," the mayor said slowly with glowing affection. "She finished at the top of her class at Howard University with degrees in both Business Administration and Marketing. Right after graduating from college, she entered the Miss Black America beauty pageant and won first place. She went on to work for the Coca Cola firm here in Atlanta and advanced very rapidly within the organization. She came to work within my administration a couple of years ago as the Director of the Equal Opportunity Program, and brought about unprecedented change in the advancement of minority businesses and gender equality in this city.

"She also, as everyone probably knows, has owned one of the most popular and successful nightclubs in this city and was recently in the process of starting up her own music company." The mayor continued. "She also had other business enterprises that she was very busy with. Besides the business side of her achievements, Joletta has put her heart and soul into many social causes and issues around this city and was a trailblazing advocate for human rights."

"Joletta was truly extraordinary, wasn't she?" the prosecutor said with admiration when Mayor Anderson finally finished.

"Yes . . . she certainly was."

The prosecutor suddenly became grim faced as she continued to look at the mayor.

"Mayor Anderson," she said slowly, "when did you learn of the tragic death of your daughter?"

"Around four that morning when she was murdered."

"Who informed you of your daughter's murder?"

"Detective John Eagleberg called me at my home."

"I'm sure it came as devastating news?"

"It literally crushed my soul," Mayor Anderson said with pain in his throat.

"Mayor . . . were you aware of a relationship between the defendant and Joletta?"

Mayor Anderson nodded gravely. "I was aware of a previous involvement," he said reluctantly.

"What was your knowledge of that involvement?"

"Joletta told me about a year ago that they were dating. At the time, I didn't know how serious it was. Then about six months ago, Joletta told me that they had ended their relationship."

"Did your daughter say why they had ended their relationship?"

"She told me that he was becoming too possessive of her. That he was becoming too demanding and was beginning to threat and intimidate her when they began to have disagreements."

"And your daughter was beginning to fear that the defendant would soon become violent. That he was becoming a threat to her safety?"

"Objection," Michael Baldwin rose as he broke the stream of testimony. "Counselor is leading the witness."

"Sustained." Judge Foster declared. "Redirect your questioning."

"Mayor Anderson," the prosecutor said slowly, "when Joletta told you of the defendant's irrational aggressive behavior toward her, did you become concerned for your daughter?"

Mayor Anderson looked over at Terrence sitting at the defense table for the first time, and glared a look in his direction that could cut glass. Terrence, it seemed, wasn't about to be intimidated one bit. He met the mayor straight on, eye for an eye.

"Yes . . ." Mayor Anderson said as he eyed Terrence even harder. "I most certainly did."

"And during this time when Joletta told you of the defendant's behavior toward her, did you warn her that she should discontinue seeing the defendant?"

"Yes, I did," Mayor Anderson said with heated passion. "I told Joletta she needed to break it off with him as quickly as possible because I knew he was nothing but trouble, and she did."

"And when Joletta broke off their relationship, did she begin seeing anyone else?"

"Yes."

"And when she began seeing this other person, did she ever tell you that the defendant tried to reappear in her life to renew their relationship?"

"Yes, several times."

"When was the last time she informed you that the defendant tried to re-enter her life?"

"About a week before she was murdered. She said he was constantly calling her, coming over to her condo uninvited, and just making her life a mess. She said he was constantly jealous of her relationship with her new boyfriend. She said she began to feel like she was constantly being stalked."

"Joletta said she was being stalked by the defendant?"

"Yes."

The prosecutor looked over at Terrence sitting at the defense table as she let her ominous gaze hang for a few seconds. "No further questions," she finally said.

The prosecutor retrieved her notes from the lectern as she returned to her table. Michael Baldwin got up slowly from the defense table as he positioned himself at the podium. He looked at Mayor Anderson on the witness stand and gave a polite smile.

"Good morning, Mayor," he said appropriately.

Mayor Anderson merely nodded.

"Mayor Anderson, how did you feel when your daughter first told you that she was dating Mr. Terrence Jackson?"

"I wasn't very pleased if you have to ask," Mayor Anderson said rather tartly.

"Was it because you thought that Mr. Jackson was beneath her standards, or yours?"

"I just didn't think he was suited for my daughter," Mayor Anderson said tersely.

"Did your daughter ever bring Mr. Jackson over to your place for you to meet?"

"Once."

"And how did you perceive Mr. Jackson? What was your first impression of him?"

"Not very flattering," Mayor Anderson said matter of fact.

"Was it the way he dressed, or his style of hair, or the way he talked that made you have an unfavorable opinion of Mr. Jackson?"

"Objection Your Honor," the prosecutor rose. "This line of questioning is irrelevant."

"Sustained. Move along with your questioning."

Mr. Baldwin nodded accordingly to the judge. "Mayor Anderson, you stated that your daughter informed you that the relationship between her and Mr. Jackson had terminated. That they had nothing to do with one another anymore. But during this time when they were *supposed* to have had no contact with one another, didn't Joletta inform you that Mr. Jackson was still employed at the nightclub Seven Flavors. A nightclub that your daughter owned and ran?"

"No . . . well . . . yes." Mayor Anderson recanted. "I knew he worked at the place."

"And did your daughter inform you that she had signed Mr. Jackson to be an artist at her new music company just a mere month ago?"

"No, she didn't."

"Well, wouldn't you say that Joletta wouldn't have kept Mr. Jackson on as an employee at Seven Flavors, and certainly wouldn't have brought him along with her to the new music company she was forming, if she didn't feel comfortable being around the presence of Mr. Jackson?"

"I don't see the connection."

"Oh, I believe there's a very good connection, Mayor Anderson," Michael Baldwin said as his voice rose with authority. "Your daughter, Joletta, and Mr. Jackson had a mutual business interest together which was why they were frequently around each other's company so much, even after their love interest had ended. Wouldn't you say?"

"Not necessarily?"

"And wouldn't you say that implies that my client wasn't stalking your daughter, but was having a meaningful business relationship with her?"

"Not according to my daughter he wasn't," Mayor Anderson said forcefully.

"Well, maybe you didn't know your daughter as well as you thought you did. Maybe your daughter was just telling you these things about Mr. Jackson because she knew that you disapproved of him. And maybe she didn't want you to know that they were having more than just business relations. Maybe she was trying to hide the fact that they were still having *intimate* relations."

"Objection!" the prosecutor rose quickly.

"Sustained. Mr. Baldwin—"

Michael Baldwin quickly nodded before Judge Foster could admonish him. "Sorry, Your Honor. No further questions."

After Judge Foster excused Mayor Anderson from the witness stand, the prosecution called forth Joyce Griffith, chairman of Atlanta's Hip Hop Summit Organization. The twenty-seven-year-old woman, dressed conservatively in a blue skirt, a white blouse, and a matching blue business jacket, took the stand as she raised her right hand and was sworn in. She looked comfortable and composed as she sat attentively in the chair.

"Would you state your entire name for the record?" the prosecutor said.

"Joyce Ellaine Griffith."

"And what is your occupation?"

"I'm head of the music talent division at Urban Roots Music here in Atlanta, and I'm also chairman of Atlanta's Hip Hop Summit Organization."

"Ms. Griffith, did you know Joletta Anderson?"

"Yes, we were good friends. I'd known her as far back as high school."

"Could you tell the court when was the last time you saw Joletta Anderson?"

"It was at the Civic Center for the Hip Hop Summit the night that she was murdered."

"And why was she at the Hip Hop Summit?"

"Well, she was getting into the music business, and if you're anybody in the music business here in Atlanta, then the Hip Hop Summit is an event to meet people on the inside, new artists, producers, and so forth."

"Ms. Griffith, did you know of a relationship between Joletta and the defendant, Terrence Jackson?"

"I knew some months ago that they dated. But recently I knew that Joletta had signed Terrence as an artist to appear on her new music label, along with a few other artists she'd signed."

"She'd signed the defendant to her music label as a rap artist?"

"Yes."

"Ms. Griffith, did you see the defendant at the Hip Hop Summit that night when Joletta was there?"

"Yes, I did."

"Did you see them together at any point that night."

"Yes, I saw them together."

"What was their demeanor that night when they were together?"

"Objection, Your Honor." Michael Baldwin rose quickly. "Calls for speculation."

"Overruled," Judge Foster answered.

"They were arguing most of the time." The witnessed continued. "At one point, I saw them off in a corner and they were really having a very heated discussion."

"Did you hear what they were arguing about?"

"When Joletta stormed off from Terrence and headed into the lady's room, I went in after her to see if she were okay. That's when she told me that Terrence was demanding that she give him some more advance money."

"Joletta paid the defendant advance money for signing with her label?"

"Yes, she did."

"How much advance money did Joletta say she'd already given the defendant?"

"Ten thousand dollars."

"How much more advance money did the defendant want?"

"Ten thousand more."

"Did Joletta say the defendant demanded the money in a belligerent, threatening manner?"

"Yes. She told me that if she didn't give him what he wanted, then he told her that she'd be one sorry sister."

A couple of moans and groans began to echo around the courtroom. Frances and her family sat stoic amid the mild ruckus that erupted around them. The prosecutor was in no hurry to proceed. She seemed to want to milk the scene for all that it was worth.

"No further questions, Your Honor," she finally said as she left the podium and returned to the prosecution table.

Terrence's lawyer slowly got up from the defense table as he approached the podium. He looked at Ms. Joyce Griffith sitting on the witness stand as he prepared his attack.

"Ms. Griffith, you contend that Mr. Jackson and Joletta were arguing. Is that correct?"

"Yes, they were."

"What do you constitute as arguing?"

"Very loud talking, swearing, angry words between each other."

"You've seen many people argue before, haven't you?"

"Yes."

"You've seen many couples arguing before, haven't you?"

"Objection." The prosecutor quickly declared. "It's been established that the defendant and Ms. Anderson were no longer a couple."

"Sustained."

"Ms. Griffith, after you talked with Joletta, did you see Joletta and Mr. Jackson together anymore that night?"

"Well . . . yes. Much later that night."

"Did they appear to be in a brawling, argumentative mood at that point?"

"Well. . . no," Joyce Griffith said slowly.

"So, they seemed to be over the spat they had earlier. They seemed calm and at ease?"

"Well . . . somewhat."

"Was that the last you saw them that night, when they seemed calm and at ease?"

"Yes."

"So, from your perception, you believed everything was alright with them. You didn't think another thought about the spat they had earlier?"

"Well, I don't know if I would say I believed everything was alright with them."

"Yes or no, Ms. Griffith," Mr. Baldwin said as he persisted, "from the state that you saw them last, did you believe that any harm was going to come to Joletta Anderson?"

"No."

"Thank you. No further questions, Your Honor."

<hr />

AFTER AN HOUR-LONG lunch recess, Judge Foster reconvened the court proceedings. With the courtroom packed and both sides ready to go, the prosecution called its next witness, Allen Jones, the security guard at Joletta's condo building. When he was sworn in, the security guard had a seat in the witness chair.

"State your entire name for the record." The prosecutor began the testimony.

"Allen Randall Jones."

"And what is your occupation, Mr. Jones?"

"I'm a security officer at the Shadow Valley Condominiums."

"Mr. Jones, were you on duty on the morning of Sunday, May 30th?"

"Yes, I was."

"Could you tell the court what you saw that morning?"

"Well, I was surveying the grounds of the property around three-thirty that morning when I came to building D. That's when I saw this tall, young black man running from a blue Mercedes that was parked in the lot."

"Now this tall, young black man, did you get a good look at him?"

"Yes."

"Could you describe him for us?"

"He was around six-feet or six-feet-one inches. He was of slender build and of brown skin complexion. He was wearing baggy blue jeans, an Atlanta Falcons jersey, he had on a white head band, and he had long cornrows."

"Is that person present in the courtroom today?"

"Yes."

"Could you point him out for us?"

"He's that fellow sitting right there," the witness said as he pointed over to Terrence sitting at the defense table.

"The perpetrator you saw running from the blue Mercedes that night was the defendant, Terrence Jackson?"

"Yes."

"And it's no doubt that it was the defendant?"

"I'd seen him previously before over at the condominium, so I recognized him right off when I saw him."

"You recognized him so well that you were able to pick him out of a police lineup with no problems?"

"Yes."

"After you saw the defendant running from the Mercedes, what did you do?"

"Well, I went over to the car and discovered that Ms. Anderson's throat had been slashed. That's when I phoned the paramedics."

"And when the paramedics arrived, Ms. Anderson was pronounced dead?"

"Yes. That's when the police arrived and began interviewing me."

"And you identified to the police a description of the defendant running from Ms. Joletta Anderson's Mercedes?"

"Yes, I did."

"Thank you, Mr. Jones. No further questions."

The prosecutor left the podium and returned to her table as Terrence's attorney quickly took her place at the podium. He wasted no time plunging into his cross examination.

"Mr. Jones, you said that you saw the perpetrator running from Ms. Joletta Anderson's Mercedes at three-thirty on the morning of Sunday, May 30th. Is that correct?"

"It was around that time . . . yes."

"And it was no doubt that you saw Mr. Jackson that night running from Ms. Anderson's Mercedes," Michael Baldwin said as he turned and pointed at Terrence sitting at the defense table.

"No doubt."

"Now Mr. Jones, how far away were you from the perpetrator who was running from Ms. Anderson's Mercedes?"

"About ten or fifteen feet."

"Ten or fifteen feet," Michael Baldwin said slowly. "You sure it wasn't more like thirty, forty, or fifty feet, since the perpetrator was running *away* from the Mercedes?"

The security guard hesitated as he looked at Terrence's lawyer. "It's . . . it's possible." He conceded.

"And you said you got a good look at the perpetrator running from Ms. Anderson's Mercedes?"

"Yes . . . I did."

"But how could you get a good look if the perpetrator was running away?"

"I got a good look at him before he ran away."

"But how's that possible if all you saw of the perpetrator was his back as he was running away, and you could've been more than fifty feet from him?"

"It only takes a split second to identify someone," the witness said with an edge. "Especially one you've seen numerous times before."

"A split second?" Terrence's lawyer said incredulously. "But it was dark and the perpetrator was running away at a high rate of speed, and you were probably a good distance away from him. How can you be one hundred percent sure that the perpetrator you saw running away from Ms. Anderson's car was Mr. Jackson?"

The witness glared hard at Terrence's lawyer. "Because I'm sure," he said in an irritated tone.

"Are you sure simply because you've seen Mr. Jackson in the past coming and going from Ms. Anderson's condo, and you just assumed it was him because he maybe resembled the perpetrator that night?"

"No, I'm not."

"But it was dark, Mr. Jones, and you were standing a great distance away. How can you possibly say that you're one hundred percent sure that the perpetrator you saw running away that night was Mr. Jackson? Your eyesight cannot be that good."

"Objection, Your Honor." The prosecutor rose hastily. "Counselor is badgering the witness."

"Sustained."

"Sorry, Your Honor," Michael Baldwin said as he gathered his stuff from the podium. "No further questions."

"Very well," Judge Foster said as he looked at the big clock on the courtroom wall. "Court will stand at recess until 9 a.m. tomorrow morning when the prosecution will continue with its witnesses. Until then, court is adjourned."

Judge Foster banged his gavel as the courtroom began to clear.

Chapter 28

When court adjourned for the day, Frances and the rest of her family headed back to her house as they sat around in the living room and watched the nonstop news coverage of today's events of Terrence's trial on TV. The house was literally a beehive of activity. If it weren't friends dropping over or church members stopping by to give their support, then the phone constantly rang off the hook.

Frances fielded calls from reporters around the country wanting and demanding interviews concerning the trial and their family, and she turned them all down flatly. The calls quickly became a headache as Frances became more obstinate and ruder as the reporters became pushier. When the endless irritating calls wouldn't stop, Frances thought seriously about just cutting off her phone for the night. However, when the publisher for *Ebony Magazine* suddenly called and convinced her that they wanted to do a positive piece on her family, Frances reluctantly broke from her obstinate stand and agreed to do the interview. She went into her bedroom as she locked the door behind her. She was going to make certain that she had no disturbances whatsoever.

While Frances was locked away in her bedroom on the phone conducting the interview, her family sat quietly in the living room glued to the events on TV. By now, all of the friends and guest who'd trampled in and out of the house had finally ceased, and now only family remained. Willie Joe, Patricia, Carolyn, and Ernestine were all exhausted from the long day of court. The TV, with the constant coverage of the details of Terrence's trial still being analyzed and talked about, was the only thing keeping anyone company.

"Why the hell they keep talking about the prosecution hammered home some good points today," Ernestine said hastily as she listened to one of the commentators on TV analyzing the case. "They ain't got no proof that Terrence killed that girl."

"Don't let that stuff upset you," Willie Joe said without taking his eyes from the TV. "Them folks get paid to make it seem like they know what's going on. It ain't nothing but talk."

"Well, I ain't heard one damn word they said since we been sitting here in defense of Terrence. The way they talk, they *want* to see my boy found guilty."

"Like I said, Sis . . ." Willie Joe turned from the TV and looked at Ernestine, "it ain't nothing but a lot of babbling talk."

"Well, it just ain't right!" Ernestine scoffed.

"*Right* . . ." Carolyn said in a derisive tone as she looked over at Ernestine. "And just what do *you* know about what's right?"

Ernestine looked over at Carolyn with hooded eyes. By her glaring look, she was in no mood for games. "Don't you dare start with none of your mess," she said angrily. "My son is on trial here remember, or didn't you know."

"Uh . . . why don't we turn to something else," Patricia suddenly said as she seemed to perceive a fight beginning to brew. "I think we've all seen enough of this."

"Of course, I know he's on trial," Carolyn said hastily as she ignored Patricia. "I was there—*wasn't I*?"

"What you want . . . brownie points for showing up at court today and sitting with the family?" Ernestine countered. "The only reason you even came today is because Franny begged you to support the family and be with us in court. I know it must've really been embarrassing to march with us in court today with all those cameras and reporters shouting out all those scandalous questions and asking about our wonderful family history. I know you just wanted to run as far away as you possibly could from your *jinxed* family."

"Look, I canceled all of my classes today to make sure I could be there with the family in court." Carolyn fumed. "Franny didn't have to beg me—*I* made the choice to be there today. At least I was in court to support the family, which is more than I can say for your other trifling no a count son. Where was he?"

"Don't you think you could be a little more considerate, Carolyn!" Willie Joe snapped. "Ernestine's son is on trial for murder and all you want to do is stir up a lot of hell. You know, you beat everything."

"Considerate," Carolyn said with a jolt as she glared over at Willie Joe. "I'm the only one around here who seems to care that Franny has been under tremendous stress lately. She's been running around here these last few days worried more about you, Terrence, and Ernestine more than she has about the destruction of her own restaurant. You two seem like you don't give a damn that she's lost everything that she's worked for."

"She's got insurance, Carolyn." Ernestine flared. "It's going to get rebuilt."

"Yeah, and it's no skin off your back just as long as she keeps taking care of your ass!"

"Guys, please." Patricia stood up as she tried to be the peace maker. "Can we all just settle down and stop all of this bickering."

"You know, Carolyn," Willie Joe said forcefully as he suddenly rose from the sofa and literally pushed Patricia out of the way. "All of these years you ain't been nothing but an instigator. Everything we've ever done you've look down on, criticized, and belittled. You act like your life has been one perfect straight ass road, and you've never had obstacles in the way. Well, even if your path has been *smoother* than ours, that gives you no right to look down on us."

"I've never said my life has been perfect." Carolyn shot back. "Whenever obstacles have appeared in my path, I've dealt with them in a rational, reasonable fashion. I certainly didn't resort to no dope or booze to try to straighten out my problems. You two have done nothing but create all kind of havoc for everyone and have dragged this family down."

"Go ahead, get it all out," Ernestine said furiously. "Blame us for being such an embarrassment on your precious little organized life. I bet you can't stand when one of your colleagues down at that university brings up something about our family. I bet you just cringe and shudder all over."

"Well, I wouldn't have to cringe so much if I didn't have a sister on some porno tape getting screwed from behind while she was giving another man a blow job!" Carolyn ranted. "I got horny male students coming up to me dropping little innuendoes and insinuating what they would like to do if they only had the opportunity. And all of this is due because of your whorish, stank ass!"

"Shut up, Carolyn!" Willie Joe roared as he pointed a finger over at Carolyn. "We don't need none of that mess, so just shut up!"

"No . . . no, it's alright." Ernestine rose from the couch like a fighter who'd just gotten up from the canvas after a crushing blow. "Instead of worrying about me, maybe you need to try it yourself one of these days." She seethed. "Then just maybe George wouldn't have to go out looking for what he ain't getting at home!"

Carolyn jumped up and lunged at Ernestine as the two embittered sisters exploded into a vicious fight. Willie Joe quickly jumped into the middle of their melee and did all he could to pry them loose. The three of them together going back and forth, flaying and swinging, looked like a heap of clothes inside a Laundromat dryer tossed round and round.

"Break it up! Break it up!" Willie Joe roared as he finally pried his two squabbling sisters apart. "Just stop it!"

"What in the world is going on in here?" Frances yelled as she stormed into the living room. "I'm on the phone trying to do an interview and it sounds like a damn elephant trampling around in here! What the hell is going on?"

Carolyn and Ernestine glared at each other with vengeance in their eyes as Willie Joe held them at arm's length. All three were breathing rather heavily.

"I've had it with this damn family!" Carolyn shouted as she glared over at Ernestine. "I've had it!"

Carolyn turned and stormed out of the house as she headed straight for her car. Frances followed her out the door as she tried to get her to stop and talk, but Carolyn didn't want to hear any of it. When she jumped into her car and sped off, Frances came back into the house to find only Willie Joe and Patricia standing in the living room. Ernestine had gone to her bedroom and had slammed the door.

"What in the devil is going on around here?" Frances said desperately as she walked up to Willie Joe.

Willie Joe wiped the perspiration from his face as he slowly shook his head. "Just a little fight, Franny, that's all," he said in a nonchalant voice.

"A fight!" Frances blasted. "What the devil about?"

Willie Joe hung his head as he slowly rubbed his brow. When he didn't say anything, Patricia slowly grabbed his hand.

"We better be going, too, Willie Joe. It's getting late."

Willie Joe nodded slowly in agreement. "I . . . uh . . . I'll see you tomorrow, Franny."

"Patricia, will you be able to go with us tomorrow to court?"

"I've got to be at the hospital at eight in the morning, Frances. I'm sorry. I'm afraid I just won't be able to go with y'all tomorrow."

"That's quite alright," Frances said understandingly. "Thanks for coming today. I really appreciate it."

Frances watched as Willie Joe and Patricia headed out the door. Still too stunned and flabbergasted over the heated altercation that Carolyn and Ernestine had just engaged in, she couldn't even move. Finally, when she realized that everyone had left and she stood all alone in the living room, she headed back to her room.

When Frances came back into her bedroom and saw the phone still lying on the dresser off the hook, she suddenly remembered she'd put the publisher from *Ebony Magazine* on hold when she heard the loud ruckus out in the living room. Frances quickly picked the phone back up to continue the interview, but when she put the receiver to her ear, she realized that her heart just wasn't in it anymore as she slowly hung the phone up.

Instead, with her stomach filled with nothing but pain and sorrow, she slowly dropped to her knees beside her bed. With her heart aching, she began to pray a heart-rending prayer that God would somehow put an end to the bitter hatred and the deep divisiveness slowly choking the life out of her embattled family.

Chapter 29

The strippers at the Flamingo Exotic Palace were all over Travis. They smelled money and Travis gave them good reason to. All night long, Travis had spread hundred dollar bills around like raffle tickets at a giveaway. The women literally fought over one another to give this prime-time player their undivided attention, and to get a couple of Benjamins slipped between their G-strings. Nothing he wanted to fulfill his erotic fantasy was out of the question. Travis was the man, and every stripper in the exclusive VIP room treated him like the ultimate king.

To Travis, money grew on trees, and he was about to reap the biggest harvest in his life. The major cocaine deal that he'd set up, organized, and meticulously planned for the last couple of months was finally about to go down. Twenty kilos of Columbia's best were about to be shipped into his hands via Miami, and Travis could already count the loot he was going to make when he cut the shipment up and sold it on the streets.

Since his release from prison three years ago, he'd steadily moved up the chain and was fast becoming a major player. This deal, however, was finally going to push him into the big time, and it was only the beginning. Bigger deals were around the corner, and the money was just going to keep rolling right in. Mansions, yachts, a fleet of expensive cars, a swank restaurant or two, even a private leer jet didn't quite seem out of the question. Travis was dreaming big, but now he could afford to. He was on the cusp of having it all, and absolutely nothing was going to stop him from getting it.

By 2 a.m., Travis had finally had enough. He called it a night as he said so long to the entourage of females who surrounded him as he left the VIP room and departed from the strip club.

Feeling high and loose, Travis strolled through the parking lot as he made his way over to his Hummer and got in. He made a quick call on his cellphone to his boys on the street to check on how business was doing. When he hung up, he started up his Hummer and began to pull out of the parking lot. As soon as he began to back out, a white van suddenly pulled in front of him and blocked his path.

Three men jumped out of the van and quickly surrounded his Hummer. With their weapons brandished, they ordered Travis out of his truck. Travis, confused and startled, slowly opened his door. The men with the automatic weapons, however, weren't about to wait around for him to ease out of the truck. They quickly dragged Travis out of the driver seat and slammed him up against his Hummer. They kicked his legs apart and told him to put up his hands.

"Hey, what the hell is this—"

"Shut up!" the man with the automatic to Travis' head growled. His partner pulled out a badge and flashed it in Travis' face.

"Drug Enforcement Administration—DEA. We want you to take a little ride with us."

"Man, I ain't going nowhere with y'all." Travis complained. "I ain't done a damn thing. Y'all ain't got no right to do this."

The DEA agents ignored Travis' gripe as they quickly slapped handcuffs onto his wrists. They quickly hauled him into the van, slammed the doors, and sped out of the parking lot.

TRAVIS WAS TAKEN TO the DEA bureau downtown as he was seized from the van and taken to a secluded room inside the complex. The room had no windows or furnishings whatsoever; just a lone folding chair occupied the empty space. Travis, still handcuffed, was placed in the folding chair in the middle of the room. Two of the DEA agents took up positions along the wall and by the door, as the other agent, the lone black enforcement officer, hovered ominously over Travis. Travis looked up at his hardened face but was unmoved by all of the bluster and theatrics.

"Man, what the hell y'all bring me here for?" Travis blurted out when he got tired of their pretentious silence. "What's this all about?"

"I think you got a good idea why you're here, my man," the agent said sternly. "We know all about the major deal that's going down tomorrow. You want to come clean before we bust your ass."

"Man, I don't know what the hell you talking about!" Travis fumed. "What deal?"

"The deal you got with the Carruth brothers," the agent said as he leaned down and got into Travis' face. "Those twenty kilos you been waiting to purchase. We've been watching your ass for weeks. We know what's about to go down, my man. We know exactly what's about to happen."

Travis began to squirm, but he wasn't about to surrender to their pressure.

"Man, I want to call my lawyer." He protested. "This crap is unlawful."

"Go right ahead," the agent said calmly. "But when you make that deal with the Carruth brothers and we move in and bust your ass, the only good a lawyer will do you is to try to reduce your time. And that's *if* he can do that."

Travis' chin slowly dropped to his chest. He was beaten before he even got started and he knew it. All of his big plans and dreams had suddenly been thrown out the window. Now as he sat there handcuffed and surrounded by federal agents, he had nothing, absolutely nothing, to stand on.

"Now, you can either make one of two choices, my man," the agent finally said when he sensed Travis realized he had no way out. "You can either work with us, or you can just rot in prison for the rest of your life when we move in and bust your ass. The choice is yours, my man."

Travis remained silent for what seemed like a half an hour. He tried desperately not to give in, to hold out as long as he could. However, the longer he held out, the more he realized that he was cornered.

"What do you want?" he finally said.

"We've been trying to bust the Carruth brothers for some time now. Every time we've tried, they've alluded our efforts. But now we've got them right where we want them, and we know they're sitting on a mighty large supply. What we want from you is to go along with the deal, but we want you to wear a wire. A couple of agents will be stationed nearby, and at the appropriate time, we'll move in and make the bust. But instead of twenty kilos, we want you to arrange to buy forty keys. We'll front the buy money. The only thing you have to do is make the purchase. Then when the trial comes, you'll testify for us in court."

"And what the hell do I get out of this?" Travis said heatedly when he saw his big deal was crushed.

"You'll enter our witness protection program," the agent said as he leaned down once again into Travis' face. "And you get to stay out of prison."

Travis breathed deeply, then exhaled out of pure frustration. When he was finally able to grasp that his big dreams had been crushed, he slowly nodded agreeing to their terms.

Chapter 30

Court resumed on the second day of testimony as the prosecution continued with their line of witnesses. Frances, Ernestine, and Willie Joe sat in their same spot on the front row and watched intensely as the chief homicide detective of the Atlanta Police Department was sworn in and seated. The courtroom was once again packed with reporters, family, and those fortune enough to arrive in time to obtain a seat. The buzz was once again in the air. There wasn't a single sound uttered as everyone waited anxiously for the prosecutor to begin her line of questioning.

"Could you state your entire name and occupation for the record?" the prosecutor began.

"John Eagleberg. I'm a senior homicide detective for the Atlanta Police Department."

"And how long have you been a detective for the Atlanta Police Department, Mr. Eagleberg?"

"For thirty years."

"Thirty years," the prosecutor said with admiration. "So, you're considered an expert. I presume you are the most experienced detective in the Atlanta Police Department's homicide division?"

"I have a few more years of experience than some of the others," the detective said as he smiled modestly.

"Mr. Eagleberg," the prosecutor said with a serious face as she paused and looked over at the jury, "when you arrived at the Shadow Valley Condominiums on the morning that Joletta Anderson was murdered, describe to us the manner in which you found Joletta's body?"

"We found her body slumped over the steering wheel of her Mercedes with her throat slashed."

"And a police photographer came to the scene and took photographs of the murdered body?"

"Yes."

The prosecutor walked over to the prosecution table and grabbed the crime scene pictures lying on the table. "The state would like to introduce these into evidence, Your Honor," the prosecutor said as she handed the pictures to the judge.

"So ordered." Judge Foster acknowledged.

The clerk assigned them as—Exhibit A—as the prosecutor took the enlarged pictures of Joletta Anderson's dead body to the witness stand and handed them to Detective Eagleberg.

"Was this the manner in which you found Joletta Anderson's body, Detective Eagleberg?"

Detective Eagleberg slowly looked at the grisly pictures of Joletta's throat slashed viciously from ear to ear. He took his time and was in no hurry. "Yes, it was," he said as he continued to study the pictures.

Detective Eagleberg handed back the pictures to the prosecutor as she took them over to the jury as each member slowly looked at the pictures.

"Now, Detective Eagleberg," the prosecutor said as she returned to the podium, "during your investigation, was a weapon found on the morning that Joletta was murdered?"

"Yes, we found a knife in a field not far from the Shadow Valley Condominiums."

The prosecutor went over to the prosecution table as her assistant handed her a knife contained in a clear bag and marked as evidence. She took the knife over to the witness stand and handed it to Detective Eagleberg.

"Was this the knife you found on the morning that Joletta was murdered?"

Detective Eagleberg looked closely at the knife in the exhibit bag. "Yes, this is the knife we found in the field."

"And was it determined that this knife was the weapon used to murder Joletta Anderson?"

"Yes, it was."

"And how were you able to determine that?"

"The blood that was on the blade of the knife matched Joletta's blood."

"Now, detective," the prosecutor said as she retrieved the knife, "what else did you discover during your investigation of the crime scene?"

"We found fingerprints other than the victims on the steering wheel, the dashboard, on the window, and on the driver and passenger seats. We also found a cigarette lighter with the same fingerprints on it."

"And were these fingerprints analyzed?"

"Yes, from our crime lab we were quickly able to determine that the prints matched those of Mr. Terrence Jackson."

"And how were you able to determine that?"

"His data was already in our records from a previous conviction several years earlier."

"Because of his prior rape conviction?"

"Objection!" Terrence's lawyer rose quickly. "The record of my client is inadmissible."

"Overruled."

"But, Your Honor—"

"Continue Mrs. Brown," Judge Foster said as he cut off Terrence's attorney.

"Detective Eagleberg, were there any other findings during your investigation of the crime scene?"

"Yes, we found traces of dried blood under the fingernails of the victim."

"Traces of blood?"

"Yes."

"So, you're saying Joletta struggled with her perpetrator before she was murdered, and she maybe could've scratched her killer during the process of trying to feign him off."

"Exactly."

"Objection, Your Honor." Terrence's attorney rose again. "The gender of Ms. Anderson's murderer hasn't been established."

"Sustained."

"Detective Eagleberg," the prosecutor said as she continued. "When was the defendant, Terrence Jackson, arrested?"

"A few days after Ms. Anderson's murder."

"And were you the one that issued the arrest of Mr. Jackson?"

"I was part of the arresting party."

"And did you notice any scratch marks on the defendant's face, neck, or any other place?"

"Yes," the detective answered. "There were some long scratches along the right side of Mr. Jackson's neck."

The prosecutor looked over at the jury. "Thank you, Detective Eagleberg. No further questions."

Mrs. Brown retrieved the pictures from the jury as she headed back over to her table. Michael Baldwin slowly got up from the defense table as he approached the podium.

"Detective Eagleberg, were there any fingerprints found on the knife that you discovered from that field?"

"No, there wasn't."

"Well, that seems rather strange that no fingerprints were found on that knife, wouldn't you say, Detective?"

"Well, not at all," the detective said with confidence. "The perpetrator could've easily been wearing gloves."

"But you believe the fingerprints that were found inside Joletta's car were also those of the killer. Is that correct?"

"Yes. That's correct."

"Well, wouldn't it seem strange for the killer to have prints all through the victim's car, then suddenly put on a pair of gloves to commit a murder?"

The detective hesitated before he answered. "Yes . . . it would seem somewhat strange," he said slowly.

"I'd say it would seem *very* strange, Detective." Michael Baldwin emphasized.

Terrence, who paid close attention to the testimony, slowly nodded in agreement. His eyes were riveted straight on Detective Eagleberg's face as if he had a couple of questions he wanted to ask the witness himself.

"Now, Detective Eagleberg," Terrence's lawyer finally said after he got his point across, "wouldn't you concur that a murder of this nature would be attributed more in line of a professional hit, instead of a crime of passion?"

"No . . . not necessarily."

"And why would you disagree?"

"Because most professional hits are carried out with a gun. Rarely is a knife ever used to carry out a professional hit."

"Yes, but it's possible that this murder could've been carried out by a professional."

Detective Eagleberg hesitated as he looked out over the packed courtroom. "Anything is possible," he finally said.

"Detective Eagleberg, where was it determined that the assailant committed this murder?" Michael Baldwin said as he eyed the detective. "From inside the car or from outside?"

"From inside the car."

"But from the police report, it says that the window on the driver's side was shattered. Wouldn't this indicate that Ms. Anderson's attacker sneaked up and surprised her and smashed in her window and committed the murder from outside of her Mercedes? So, the murder couldn't happen inside the vehicle as you stated."

"That's not likely."

"And why's that, Detective Eagleberg?"

"On the back of the victim's left arm, there were heavy lacerations and bruises. This would indicate that when the perpetrator was attacking her, Ms. Anderson had swung her arm, perhaps out of fear or excitement, and during the adrenaline rush of being attacked, she swung a blow against the window causing it to shatter. And in the process, cutting her arm from the broken glass."

"But Ms. Anderson was a very petite woman. You actually believe she could break out the window in that fashion, Detective Eagleberg?"

"During the course of being attacked, and with her adrenaline rushing, yes, Mr. Baldwin, very much so."

Terrence's lawyer briefly became silent when Detective Eagleberg said those last words with resounding confidence. Frances, sitting along with Willie Joe and Ernestine, looked straight at the witness stand with a deep furrow on her face.

"Detective Eagleberg," Michael Baldwin said after he regrouped, "how well do you know Mayor Anderson?"

"I've met him a couple of times."

"You've been seen at various functions where the mayor has been at, and you've had your picture taken with the mayor numerous times. So, wouldn't you say you know Mayor Anderson fairly well?"

"Maybe . . ." Detective Eagleberg shrugged.

"So, when you heard that Joletta Anderson had been murdered on that night in May and you were called to the crime scene, you rushed to call Mayor Anderson, didn't you?"

Detective Eagleberg seemed to quickly detect the subtle meaning behind his question as he hesitated answering. "I called the mayor, but only after all the evidence was collected," he finally said.

"And what did you tell the mayor?"

"I told him that his daughter had been murdered," Detective Eagleberg said testily.

"And how long did you talk to the mayor?"

Detective Eagleberg shrugged. "Maybe five minutes," he said slowly.

"Five minutes?" Terrence's lawyer said with a raised eyebrow. "And what did the mayor say to you?"

"Well . . . he just wanted to make sure that the investigation got quickly underway and that we left no stone uncovered to catch the killer."

"And during that five-minute conversation, Detective Eagleberg, Mayor Anderson didn't try to hint to you his deep dislike and suspicion of my client?"

"Objection!" The prosecutor quickly rose.

"He didn't try to implicate Terrence Jackson just because he disapproved of him having a relationship with his daughter in which he just couldn't accept?"

"Objection!" the prosecutor shouted again.

"Sustained!" Judge Foster said as he crashed his gavel.

"You're sure you didn't go after Mr. Jackson because Mayor Anderson *wanted* him apprehended, Detective Eagleberg!"

"Objection, Your Honor! Objection!"

"Sustained!" Judge Foster said heatedly. "Mr. Baldwin, you are out of order!"

Terrence's lawyer slowly picked up his notes from the podium. "Sorry, Your Honor. No further questions."

After Detective Eagleberg stepped down from the witness stand, the coroner who came to the crime scene the night Joletta Anderson was murdered was brought to the stand as the prosecution solidified the cause and the actual manner right down to the precise detail of how Joletta was murdered on that night. That paved the way for the knife store owner on Pine Street to be brought to the stand. He was quickly called and sworn in as he had a seat on the witness stand.

"Would you state your entire name for the record." The prosecutor began.

"Bob Fentress," the middle age gentleman said.

"And what is your place of occupation, Mr. Fentress?"

"I own and run Fentress Knife Shop on Pine Street. I sell and buy all manner of knives, whether they're camping, military, utility, rare handmade knives, you name it . . . ."

"Mr. Fentress," the prosecutor said as she pointed over at Terrence sitting at the defense table, "do you remember seeing the defendant at any time come into your establishment?"

"Yes." He nodded as he looked over at Terrence. "He came into my store several times."

"And did he purchase a knife?"

"Yes, he did. I remember very clearly. He purchased one of my Bowie style knives."

"And describe to us what a Bowie style knife looks like?"

"Well, the one the gentleman sitting over there purchased was a fine homemade knife with a blade three by sixteen inches wide and eight inches long. The guard and spacer were German Silver, with Rope Filework along the guard. The handle was five inches long, made from a polished Desert Ironwood. The Ironwood was reddish brown with a nice grain pattern."

The prosecutor once again went over to her table as she retrieved the knife in the exhibit bag and carried it to the witness stand.

"Mr. Fentress, is this the knife that the defendant came into your shop and purchased?"

The knife owner held the knife as he carefully studied every inch of it. "Yes, this is the Bowie Knife that the young man sitting over there purchased."

"I see," the prosecutor said slowly as she looked over at the jury. "How much did the defendant pay for this knife?"

"I sold it to him for three hundred dollars."

"Three hundred dollars," the prosecutor said with admiration.

"It's a very fine made knife."

"And the defendant came in and paid cash for it?"

"Yes, he paid cash for the knife."

"And Mr. Fentress, when did the defendant come into your shop and purchase this knife?"

The witness reached into his suit coat and pulled out a small itemized booklet. He slowly flipped through the pages of his booklet until he found what he wanted.

"I sold a Coilte style Bowie knife, serial number 831506, to a Mr. Terrence Jackson on May 21st of this year."

"May 21st . . . only a week before Joletta Anderson was murdered," the prosecutor said as she gave the jury another dubious stare. She then came back to the witness stand as she retrieved the knife. "Thank you, Mr. Fentress. No further questions, Your Honor."

"Does the defense have any questions for the witness?" Judge Foster said as he looked over at the defense table.

Michael Baldwin knew Terrence had purchased a knife from Fentress Knife Store on May 21st. He knew there wouldn't be anything to gain by questioning the purchasing of the knife.

"No questions, Your Honor," Michael Baldwin finally said.

"Very well." Judge Foster proclaimed. "Court will stand adjourned until nine a.m. tomorrow morning."

THE SUN BEGAN TO SET over the late afternoon sky as DEA agents took up their positions near the abandon warehouse building located on the outskirts of the city. Three unmarked vans with four agents each sat concealed, listening, and waiting for their pigeon to arrive. The Carruth brothers were already there inside the warehouse. The only thing the DEA had to do was just wait and be patient.

An hour later when darkness had descended over the horizon, their pigeon arrived. Travis, along with three of his boys, pulled up in his Hummer to the entrance of the warehouse and parked. Nervous and still frustrated that his deal had been snatched away from him, Travis looked around as he stepped out of the Hummer to see if he could spot any agents nearby. He couldn't spot a one, but he knew without a doubt that they hovered close by, listening and waiting.

Wired and with the money in his possession, Travis and his posse—who were clueless of the deal he'd made with the DEA—headed into the warehouse for their appointed rendezvous with the Carruth brothers. The place was pitch black when Travis and his boys entered the warehouse. Then suddenly, the lights were switched on. The Carruth brothers, dressed in matching black Armani suits, immediately appeared from an office as they approached Travis and his posse. The two parties suddenly stopped when they got fifteen feet from one another. There were silent stares from both sides as each party gauged the other.

"On the phone you said you wanted forty kilos instead of twenty. Is that right, homie?" Big Bam Carruth said as his brother stood silently by his side. Travis, standing at the head of his posse, slowly nodded.

"That's right," he said forcefully, but with a twitch of nervousness in his voice.

"That's going to cost you another half a mil homie. You got the dough?"

"Yeah dog . . . I got the roll to cover that."

Big Bam Carruth looked down at the brown leather satchel in Travis' hand. "Is that it?" he pointed to the satchel.

"Yeah . . . I'm holding the money."

"Then step over here," Big Bam said as he pointed over toward a table, "and we'll get down to business, little homie."

Travis and his posse headed slowly over to the table as the Carruth brothers followed suit. There was a briefcase already placed in the middle of the table and Travis assumed that it was the forty kilos he was about to buy.

"Well, homie, why don't you show me that million in cash and we can get started with our business," Big Bam Carruth said as he and his brother stood on the other side of the table and eyed Travis. Travis eyes went straight to the briefcase.

"Why don't you show me what I'm getting first," he said as he stared at the briefcase.

"No problem, homie."

Big Bam Carruth opened the briefcase as Travis immediately saw the bags of cocaine. He handed the satchel over to one of his boys as he reached into the briefcase and opened one of the bags. He dipped his fingertip into the bag, then raised his finger and snorted the white powder. He quickly nodded with satisfaction.

"Yeah . . . that's the real deal."

"Ain't no doubt, little homie," Big Bam Carruth said with an arrogant smile. "The best stuff you'll ever find. So, if you're satisfied, then let's finish the rest of our business."

Travis nodded as his partner handed him back the satchel. The Carruth brothers eyed Travis as he opened the satchel and began to lay the thick rubber band wads of cash onto the table one after another. When he laid the last wad of cash down on the table, he looked up at the Carruth brothers and gave a nod.

"A cool million . . . just like we said. Y'all can check it out, it's all there."

"No need to, little homie," Big Bam said as he and his brother, Romeo, both pulled out 9 mm Glocks from their suit coats and pointed their weapons at the party across the table. Travis' boys quickly reached for their guns, but they were immediately halted.

"Reach and I'll blow your heads off!" Big Bam growled as Travis' boys slowly took their hands away from their guns. Before they realized it, they were surrounded by five other men with A-K 47's pointed at their backs. The men quickly stripped them of their weapons as Travis and his boys stood helpless against the Carruth brothers and their men.

"Yo, what the hell is this?" Travis yelled as he looked around at all the guns pointed at them.

"What do you think, homie. We taking the damn money!" Big Bam Carruth sneered. "Now you and your boys are going to come with us. We're going for a little ride."

"Where the hell are we going?" Travis asked fearfully.

"Shut up and move, I said!" The big man growled again.

Travis and his boys had no choice as they obeyed their captors. With weapons pointed at them in every direction, they slowly began to head with the Carruth brothers and their men toward the back door.

Travis and his boys took no more than five steps when all hell broke loose. The DEA agents busted in on the warehouse in every direction, creating instant panic and bedlam. Travis and his boys, fearing for their lives, tried desperately to scatter and run for cover. The vicious gun battle that quickly erupted was more hectic than any battlefield engagement. Bodies quickly fell one after another as the shooting was fast and fierce. The rapid blast of gunfire that exploded through the warehouse, sounded louder than a million cannons going off at the same time.

When the shooting was finally over, there was hardly a soul standing. The Carruth brothers and their men, Travis and his posse, along with a number of federal agents, lay motionless on the warehouse floor. With the rank smell of gunfire hovering over the air, the remaining agents began to search the bodies that lay motionless on the floor. There wasn't much life found as one body after another was pronounced dead and gone. Only one of the bodies riddled with bullets wasn't quite gone yet. Travis, with death probably only seconds away, still had a pulse.

Chapter 31

By the next morning, news of the DEA drug raid of the Carruth brothers and the big shooting that erupted at the abandon warehouse on the outskirts of Atlanta overnight began to make news. The death toll in the devastating gun battle had reached thirteen, and many unanswered questions still needed to be answered. Ordinarily a drug bust with a blazing gun battle and multiple deaths would create plenty of talk around many breakfast tables, but the fact that a member of the Jackson family was right smack in the center of it all during the middle of the most scrutinized murder trial in the city of Atlanta, created an avalanche of rumors, gossip, and controversy.

The Atlanta newspaper carried bold headlines of the incident that occurred overnight, and the news media had a field day with it. Once again, the Jackson family name was entangled in a scandalous story. Only this time, the negative press heaped upon their already tainted family name, seemed even more slanderous and villainous than ever before.

Frances, Ernestine, Willie Joe, and Patricia tried to ignore the barrage of questions shouted at them by reporters as they entered the courthouse. The questions were offensive enough to make anyone's blood boil.

"Does your entire family sell drugs?"

"How many scandals does this make for your family?"

"Mrs. Jackson, does your family have a genetic imbalance for deviant crimes?"

"What's the next episode for this family—to rob a bank?"

The torrid of snipes and questions from the aggressive, hounding reporters nearly made Frances snap, but somehow, she held her anger in check as she and her family headed on into the courthouse.

The courtroom quickly became packed once again as Terrence was soon brought in and placed in his seat at the defense table beside his attorney. A buzz swirled around the courtroom as everyone seemed to want to know all about the gun battle that had occurred last night, and Terrence was no different than anyone else.

He immediately turned around when he spotted Frances and the rest of the crew sitting on the front row as he mouthed the question, "How's Travis?" with desperate concern on his face. However, there was no time for any reply, least not any family conversation as Judge Foster promptly entered the courtroom. After the bailiff ordered everyone to rise, the judge quickly put the court proceedings back in session.

"Mrs. Brown, call your next witness," Judge Foster said off the bat as he had a seat and the courtroom came to order.

"Your Honor, the state calls Vanessa Baxter to the stand."

Terrence's stomach grumbled and pained when he heard his ex-girlfriend called to the stand. He knew for days that she would testify and he'd dreaded it since.

Their break-up two years ago ended in such a heated, nasty affair, and Terrence knew that Vanessa definitely couldn't wait to get back at him. His arrest for domestic battery and their tumultuous three-year relationship were about to be aired for everyone to hear. Terrence's lawyer tried to persuade the judge not to allow her to testify on the grounds that her testimony would inflame the jury and that it wasn't germane to the current case.

Judge Foster, however, overruled Terrence's lawyer, stating the fact that since Terrence was arrested and sentenced to thirty days in jail for domestic battery—and that a knife was used against his ex-girlfriend—that her testimony was very much relevant to this case. She could indeed testify, and there was absolutely nothing that neither Terrence nor his lawyer could do about it.

Vanessa Baxter, dressed in a starched white blouse and blue skirt, took to the witness stand as she was sworn in and seated. The attractive young woman of early twenties looked over at the defense table at Terrence, and by the hateful, scornful look that she gave him, it was clear that today she was going to get her payback.

"Could you state your entire name for the record?" The prosecutor began.

"Vanessa Shantella Baxter," she said like a charming receptionist.

"Now, Ms. Baxter," the prosecutor hesitated after her opening words as she looked over at the defense table, "when did you first meet the defendant, Terrence Jackson?"

"We met at a party one night about four years ago."

"And did you two start dating after that?"

"Yes, we did."

"And how long was it when your relationship finally became serious?"

"We were seeing one another on a regular basis for a couple of months, then about a year later, we moved into an apartment together."

"And how were you two earning income?"

"I was working at a bank as a teller, and he was working at several clubs around the city deejaying."

"And how was your relationship when you two first moved in together?"

"At first . . . it was good," Vanessa said slowly.

"I see," the prosecutor spoke as she once again glanced over at Terrence sitting at the defense table. "Now, Ms. Baxter, when did you first realize your relationship with the defendant began to grow troublesome?"

"About six months after we moved in together."

"And how did your relationship begin to change?"

"Terrence started to become jealous when I used to stay out late at night with my girlfriends. He thought I was fooling around on him."

"And did his jealousy toward you turn to violence?"

"Not at first . . . but eventually it did."

"And when did he become violent?"

Vanessa looked over at Terrence with anger in her eyes. "One night I came home from a birthday party that one of my friends was having," Vanessa said slowly. "My car had stalled and I had to get a ride home with a male friend who was at the party. So, when we pulled into the apartment complex and my friend parked to let me out, that's when Terrence pulled up beside us."

"And what happened after that?"

"When I got out of the car, Terrence charged out of his car and jumped in my face. We got into a big argument and things were getting really heated. Then all of a sudden, Terrence hauled off and slapped me so hard that I fell to the ground."

"He slapped you outside of your apartment?"

Vanessa nodded. "Yes. That's when the guy who gave me the ride home got out and tried to come to my aid, but Terrence pulled a gun on him."

"He pulled a *gun* on your friend?" the prosecutor said with an astonished look.

"Yes."

"Then what happened?"

"I told the guy just to leave. That I'd be okay."

"And did he leave?"

"Yes . . . he left."

"And then what took place after that?"

"We went on into the apartment and we ended up arguing some more, for quite a long time."

"Weren't you afraid of the gun he had on him, that he might try to use it on you?"

"No," she said slowly as she looked down. "I didn't think he would try to harm me at the time."

"So, you didn't try to press charges for him striking you at the time?"

"No."

The prosecutor looked down at her notes, then glanced over at the jury as if to make sure she had everyone's attention; all twelve stared intently at Vanessa Baxter sitting on the witness stand.

"Now, Ms. Baxter, after the time when he struck you in front of your apartment, were there other altercations in your relationship when he struck you or threatened you?"

Vanessa glared once again over at the defense table at Terrence. "Yes . . . he did," she said with vengeance in her voice.

"Could you describe to the court those altercations?"

She slowly took her eyes away from Terrence as she focused once more on the prosecutor. By her vengeful look, she was ready to drop the bomb on Terrence.

"After that initial altercation, the relationship between Terrence and me slowly began to grow worse," Vanessa said with pain in her voice. "There were times when he'd come home from working late at the club and he'd be drunk. He'd start a fight with me over anything, and the next thing I'd know, he'd be hitting me."

"So, Mr. Jackson was continually striking you and abusing you as your relationship went on?" The prosecutor said as she looked over at the jury.

"Yes . . . he was."

"Please continue, Ms. Baxter."

"Well . . . one night I'd finally had enough of all his abuse and decided to just pack up my stuff and leave. So, when I was about to head out of the apartment, Terrence walks in and blocks me from leaving. We get into this heated argument, then he starts hitting me. I try to protect myself. So, I end up kicking him in his groin and try to fly out of the apartment as fast as I can, but Terrence yanks me by my hair and drags me into the kitchen where he gets a knife and presses it against my throat saying that he was going to kill me."

"And you feared for your life?"

"Yes."

"And what happened after that?"

"Well, the neighbors called the police because of all the noise that was going on. When the police finally came to our apartment, they arrested Terrence."

"And you filed charges against him?"

"Yes . . . I did."

"And he was sentenced to serve a month in jail and was ordered not to come within a hundred feet of you again?"

"Yes."

"Now, Ms. Baxter, when you heard that Terrence Jackson had been charged in the stabbing death of Ms. Joletta Anderson, did you believe, based on the experience you endured with Mr. Jackson threatening you with a knife, that he committed this crime?"

Vanessa glared over at Terrence sitting at the defense table. "Yes . . . I did."

"And did you feel that if you stayed in a relationship with Mr. Jackson, possibly that could've been you who was stabbed and murdered so viciously?"

Vanessa kept her steady glare dead on Terrence, as Terrence kept his steady glare dead on her. "Yes," she said with anger pulsating in her voice. "I most certainly do believe that could've been me."

The prosecutor looked over at the jury and saw all of their undivided attention square on Vanessa Baxter's pain, wrenched face. "No further questions, Your Honor," she finally said as she retrieved her notes from the podium and headed back to her table.

Terrence's lawyer got up from the defense table and took the place of the prosecutor at the podium.

"Ms. Baxter, you and Mr. Jackson lived together for two years. Is that correct?" Mr. Baldwin said slowly.

"Yes . . . that's correct."

"And during that time, you stated that your relationship with Mr. Jackson was often contentious and abusive?"

"Yes . . . it was."

"But it certainly wasn't one-sided as you have made it seem, was it Ms. Baxter?"

"What do you mean?"

"There were numerous times when you, Ms. Baxter, initiated the abuse. Times when your jealousy and mistrust caused you to lose the betterment of *your* judgment."

"I don't follow you," Vanessa said hastily.

"Well, let me refresh your memory then, Ms. Baxter," Michael Baldwin said as he pulled out a police report from a folder.

"Two years ago, one night at a restaurant, you saw Mr. Jackson and another young woman out having dinner together and you approached them and had some very heated words. Things quickly got ugly and witnesses stated that you threw a beverage into the face of Mr. Jackson and a nasty brawl took place with you and the other young woman inside the restaurant. And you were both arrested, isn't that correct, Ms. Baxter?"

"Well . . . yeah . . . maybe."

"And on another particular night, you came to the club where Mr. Jackson was working and had a very loud and ruckus argument with Mr. Jackson. You accused him of cheating on you, and you proceeded to go out into the parking lot and smash out all of the windows to his brand-new Mazda with a bat. And you were still shouting and cursing in the middle of the parking lot like a raving lunatic when the police arrived. Isn't that correct, Ms. Baxter?"

"It . . . it wasn't like—"

"Isn't that correct, Ms. Baxter?" Mr. Baldwin pressured the nervous witness.

"Yes!" Vanessa snapped with anger.

"And furthermore, Ms. Baxter, isn't it correct last year when you found out that Terrence Jackson was dating Joletta Anderson, that on several occasions you followed and stalked them when they were out and about on the town. And on one particular occasion, you were caught trying to flatten the tires of Ms. Anderson's Mercedes because you were jealous of their relationship and couldn't take the fact that you and Terrence were no longer together anymore?"

Vanessa Baxter stared out at the packed courtroom with a silent, blank expression, as if she didn't want to answer the question.

"Ms. Baxter, is it, or is it not true, that you tried to flatten Ms. Anderson's tires?"

Vanessa remained silent.

"Please answer the question, Ms. Baxter." Judge Foster demanded.

"Yes . . ." she finally said in a defeated voice.

Michael Baldwin stared at the witness, then slowly gathered his notes from the podium. "No further questions, Your Honor."

"Any redirect?" Judge Foster said to the prosecutor as she slowly shook her head.

"Then the witness may be excused."

Vanessa Baxter rose slowly from the witness stand and headed dejectedly out of the courtroom.

"You may call your next witness," Judge Foster said after Ms. Baxter had departed the courtroom.

The prosecutor rose as she stood behind the table. "Your Honor, the State rests."

"Very well," Judge Foster said. "We will recess until 9 a.m. in the morning when the defense will begin calling its witnesses. Until then, court's adjourned."

WHEN COURT WAS ADJOURNED Frances, Ernestine, Willie Joe, and Patricia headed over to the Atlanta County Hospital to check on Travis' condition. The hospital literally swarmed with reporters when Frances and her crew arrived at the information desk. When they spotted Frances and the family, they quickly surrounded them like a pack of hungry dogs salivating over a fresh mound of raw meat. Frances fought off their incessant questions until a DEA agent suddenly showed up. He led the family away from the rove of reporters to a small room. Everyone waited patiently for him to speak.

"I'm agent Frank Conners," he said as he flashed his badge. "I guess by now you've heard of the situation that transpired last night on the outskirts of town at that abandon warehouse."

"What happened?" Willie Joe said as the law enforcement officer in him seemed to suddenly resurface.

"Our division was conducting a major drug sting on the Carruth brothers. We knew they were sitting on a major shipment of cocaine, and our unit was prepared to bring down their operation. But a problem developed during the conducting of the sting and our people had to act."

"And Travis was part of the sting?"

"Yes . . ." the agent said reluctantly. "We discovered some weeks back that he was about to make a major transaction with the Carruth brothers. Our people apprehended him a few days before the transaction was to take place and we offered him a deal if he helped us set up the Carruth brothers, and he took it. Unfortunately, the sting didn't go as we planned."

When a surgeon opened the door and entered the room, everyone's attention was suddenly drawn to him. Agent Conners left from the room as the family waited eagerly for the surgeon to speak.

"I'm Dr. Gerald Synder," he said as he looked around at the family. "You're the Jackson family, I presume?"

"Yes . . . how's my son?" Ernestine quickly said.

"Travis was admitted to our hospital last night with multiple gunshot wounds. We were in surgery most of the night, and as of early this morning, we were able to remove all but one of the bullets. Right now, he's stable, but there's serious concern."

"What kind of concern?" Frances said in a troubled voice.

"Travis has sustained significant damage to his spinal cord from one of the bullets that entered through his side. If he does indeed survive, it's most likely that he'll never be able to walk."

"You mean . . . that he's paralyzed," Ernestine said with reluctance.

"Yes, ma'am, it looks that way."

Everyone slowly cast their eyes to the floor. Frances, who'd long ago given up on Travis, couldn't help but to feel pain and sympathy for her grandson.

"What . . . what can we do?" Frances finally said as she looked at the doctor.

"There's not much anyone can do. Just wait . . . and be patient," he said as he looked around at everyone. "I'm sorry."

The doctor quickly left from the room as Frances and her family stood in silence. When they finally came out of the room to head home, the reporters once again surrounded them as they prodded and goaded them with question after question.

Chapter 32

The next morning Frances and her family headed back to the courthouse as Terrence's trial continued. Today the defense would begin calling its line of witnesses, and the first to be called to the stand was Frances herself.

Frances wasn't up to testifying in front of a packed courtroom, but Terrence's lawyer insisted that she say a few words to help establish a positive image for her grandson. She felt low today, and it wasn't just the devastating news about Travis.

Yesterday when Frances returned home from the hospital, she received the news in the mail from the Department of Children Services rejecting her appeal to adopt Trinika's sixteen-month-old child. The news came as a crushing blow, along with all the other crushing blows that had occurred over the course of the past couple of months. Frances told herself that she wasn't going to despair. She wasn't going to let this blow, or any other future blow, drain her spirits. She still believed that God would somehow make a way to bring unity and harmony to her besieged family. With that in mind, she knew she had to keep going and stay strong, for herself, and for her family.

When Frances took the stand and laid her hand on the Bible and swore to tell the truth, she did it with the utmost sincerity than anyone before her. She then had a seat and waited for Mr. Baldwin to address her as he stepped to the podium.

"Mrs. Jackson, how are you feeling today?" Mr. Baldwin said with a pleasant smile.

"I'm making it alright," Frances said in a strong voice.

"You and your family have certainly endured a lot over the last couple of months, haven't you?" the attorney said sympathetically.

"Yes, we have," Frances said slowly. "But we're a strong family and we'll survive."

"Indeed, you shall," Mr. Baldwin said optimistically. "Now, Mrs. Jackson," the attorney said as he pointed over at Terrence sitting alone at the defense table. "You indeed know the young gentleman who's sitting over there at the table and who's currently on trial, don't you?"

"Yes, I do. He's my grandson."

"And you certainly know this young gentleman better than anyone, don't you?"

"Yes . . . you can say that," Frances said as she looked over at Terrence, and as Terrence looked back at her. "I've pretty much raised him since he was a small child."

"And how would you describe the character of your grandson?"

Frances once again looked over at Terrence. "He's a smart young man that can do anything he put his mind to," she said with reverence. "A young man that I've raised to know right from wrong, and knows that hard work will take you where you want to go in life."

"So, you instilled some good wholesome values in your grandson?"

"Indeed, I have," she said without doubt.

"Now, Mrs. Jackson, when you heard that Joletta Anderson had been murdered, how did you feel?"

"I thought it was such a shame," Frances said in a heartfelt voice. "I thought she was so young and had so much promise going for her to depart from this world like that. I thought it was really a tragedy."

"Now, Mrs. Jackson, did you know that Terrence and Joletta Anderson had had a relationship?"

"Yes, I did."

"And you knew at one time that they were really close?"

"Yes . . . I knew of it."

"How much did you know of their relationship?"

"Well, I knew that she and Terrence were working together at that dance club, but not much beyond that. I try not to meddle too much in Terrence's own social life."

"But when you heard that Joletta had been murdered, did you think, even for a split second, that Terrence could've had anything to do with it?"

"Absolutely not!" Frances said in a riled voice.

"And you were one-hundred-percent sure he could no way commit such an act?"

"I know my grandson, Mr. Baldwin," Frances said in a heated voice, "and he's *certainly* no murderer."

Michael Baldwin slowly nodded his head. "Well, thank you, Mrs. Jackson. I have no more questions."

"Does the prosecution have any questions for the witness?" Judge Foster asked as Mrs. Brown quickly declined. "Very well, Mrs. Jackson, you may step down."

———————◦———————

CAROLYN ARRIVED HOME tired and in need of a hot bath after a long day of lecturing classes at Georgia Tech. She went straight up to her bedroom as she laid down her briefcase and checked the messages on the phone. After listening to the five or so meaningless messages on the recorder, she picked up the phone to call Frances to see how her day in court went. Before she could dial the number, she heard the front door downstairs open and close back.

George had left the house nearly two weeks ago, returning only once or twice to get a fresh change of clothes, or to retrieve some important files he needed for the office. Carolyn, with her heart racing, quickly hung up the phone as she heard George coming up the stairs. She desperately hoped that he had decided to end his brief separation and was finally coming back home for good, but when she saw the look on his face as he slowly walked into the bedroom, her heart began to sink.

"So, have you finally decided to come back home, or are you some kind of burglar that's come to terrorize me." Carolyn slowly smiled as she tried an ill attempt at humor.

"No . . . I . . . uh," George said as his words trailed off. Both Carolyn and George stared at one another until the sight of one another became uncomfortable.

"Look, George, whatever problems we have between us—"

"No, Carolyn," he said as he quickly cut her off. "No more. Not any longer."

"What . . . what are you trying to say then?"

George looked away. "Carolyn, I'm trying to say . . . I'm saying that it's over," he said as he turned back to face her once again. "I think it's time that we go our separate ways."

"Why?" Carolyn steamed. "Because my family keeps embarrassing you, bringing down your prestige and ego around your precious peers. You afraid you won't get your damn picture on the cover of *Time* magazine if you stay connected with my family?"

"No, Carolyn." George sighed as he shook his head. "That's not it."

"Oh, how silly of me," Carolyn said in a mocking voice. "If that's not it, then it must be that whore of a nurse who you can't seem to stop sleeping with, isn't it?"

"Carolyn . . ."

"No, I want to hear it from your mouth." Carolyn demanded. "Is it because of her?"

"Look, Carolyn—"

"Don't lie to me, George!"

"Yes!" George finally shouted. "You want to know the truth, then yes! It's because of Julie."

George stared at Carolyn as they both grew silent. The dreaded silence seemed to pain both of them the longer they stared at one another.

"Look, Carolyn, there's nothing left between us," George finally said as he broke the silence. "We've been drifting apart for a long time. We've simply just been hanging on, going through the motions."

When they grew silent once again, George slowly stepped to Carolyn and gently handed her some papers.

"What's this?" Carolyn said as she took the papers.

"I went to see my attorney," George said slowly. "I'm willing to give you the house, and I'm sure we can come to an equitable agreement over alimony. I just want to make this as smooth a transition as possible," he said as he suddenly became silent. "I'm sorry."

George slowly turned and headed out of the bedroom as he went back down the stairs and out of the house. When Carolyn heard the door close, she slowly sat down on the edge of the bed as she stared down at the papers in her hand. The weight, the pain, and the burden on her shoulders suddenly became too much to bear as the papers that George had given her slowly fell from her fingers, along with the tears that fell from her eyes.

Chapter 33

C ourt reconvened the next morning as the defense called the bartender to the stand who worked at the Seven Flavors nightclub. The heavy set muscular gentleman raised his right hand and swore to tell the truth as he had a seat on the witness stand.

"Would you state your entire name for the record?" Mr. Baldwin began.

"Lucas Alexander."

"Now, Mr. Alexander, you worked as a bartender at the nightclub Seven Flavors, is that correct?"

"Yes."

"How long were you a bartender at Seven Flavors?"

"Since the club first opened up three years ago."

"Then you certainly know the gentleman sitting over there then, don't you?" Mr. Baldwin pointed over at Terrence sitting at the defense table.

"Definitely."

"He was the DJ at the club, isn't that correct?"

"Yes, and one of the best DJ's around, I might add," the bartender said as he looked over at the defense table as he and Terrence exchanged quick smiles.

"How was your relationship with Terrence during the time that y'all worked together at the club?"

"At first, we had somewhat of a casual relationship. But as time went by we became closer, then later on, we became good friends."

"Did Terrence ever come and talk to you about personal issues as close good friends often do?"

"Yes, he did."

"So he was quite open with you about his personal life?"

"Yes, he was."

Mr. Baldwin nodded.

"Now, Mr. Alexander," he said slowly, "did you know of a relationship between Terrence and the owner of the club, Ms. Joletta Anderson?"

"Of course . . . everyone knew."

"So, you knew that they were romantically involved?"

"Yes."

"Now, Mr. Alexander, on the days leading up to Joletta's murder, did you ever see Terrence and Joletta interact much during the club hours?"

"Yes, quite often."

"Was there any anger or hostility between them?"

"You mean were they ever arguing or fighting?"

"Yes?"

"No . . . never."

"Did Terrence ever confide in you that he was by anyway upset with Joletta during the days leading up to her murder?"

"Absolutely not."

"So in your view, being close friends with Terrence and working in so close of a space with both Terrence and Joletta, you didn't see any kind of ill will between them?"

"No," the bartender said as he shook his head firmly. "There *was* no anger, hostility, ill will, or no kind of outward rage between them. Absolutely none."

"Thank you, Mr. Alexander," Michael Baldwin said. "No more questions."

Mrs. Brown got up and replaced the defense counselor at the podium.

"Mr. Alexander, you said you saw no outward signs of hostility between the defendant and Joletta leading up to her murder, is that correct?"

"Yes."

"But how do you know there was no hostility between them just because you didn't *see* any outward signs of it?"

"Because I know Terrence, and know that he and Joletta were not fighting or angry about anything."

"That which you know of," the prosecution quickly said. "What about the additional advance money that the defendant was demanding from Joletta. Did the defendant ever talk to you about that?"

The bartender hesitated. "No . . . he didn't."

"The defendant *never* mentioned anything to you about it?" the prosecutor asked in a startled voice.

"No . . . he didn't."

"I kind of find that hard to believe, Mr. Alexander, since you said that you and the defendant were *really* close."

The witness shrugged. "It's just something he never talked about."

"Well, perhaps, Mr. Alexander, the defendant never talked about it because he was trying to hide the true anger and rage that was boiling down deep in him, and he didn't want you to discover what he really felt about Joletta Anderson, wouldn't you say, Mr. Alexander?"

"Objection, Your Honor," Michael Baldwin said in defense.

"Sustained."

"Perhaps the defendant was trying to hide his true intentions from you that he was all the while plotting and planning to kill Ms. Anderson, wouldn't you say, Mr. Alexander?" The prosecutor rolled on.

"Objection."

"Sustained."

"And perhaps you really don't know the defendant as well as you thought you did, wouldn't you say, Mr. Alexander? He could've been a mass murderer and you wouldn't know it."

"Objection!" Michael Baldwin roared.

"Sustained. You're out of order, Mrs. Brown," Judge Foster said as he banged his gavel.

"Sorry, Your Honor," the prosecutor said as she began to leave the podium. "No further questions."

After Judge Foster dismissed the bartender from the stand, the defense called the drive-in market attendant who worked at the store located only a block from Terrence's apartment. The drive-in market worker took the witness stand and was quickly sworn in.

"Would you state your entire name for the record?" Mr. Baldwin began.

"Lance Stewart," the young nineteen-year-old with multicolored hair said.

"And where do you work?"

"I work the night shift at the Zip and Go Market located on Memorial Drive."

"And were you working the store on the early morning of May 30th of this year?"

"Yes, I was."

"Do you remember seeing the gentleman sitting over there come into the store on that early morning?" Mr. Baldwin said as he pointed over at Terrence sitting at the defense table.

"Yes, I remember him coming into the store."

"On the morning of May 30th of this year?"

"Yes."

"Do you remember what time it was when Mr. Jackson came into the store on that early morning?"

"It was around three-thirty or so," the witness said as he looked over at Terrence.

"Around three-thirty . . . are you sure?"

"Oh, yes, I remember exactly. He came into the store right when the patrol officer who normally comes in and makes the security rounds at the store at night. And every night, he makes his checks around three-thirty."

"So, Mr. Jackson came into the market at three-thirty, the same time as the police officer came into the store, is that correct?" Mr. Baldwin said as he looked over at the jury.

"Yes . . . he did."

Michael Baldwin purposely halted his line of questioning as he let his point that he tried to get across to the jury sink in. The prosecution, during the presentation of their case, brought witnesses to the stand—in particular the security guard at the Shadow Valley Condominiums—who testified that they witnessed Terrence running from Joletta Anderson's Mercedes at three-thirty on the morning of May 30th. The defense counselor let it sink in that Terrence couldn't be at the Shadow Valley Condominiums committing a murder at three-thirty that morning, and also be at the Zip and Go Market on Memorial Drive some ten miles away all at the same time.

"Now, when Mr. Jackson entered the Zip and Go Market at three-thirty on the morning of May 30th," Mr. Baldwin said as he continued, "did he appear anyway nervous, agitated, or in a hurry?"

"No . . . I don't recall him being nervous or anything."

"So, you're saying that he was perfectly normal the entire time he was in the market?"

"Yes."

"What did he purchase while he was in the market?"

"If I recall correctly, he purchased a six pack of beer and a bag of Cheetos."

"Thank you, Mr. Stewart. No further questions."

The prosecutor took the place of the defense counselor at the podium.

"Mr. Stewart, you said the defendant came into the market at three-thirty on the morning of May 30th?"

"Yes . . . he did."

"And that he seemed normal and at ease, is that correct?"

"Yes, that's correct."

"Mr. Stewart, did the store have the surveillance camera operating on the morning of May 30th?"

The witness hesitated as he looked out at the packed courtroom. "Uh . . . no we didn't."

"And why didn't the Zip and Go Market have its surveillance camera operating?"

"Uh . . . because it wasn't working."

"So, the surveillance camera wasn't working at the Zip and Go Market on Memorial Drive on the morning of May 30th?" the prosecutor said in a flabbergasted voice as she gave the jury a critical look.

"No, it wasn't."

"Had the surveillance camera been out of order the previous nights?"

"No."

"But it just so happened that it wasn't working on the morning of May 30th?" the prosecutor said again in an astounded voice.

"Yes."

The prosecutor gave the jury another cynical look.

"Now, Mr. Stewart," Mrs. Brown said as she continued, "you stated that the patrol officer made his security check of the store at exactly three-thirty on the morning of May 30th, and that the defendant entered the store at exactly the same time that the patrol officer came into the store. Is that correct?"

"Yes, that's correct."

"And you're positive that it was three-thirty that the patrol officer came into the store on that morning?"

"Yes, absolutely," the drive-in attendant said with confidence. "Every night he makes his check of the store at 3:30 a.m. At least it's been that way ever since I started working."

"But not on the morning of May 30th," the prosecutor said firmly. "Because I have an affidavit from Officer Karl Wiggins, the security patrol officer, stating that on the morning of May 30th, he didn't arrive at the store on Memorial Drive until 4 a.m. because of a prior emergency at another store. So, it's possible that you only *thought* that the defendant came into the store at three-thirty because you saw the security patrol officer arriving, which in fact was a whole thirty minutes later than three-thirty. Is that possible, Mr. Stewart?"

The drive-in attendant slowly shrugged. "I guess . . . I guess it's possible."

"And isn't it possible, Mr. Stewart," the prosecutor drilled on, "that you were fired later that same morning on May 30th because you were caught smoking a joint in the store's bathroom, and you were only given another chance and rehired just a couple of weeks ago?"

Terrence's lawyer almost slumped in his seat. He thought he'd checked his witness out thoroughly, but undoubtedly his background check had a gaping hole in it. He looked over at the jury and saw a couple of the jurors shaking their heads.

"Yeah . . ." the drive-in attendant said reluctantly.

"So, now we all know, Mr. Stewart, that you were intoxicated when you were working on the morning of May 30th. You could've thought you seen an elephant come walking into that store and thought it was the defendant. Isn't that correct, Mr. Stewart?"

"Objection, Your Honor." Michael Baldwin rose slowly as he tried to save his witness. "The prosecution is trying to belittle the witness."

"That's alright. I'll withdraw the question," the prosecutor said before the judge could respond. "I'm finished with this witness, Your Honor."

<hr />

MICHAEL BALDWIN AND Terrence sat at a table in a small guarded room on the second floor of the Atlanta jail as they rehearsed and prepared for Terrence's testimony. Tomorrow was going to be an important day, and Terrence's lawyer wanted everything to go as smoothly as possible. They'd already suffered a major hit today as the prosecution tore into the credibility of the drive-in market worker who testified on the stand, and they didn't need any slip-ups tomorrow when Terrence's scheduled testimony began.

After the fiasco of today's testimony, Terrence's whereabouts on the morning of May 30th were still not clear, and even more, his innocence was now in serious jeopardy. If Terrence had any chance at all of getting an acquittal, then his performance tomorrow on the witness stand had to be not only convincing, but it had to be downright perfect.

After nearly two hours of nonstop rehearsing and practicing for Terrence's testimony, Terrence and his lawyer finally decided to call it quits. When the session ended, the guard took Terrence back to his cell as his lawyer left the jail and headed back to his office.

When Michael Baldwin returned to his office, he had a seat at his desk as he began to finish up some more work for Terrence's testimony tomorrow. After a couple of minutes or so of undisturbed peace, his secretary suddenly buzzed his inner office and informed him that he had a long-distance call waiting. He reached across his desk and picked up his phone.

"Hello, Michael Baldwin here," he said as he continued working.

"Yes, this is Yolanda Evans," the woman said in an almost nervous, shaken voice.

Michael listened patiently. "How can I help you, Mrs. Evans?"

"I was calling you about the trial," the woman said slowly. "You see I knew Joletta. We were roommates in college."

"Yes . . ." Michael Baldwin said patiently as he tried to coax the nervous woman along to the point.

"Well, right before she was murdered, I was receiving some disturbing phone calls from her."

"Disturbing phone calls . . . about what?"

"About her involvement with the Carruth brothers."

"The Carruth brothers!" Michael Baldwin said with shock.

"Yeah . . . I heard about that big drug raid there in Atlanta a couple of days ago. And I figured that now the Carruth brothers were dead and gone, that it was alright to tell someone what I knew. I was just too afraid to say anything before I heard about the drug raid."

"Exactly what is it you know, Mrs. Evans?"

The voice on the other end of the phone suddenly became silent; then, the caller let out a long nervous sigh.

"Joletta and I have been very good friends since our days in college. She often liked to call and confide in me whenever she was troubled or feeling low," she said slowly.

"Yes . . . go ahead, Mrs. Evans." Michael Baldwin prided her on.

"Well, the days leading up to her murder, Joletta was calling me quite often and telling me that she was getting pressured by the Carruth brothers. They wanted the money that she owed them, and when she couldn't come up with it, she said they were beginning to threaten her."

"You mean threatening to kill her?"

"Yes . . . and the times when I talked to her on the phone, she sounded really scared. She was really agonizing over how she was going to come up with the money."

"How much money?"

"She said it was close to ten million dollars."

"Ten million dollars!" Michael Baldwin said in disbelief. "How did Joletta ever get tangled up owing the Carruth brothers ten million dollars?"

"The Carruth brothers had loaned her money several times over the last couple of years. Joletta had been steadily sinking the money into her club and forming her music company. She said she'd been paying the Carruth brothers back in sort of small payments. But all of a sudden, she said they began to pressure her to pay them everything that she owed them all at once. That entire week before she was killed, I talked to her every night on the phone. Each time we talked, I could tell she was becoming more and more tense about the situation. Then the next thing I know, I turned on CNN one morning and find out she'd been murdered."

"And you believe the Carruth brothers murdered her?"

"Yes, I do."

"Mrs. Evans, how do I know that all what you're telling is the truth?"

"Mr. Baldwin, I have absolutely no reason to tell you some phony, cockamamie story," the woman said sincerely. "I only called you because I know you're defending that Jackson guy that she used to date. From what she was telling me about the Carruth brothers and how she was behaving those last few days, I just don't think that he killed Joletta," she said candidly. "And

204

if you don't believe me, I always record all of my phone conversations. And every single one of those conversations I had with Joletta that week before she was murdered were recorded."

"You have the phone conversations with Joletta recorded?" Michael Baldwin asked sharply.

"Yes."

"And you still have the tapes?"

"Yes, I do."

Terrence's lawyer mind suddenly raced all over the place. "Mrs. Evans, where are you right now?"

"I'm in Phoenix."

"If I could get you on a plane to Atlanta, could you be here by tomorrow?"

"Mr. Baldwin, I don't know if I want to be testifying or anything like that?"

"Please, Mrs. Evans." Michael Baldwin pleaded. "If you have what you say you have recorded on those tapes, then I think that it's imperative that you be here."

"Well . . . alright." The woman sighed as she slowly relented. "I can be there."

When Michael Baldwin got off the phone with Joletta's college roommate, he quickly dialed the number to the *Atlanta Sentinel Newspaper*. If Joletta's old roommate had told him the truth during their phone conversation, then he wanted to throw out the seeds to a story that could very well lead to the acquittal of his client.

Chapter 34

Frances finally shut off her light and closed her eyes as she snuggled under her covers and began her descent into some well-deserved sleep. She craved and desired for some rest and sleep after the long, tedious day of sitting through Terrence's trial, going to the hospital and agonizing over Travis' condition, and then coming home and listening to Carolyn lament on the phone for several hours about the bombshell George had dropped on her the other day wanting to end their marriage.

Frances knew that she was the anchor and pillar of the family, but over the last couple of days, the weight and burden that came along with being the stalwart of their contentious family began to wear her down. A long getaway to a faraway place like the sandy beaches of Jamaica, or the Virgin Islands, seemed the prescription to the headaches, ills, and worries that had her nerves all twisted up in knots. Frances, however, knew that a getaway was only a placebo for the cure she needed. She knew she simply needed more faith in the Almighty that everything would turn out alright.

When Frances finally drifted off to sleep, the phone suddenly jarred her awake. She looked over at the alarm clock on the night stand and saw that it was two minutes before midnight. She hoped that it wasn't Carolyn calling once again to cry and boohoo over her failed marriage. Frances had heard enough of that for one day, and maybe even heard enough to last a lifetime.

"Hello?" Frances said in a groggy voice as she picked up the phone.

"Yeah, is this Frances Jackson?" the gruff voice said on the other end.

"It is . . . and who's this calling?"

"You mean you don't recognize me?"

Frances tried to clear the cobwebs as she gripped the phone tighter. "Who in the devil is this?" She hissed.

"I'm the sucker that burnt down that restaurant of yours and sent your ass running to the unemployment office."

Frances felt a raging fire beginning to burn deep in the pit of her stomach. She could almost see Daddy T.'s evil, conniving face on the other end. "How dare you call this house after all the trouble you've caused me!" She sneered through the phone. "And I hope you know the police are going to track down your trifling tail!"

"Please, lady, don't make me laugh," Daddy T. said as he let out a boisterous laugh. "And as far as me causing you trouble, I ain't even got started yet. I'm just getting warmed up."

"And what in the devil is that supposed to mean?"

"It means if I were you, I would check my closet. You just might find a little special present."

The line suddenly went dead as Frances realized that Daddy T. was no longer there. As she slowly hung up the phone, she stared over at her closet through the darkness with fear cringing at her chest. She had no idea what was going on, but the longer she stared over at her closet, the more fear began to grow.

Finally, Frances got up enough courage to throw back the covers as she got out of bed. She switched on the lamp on her night stand as she slowly ventured over to her bedroom closet. The closet door was already slightly opened, and for a second, Frances was almost too frightened to touch it, but she quickly came to her senses as she went ahead and pulled back the door.

Frances quickly switched on the light in the closet and discovered that everything was just as it appeared when she came home earlier and changed clothes. There was nothing out of the ordinary then, and she couldn't find anything now. However, as she began to check closer, she heard a faint ticking sound coming from the back of the closet. Frances slowly pulled back her clothes toward the back of the closet and detected a black shoe box on the floor she hadn't seen before. As she cautiously stooped down toward the black shoe box to investigate further, she distinctly heard the ticking growing louder.

With her heart pounding in her chest like a bass drum, Frances flew out of her bedroom faster than she'd run in her life. She went straight to Ernestine's room and banged on her closed door.

"Ernestine, wake up! Wake up!"

Ernestine finally opened her door as she stood in the doorway in her gown, half dazed with sleep.

"What is it, Franny?" she said in a groggy, grumpy voice.

"Get your coat on and get out of the house quick!"

"For what?"

"There's a bomb in the house!"

———— ◈ ————

AN HOUR LATER, A LINE of police cars with flashing lights circling in every direction were crowded in front of Frances' house. The flashing lights from the police and all the commotion, brought out all of the neighbors into the street as everyone watched with curiosity as the activity took place on Frances' lawn.

Frances and Ernestine both stood in the driveway shivering in the cold, late-night air with sweaters draped over their night clothes as they waited for a response from one of the policemen busy bustling around them. A guy from the bomb squad unit finally came out of the house with the black shoe box in his hand. After he and another policeman converged and said a few words, they approached Frances and Ernestine where they both stood and waited patiently.

"Mrs. Jackson?"

"Yes," Frances quickly spoke as she peered apprehensively at the black shoe box that the guy from the bomb squad unit held.

"We've checked out the device that was in this box, and discovered that it's definitely not a bomb."

Frances continued staring at the device inside the shoe box. "Well . . . what is it?"

"It's an elaborate phony, ma'am. It seems that someone was just trying to scare you."

"We searched for evidence and didn't come up with much, ma'am," the policeman said. "Whoever broke into your house made sure not to leave any prints. Do you know of anyone who's trying to harass you, Mrs. Jackson?"

"The same low life scum that has caused me all kind of pain and grief!" Frances fumed. "He's destroyed my restaurant and now he's invaded my home!"

"Well, could you come down to the station and answer some questions. It would be beneficial in tracking down the perpetrator?"

Frances reluctantly agreed as she and Ernestine got into the back of one of the police cars. The only thing Frances wanted was for this nightmare to finally end.

Chapter 35

When daylight finally broke over the sky, the late-night bomb threat that sent Frances and Ernestine scurrying out of the house still had Frances shaken up. Frances and Ernestine knew that sleep was virtually out of the question. After they returned home from the police station at 3 a.m., the only thing that either one of them could do was keep each other company in the kitchen and drink coffee as they tried to calm their troubled, frayed nerves.

By the time Frances and her family arrived at court, the buzz about the bomb threat to Frances' home had already circulated all over Atlanta. However, the big story of the day—besides Terrence taking the stand and testifying—was the story that had hit the *Atlanta Sentinel* this morning of a possible connection between Joletta and the Carruth brothers.

Rumors of a possible drug connection between the two began to surface and questions started to come from every direction. Word that the defense had a surprise witness that had evidence that could possibly tarnish the flawless image and character of Joletta Anderson, and possibly lead to the exoneration of Terrence had everyone talking. Only time would tell if the rumors were true, and that time fast approached.

When Judge Foster entered the packed courtroom and put the proceedings in order, Michael Baldwin wasted no time as he rose from the defense table and called Terrence to the witness stand. Terrence, dressed in a conservative blue suit, raised his right hand and swore to tell the truth as he was sworn in and seated. Everyone in the courtroom became silent and glued to the defendant on the stand.

"Could you state your entire name for the record?" The questioning began.

"Terrence Eugene Jackson."

"And what is your line of work?"

"I'm a DJ and a rap artist."

"Now, Mr. Jackson, you were a DJ at the nightclub Seven Flavors, is that correct?"

"Yes."

"How did you become the DJ at Seven Flavors?"

"About three years ago when I was working at another club, I met Joletta at a party and she asked me to come work for her at a new club that she was starting up."

"Now when you started working at Seven Flavors, did you and Joletta become close?"

"Yes."

"So you two started dating and seeing one another?"

"Yes, we did."

"How long was it before you two began to develop a serious relationship?"

"It was about three months after I started working at Seven Flavors, then soon afterward, we moved in with one another."

"And how long did you two live together?"

"About six months," Terrence said as he kept his eyes glued to his attorney, "then we broke up after that and sort of went our separate ways and started dating other people."

"But you continued working as a DJ at the club and kept a mutual business relationship going with Joletta." Michael Baldwin quickly added. "She even signed you as an artist to her new music company, is that correct?"

"Yes, that's correct."

"So, there was never any hostility or bad feelings between the two of you, even though you two were not involved anymore?"

"No, there were never any bad feelings or any hostility between me and Joletta. We've always got along just fine."

Michael Baldwin paused as he glanced over at the jury. He wanted the implication to sink in that Terrence and Joletta were mutual friends.

"Now, Mr. Jackson, on the night that Joletta Anderson was murdered, you two were together, is that correct?"

"Yes, we went together to the Hip Hop Summit that was downtown at the Civic Center that Saturday night."

"And what was the purpose of attending the Hip Hop Summit?"

"Well, Joletta had just formed her music company, and I'd just been signed on to her new label. It was important for us to attend the event with us just getting our feet in the music industry."

"So, this was strictly a business outing?"

"Yes."

"And did you two leave together?"

"Yes, we did."

"And what time did the two of you leave?"

"It was around twelve midnight."

"And where did the two of you go from there?"

"We headed back to Seven Flavors. I worked the club for awhile, while Joletta took care of some business."

"And did you two leave the club together?"

"Yeah. My car was in the shop for repairs, so Joletta gave me a ride back to my apartment."

"And what time did the two of you leave the club?"

"I guess it was a little bit after one o'clock that morning."

"And did Joletta drop you off at the apartment and leave?"

"No . . ." Terrence said slowly. "I . . . uh . . . invited her up for awhile."

"And did she go up to your apartment?"

"Yes."

"And what transpired during the time she was at your apartment?"

"We talked for a while. Soon afterward, we began to have feelings for one another once again, then it wasn't long before we were having sex."

"Were there any other intimate encounters between you and Joletta since the time you and she were no longer living together?"

"No." Terrence quickly shook his head. "That night was the first time we'd been together like that since we'd broken up."

"I see," Michael Baldwin said as he scribbled something down on his notepad. "Now, Mr. Jackson, what time did Joletta leave your apartment that morning?"

"I'd say it was a little after three o'clock."

"And what did you do after she left your apartment?"

"I went down the block to the Zip and Go Market and picked up a six pack of beer and some Cheetos and came on back to the apartment. I laid around and listened to some music for about an hour, then I went on to sleep."

"So that was the last you saw of Joletta was when she left your apartment, a little after three that morning?"

"Yes."

"When did you learn that Joletta had been murdered?"

"When I woke up later on that morning. A partner of mine called me around ten-thirty that morning and told me to turn on CNN, and when I turned on the TV, I found out that Joletta had been stabbed and murdered."

"And how did you feel when you heard the news of her murder?"

"I was shocked," Terrence said as he shook his head sadly. "I was numb all over. I just couldn't believe that she was dead. We'd just been together a few hours earlier. It . . . it was just shocking."

"So you were crushed by the news?"

"Yeah, to say the least."

Michael Baldwin paused momentarily as he looked down at his notes.

"Now, Mr. Jackson, you purchased a knife from Fentress Knife Shop on Pine Street on May 21st of this year, is that correct?"

"Yes . . ." he said slowly, "I did."

"Any particular reason why you purchased the knife?"

"Well, we'd had several break-ins at the apartment complex that I live in, and I wanted a weapon to protect myself with. I . . . uh . . . was never comfortable with a gun, so I purchased a knife instead."

"I see," Mr. Baldwin said as he nodded. "So you bought it for personal protection?"

"Yes, but as it turns out, it didn't do me any good."

"And why's that?"

"Because two days later, I came home to discover that my apartment had been broken into and burglarized."

"Your apartment was burglarized?"

"Yes."

"And what was taken?"

"Some music equipment I had, some clothes, and the knife that I'd just purchased two days before."

"The knife you'd purchased from Fentress Knife Shop was stolen?"

"Yes."

"And did you contact the police?"

"Yes, I did."

"And a police report of your stolen items was filled out?"

"Yes, it was."

Michael Baldwin reached into a file and pulled out a copy of the police report as he went to the witness stand and handed it to Terrence.

"Were these the items that were filed as stolen from your apartment on the night of May 23rd?"

Terrence scanned over the copy of the police report. "Yes, these are the items."

"Could you read the items out loud to the court?"

"A Roland digital workstation, a Yamaha mixer, three Fubu jerseys, a brown leather jacket, and an eight inch Coilte Bowie knife."

"An eight inch Coilte Bowie knife," Michael Baldwin said loudly for the entire courtroom to hear as he retrieved the police report from Terrence and took it over to the jury for them to see and read. When the final jury member had finally finished reading over the items and gave it back to the defense counselor, Terrence's lawyer stayed near the jury box.

"So, Mr. Jackson, the knife you purchased from Fentress Knife Shop was stolen from your apartment. This very same knife that was claimed to have been the weapon that was used to murder Joletta Anderson, and was documented and filed in a police report a couple of days before Ms. Anderson was killed as being stolen, is that correct?" Michael Baldwin said as he kept his eyes glued on the members of the jury.

"Yes."

"And a couple of days later, Joletta Anderson was murdered with a knife—the same knife that was stolen from your apartment on May 23rd and documented in a police report as being stolen." He repeated. "Is that correct?"

"Yes."

"So, there's no way the knife could've been in your possession when Joletta was murdered on May 30th?"

"No."

"And just one final question, Mr. Jackson," Michael Baldwin said as he kept a steady watch over the jury. "Did you ever receive your stolen knife back?"

"No," Terrence answered unequivocally. "I most certainly did not."

"Thank you, Mr. Jackson. No more questions," his lawyer said as he gathered his things from the podium and returned to the defense table.

When Michael Baldwin sat down, the prosecutor got up slowly as she approached the podium.

"Mr. Jackson, you stated that there were never any bad feelings or any hostility between you and Joletta." The prosecutor began. "Is that correct?"

"Yes, that's correct."

"But on the night that you and Joletta were at the Hip Hop Summit, isn't it true that you threatened Ms. Anderson verbally?"

"No, I don't recall *threatening* Joletta about anything," Terrence said defensively.

"You don't recall demanding more money from Ms. Anderson for the record deal you signed, and if you didn't get the money you wanted, that she would be very sorry that she didn't give it to you. You don't recall saying that, Mr. Jackson?"

"I remember us discussing the subject of my advance, but I certainly wasn't threatening her."

"Telling someone that they will be *very* sorry if they didn't give them what they wanted sounds like a threat, wouldn't you say, Mr. Jackson?"

"I wasn't threatening Joletta."

"*Did* you or *did you not* tell Ms. Anderson that she would be very sorry if she didn't comply to your demand?"

Terrence looked away from the prosecutor as he seemed to search for an answer. "Yes . . ." he finally admitted, "but I didn't mean it in a threatening way."

"Well, then tell us, Mr. Jackson," the prosecutor said harshly, "exactly *what* way did you mean by it then?"

"I . . . I was only joking," Terrence said as he scrambled for the right words. "I certainly didn't mean anything threatening by it."

"Oh—you were only *joking*," the prosecutor said facetiously. "So, do you think threatening someone with murder is a joke, Mr. Jackson?"

"No, I don't."

"You were angry that night at Ms. Anderson, weren't you?"

"We'd had an argument, but later on, we resolved our differences."

"You resolved your differences how? By taking a knife and butchering Joletta Anderson as she sat helplessly in her car."

"Objection, Your Honor." Terrence's lawyer finally rose. "There's no cause for this line of questioning."

"Sustained." Judge Foster quickly ruled.

The prosecutor composed herself as she glanced over at the jury.

"Mr. Jackson, you stated that your knife was stolen from your apartment a week before Ms. Anderson was murdered, is that correct?" The prosecutor continued her line of questioning.

"Yes, it was."

"Then according to the police statement, you didn't notify the police until two days after your apartment was burglarized. Why's that?"

"Well . . . I thought since some of my music equipment was taken, that it could possibly be somebody that I knew. But when I couldn't come up with nothing, then I contacted the police."

"So, you're saying you went out *investigating* on your own?" the prosecutor said in a glib voice.

"Well . . . yes."

"That seems mighty strange, Mr. Jackson. Considering your knife was used only a week later in a murder, wouldn't you say?"

Terrence looked away from the prosecutor. "Maybe . . ." he reluctantly answered.

"Or is it possible your apartment being burglarized was all a ruse to have a nice alibi to say that your knife was stolen, Mr. Jackson?"

"Objection, Your Honor." Terrence's lawyer rose again. "The prosecution is trying to claim that my client's apartment was burglarized under false pretense, when there's clear evidence to the contrary."

"Sustained," Judge Foster slowly answered.

The prosecutor looked at Terrence on the witness stand and reloaded her gun.

"Mr. Jackson, when an autopsy was done on Joletta Anderson, there were traces of your blood found under her fingernails. And the blood very much correlates to some kind of struggle in which she had, not to mention that when you were taken into custody, fingernail scratches were found along the side of your neck. How do you explain, Mr. Jackson, your blood being under Joletta Anderson's fingernails?"

Terrence looked over at his lawyer sitting at the defense table as if he were looking for some much-needed advice. His lawyer, however, simply remained silent as he watched his client on the witness stand.

"Please answer the question," Judge Foster said when Terrence hesitated too long.

Terrence began fumbling with his hands nervously as he looked out over the packed courtroom. "Well, before we had sex that night at my apartment, Joletta had slapped me," he said in an embarrassing voice. "We . . . uh . . . we had somewhat of a fight."

"What were you fighting about?"

Terrence continued fumbling with his hands. "Well . . . uh . . . I wanted to have sex, and she kind of kept resisting. And . . . uh . . . I must've come on a little too strong, and she slapped me."

"So you demanded sex that night from Joletta?"

"No, I didn't *demand* sex," Terrence said forcefully. "I just maybe came on a little too strong for her at first."

"So, she didn't consent to having sex," the prosecutor said as she lashed out, "but you cornered her anyway and forced her against her wishes?"

"No . . . she wanted it."

"But she fought you?"

"No . . . well, she did and she didn't." Terrence sputtered. "She just wanted to be persuaded."

"She wanted to be persuaded." The prosecutor chastised. "Like the way you persuaded her—or shall I say *pressured* her—into giving you more advance money?"

"No . . . not at all."

"What else have you *pressured* Joletta into doing?"

"I've never pressured Joletta into doing anything."

"Did Joletta leave voluntarily from your apartment that night or did you *pressure* her to stay?"

"No, I didn't pressure her to stay."

"What time did Joletta leave your apartment?"

"I don't know," Terrence said hastily. "I guess it was a little after 3 a.m."

"And you say you went to the convenient store down the block when she left?"

"Yes."

"And what did you get?"

"A couple of sodas and a bag of Cheetos."

"You stated that you got a six pack of beer."

"Yes, that's right." Terrence quickly corrected himself.

"And you said you went straight back to your apartment?"

"Yes, that's right."

"And what did you do?"

"Well, when I got back to the apartment, Joletta had come back."

"Joletta had come back to your apartment?"

"Yes . . . she had left her purse."

"And what happened?"

"I gave her back her purse, and . . . well . . . I asked her once again did she wanted to stay the night."

"And what did she say?"

"She said she had to go back to her place, and we sort of got into another argument and she left."

"So, you did try to pressure Joletta into staying with you?"

"No . . . I didn't *pressure* her," Terrence said defensively.

"You said Joletta left voluntarily?"

"She did."

"You seem not to be able to get your facts straight on that night, Mr. Jackson."

"My facts are straight."

"You were angry with Joletta, weren't you?"

"No, I was not," Terrence said heatedly.

"You forced your way into her car that night because you were angry with Joletta for not staying with you, and also because you wanted more money for your record deal."

"No . . . I did not."

"And when she pulled up to her condominium, you were outraged and your anger and temper got the best of you."

"No . . . I wasn't with her." Terrence reiterated.

"And when your temper got the best of you," the prosecutor said as she rolled on, "you took your knife and killed Joletta in cold blood that night, didn't you, Mr. Jackson?"

"Objection, Your Honor." Michael Baldwin rose.

"No—I DID NOT KILL JOLETTA!" Terrence finally roared loud enough for the entire courtroom to hear.

The prosecutor glared at Terrence on the witness stand, then she finally gathered up her stuff from the podium. "I have no further questions," she said as she returned to her table.

WHEN FRANCES AND HER family returned to her house when court had adjourned, Frances went straight to her bedroom and inspected her entire closet from top to bottom. After not finding any devices, contraptions, or any foreign objects that even remotely resembled anything that looked like a bomb, Frances began to breathe a little easier.

With everything appearing normal and in order, Frances then changed out of the clothes she'd worn to court and into something more comfortable. She then left out of the bedroom as she came into the living room and had a seat along with Ernestine, Willie Joe, and Patricia. Everyone was silent and glued to the news on TV. The commentators on the tube had a field day as they wrangled and fought over Terrence's testimony on the witness stand.

Twenty minutes later, the doorbell suddenly rang as it disturbed the peaceful silence. Patricia got up to answer the door, and when she came back, Carolyn was right behind her. The constant news coverage of Terrence's trial still had everyone glued to the TV when Carolyn came into the living room and had a seat.

"Franny, what happened?" Carolyn said in an almost panicked voice. "I just heard some people down at the college talking about you had some kind of bomb scare. What happened?"

"That no good scoundrel somehow got into this house and placed a device in my bedroom closet claiming that it was a bomb," Frances said with the anger still pulsating from her face. "The whole thing liked to scared us to death."

"What scoundrel?"

"Who else?" Frances said with rage. "The same low down, dirty scoundrel that burn down my restaurant. Who else but Trinika's pimp."

"How did he break into the house?"

"The police said he got in through the back door. And he didn't leave nigh a fingerprint or a trace of nothing behind."

"How come you didn't call me and let me know what was going on?"

"Carolyn, about time me and Ernestine got back from the police station, it was near three o'clock in the morning," Frances said in an irritated voice. "We were just too tired, stressed out, and exhausted, and you certainly got enough on your mind dealing with your divorce."

"But Franny, it's not safe for you to stay here. What if he tries to come and do something tonight?"

"It's probably not safe, Franny." Willie Joe agreed. "I'd feel better if you and Ernestine come stay with me and Patricia."

"No . . . no." Carolyn quickly interjected. "I think it'd be better if Franny came to stay with me."

"Why?" Willie Joe said tersely. "Because we don't live in some *multi-million*-dollar castle like you and George?"

"No, I didn't mean it that way. I just thought that—"

"Well, what the hell *did* you mean?"

Frances quickly waved her hand to stop the bickering. "It's not necessary. The police said that they'd be sending out a squad car tonight, and a policeman is going to be stationed out in front of the house. So, we'll be just fine."

"But it still worries me, Franny." Carolyn persisted. "I'm worried about your safety."

"So you ain't worried about *my* safety?" Ernestine suddenly spoke. "My life don't matter?"

"What do you mean?" Carolyn snapped as she looked over at Ernestine.

"That's all you been talking about is Franny . . . Franny . . . Franny. Well, I live here too, damnit!"

"I know you live here. How can I forget."

"Well, you certainly don't act like it!"

"Don't worry about it, Ernestine, she can't help herself." Willie Joe jumped in. "She thinks the whole damn world revolves around her anyway."

"How dare you try to criticize me as much problems as your drunk ass has caused this family."

"Carolyn, you really could try to be more helpful and supportive," Patricia suddenly said as she gave Carolyn a wayward look, "instead of always trying to criticize Willie Joe and Ernestine. We've all had our problems."

"And maybe you should mind your own business." Carolyn snapped.

Frances suddenly got up and headed out of the living room as everyone stared and grew silent.

"Franny, where you going?" Carolyn got up as she followed her out of the room. "Franny . . . Franny."

When Frances went into her room and slammed the door behind her, Carolyn started banging on the door calling her name. Frances, however, had had enough. After a long day in court, she simply didn't need to hear any more bickering from her turbulent family.

Chapter 36

When court returned to session the following day, everyone waited eagerly for the defense to call its surprise witness to the stand. By now the rumors of a possible connection between Joletta and the Carruth brothers had circulated all through the streets, and now everyone was eager to hear the truth. The prosecution had fought hard to keep the defense witness from testifying since the story broke, but Judge Foster had struck down her motion and allowed the witness to take the stand. The courtroom, set for another day of battle, was once again wall to wall packed as everyone rose and took their seats as Judge Foster entered the courtroom and put the proceedings back into order.

"Call your next witness," Judge Foster finally said.

"The defense calls Yolanda Evans to the stand," Michael Baldwin pronounced.

The bailiff opened the door to the witness room as Yolanda Evans walked out and took the witness stand. She raised her right hand and swore to tell the truth as she had a seat. A beautiful, young woman in her own right, she resembled Joletta with her model like looks and persona. If one didn't know better, one would've sworn that it was Joletta herself sitting on the witness stand.

"Could you state your entire name for the record." The questioning began.

"Yolanda Beatrice Evans," she said in a calm voice.

"And where is your place of residence, Ms. Evans?"

"I live in Phoenix, Arizona."

"And what is your occupation?"

"I'm a paralegal for a law firm in Phoenix."

"Now, Ms. Evans, you knew Joletta Anderson very well, didn't you?"

"Yes, I did."

"How long had you known Joletta?"

"I first met her back when we were both freshmen at Howard University ten years ago. We became college roommates and developed a very close relationship."

"And were you still close with her after you graduated?"

"Yes, we stayed in close contact with one another even after she moved back to Atlanta."

"How often did you stay in contact with her?"

"Well, because of the distance, we only saw each other about once a year. But we stayed in close contact with one another over the phone, sometimes calling each other as much as twice a week."

Michael Baldwin nodded as he paused and looked down at his notes.

"Now, Ms. Evans, you've kept close tabs on Joletta's accomplishments and achievements since both of you graduated from Howard University, haven't you?"

"Yes, certainly."

"Did her quick rise to success startle you any?"

"No . . . not really," Yolanda said slowly. "I knew during the time we were in college that Joletta had what it took to make a success of herself. She was always beautiful, smart, outgoing, and she always knew how to get along with people. I knew when she won the Miss Black America beauty pageant, that it was just a stepping stone to the success that was going to come her way."

"So, even in college you knew Joletta was going to be successful?"

"Yes, very much so."

"Now, Ms. Evans, did it ever seem to you that Joletta at anytime was trying to move too fast? That she was maybe going too fast for her own good?"

Yolanda looked at Michael Baldwin with a serious face. "Yes, I did."

"And when was that?"

"About the time she was trying to form her nightclub. I remember talking to her, and Joletta was determined that she was going to build the most dynamic nightclub that Atlanta had seen. She was determined that she was going to make a splash not only in Atlanta, but she wanted the club to be recognized as one of the hippest around the country."

"And this concerned you?"

"Well, I always knew that Joletta was an aggressive go-getter. That whatever she put her mind to and persevered for, that she usually attained it. But it was the size and scale of the club that she was talking about building that concerned me. And for the type of club she wanted to build, Joletta said she needed plenty of money."

"How much money?"

"At least a million dollars to get started. She said she had a good deal of money of her own that she was investing, but she needed plenty more if she ever wanted to get it off the ground and running."

"And did she say she would be going after a loan to get her nightclub built?"

"Yes, she did. I knew Joletta had some money from the trust fund her father had set up for her, and she had a couple of business enterprises she was involved with. But I knew she didn't have the type of money that she was talking about to build the scale of club she wanted."

"But obviously she was able to raise the money she needed to build her club?"

"Well, a few weeks later she called me and said she had the money she needed to start building, and it sort of surprised me how fast she was able to do it. I just assumed because of her good standing in the city, and because of her name and reputation, that she was able to attain the resources she needed without any problems."

"Did she say how she was able to attain the money so fast?"

"At first she just said she'd found some investors to put up the money she needed. Then a couple of months later, she finally told me who they were."

"And who did she say her investors were?"

Yolanda suddenly looked over the packed courtroom with apprehension. "She said her investors were from out in Los Angeles," she said reluctantly. "She said her investors were Romeo and Barry Carruth."

"The same Carruth brothers who were killed here in Atlanta in a major drug sting only a few days ago?" Michael Baldwin asked pointedly.

"Yes . . . those were the ones."

A few groans and murmurs echoed around the courtroom.

"Did Joletta know that they were major drug dealers at the time when they became her investors?" Michael Baldwin quickly asked as the pulse of the courtroom began to come alive.

"At first, I truly don't think that she knew," Yolanda said slowly. "But she eventually found out."

"Objection, Your Honor." The prosecutor rose hastily. "This line of questioning is irrelevant, and this testimony has no bearing whatsoever to this case. I ask that this line of questioning be discontinued, and this testimony be stricken from the record and the jury to be instructed to disregard this testimony entirely."

For a couple of seconds Judge Foster remained silent. He took his time as he seemed to weigh the situation carefully before he spoke. "I'll allow the testimony to continue," he finally said. "Objection overruled. Continue with your questioning, Mr. Baldwin."

"Now, Ms. Evans," Terrence's lawyer said as he continued, "so you're saying Joletta and the Carruth brothers were equal business partners?"

"Yes," Yolanda answered. "Joletta was always the one out front, but the Carruth brothers were equal partners with her in everything they did. They always stayed in the background. They were something like her silent partners."

"I see. Now, Ms. Evans, did Joletta ever discuss with you that she was having any conflict with the Carruth brothers during the time of their business relationship together?"

"Not at first she didn't," she said slowly. "But as time went by and the deeper they became involved, she began to say different things."

"What type of things?"

"Well, after the nightclub was built and became an instant success, Joletta and the Carruth brothers began to venture into other businesses together. The music company was the next thing, and even starting a line of restaurants were seriously being discussed. But when the Carruth brothers suddenly wanted Joletta to start taking large sums of money from them and to transfer it into other enterprises, Joletta refused and things between them from then on quickly began to go bad."

"You mean the Carruth brothers wanted Joletta to launder drug money?"

"Yes," she said slowly. "They knew Joletta was very good at business and they wanted to take advantage of her."

"So, what happened after Joletta refused to launder the drug money?"

"Well, the Carruth brothers became very angry with Joletta, and for awhile, they continued their business relationship. But it wasn't long afterwards that Joletta called me one night and said the Carruth brothers wanted to end their business relationship and they wanted Joletta to buy them out."

"They wanted back all the money they'd given her to invest in her businesses?"

"Yes."

"And how much did they want Joletta to pay?"

"Close to ten million dollars?"

A few moans and groans drifted from the courtroom.

"Ten million dollars," Michael Baldwin repeated. "And did Joletta say she had the money to buy out the Carruth brothers?"

"No, not all at once. She was able to pay them back in small amounts, but as time went on, she said they began to pressure her for the whole amount."

"What do you mean by they began to pressure her?"

Yolanda swallowed hard as she looked over the packed courtroom. "Well, Joletta called me one night and said if she didn't pay the Carruth brothers the money all at once, then she said that they would kill her."

The moans and groans from the courtroom suddenly grew louder.

"Joletta said the Carruth brothers were threatening to kill her if she didn't pay them all the money at once?" Michael Baldwin said fervently.

"Yes . . . she did."

"Did Joletta say why the Carruth brothers wanted her to buy them out?"

"She said the Carruth brothers owned a chain of strip clubs out in L.A. and they'd run into money problems and had borrowed heavily from the Mafia. When they couldn't pay back the Mafia, they turned to Joletta to buy them out."

"And was Joletta upset, rattled, or nervous whenever she talked to you about the Carruth brothers pressuring her to buy them out?"

"Yes, very much so. That entire week before she was killed, she'd call me every night on the phone, and each time we talked, I could tell she was becoming more and more nervous and tense about the situation. It was driving her crazy."

"You said that entire week before she was murdered, you talked to her every night on the phone. When was the last time you talked to her?"

"The night before she was murdered was the last time that we talked. Then a day later, I heard on CNN that she'd been murdered."

"And you believe the Carruth brothers murdered her?"

Yolanda slowly cast her eyes down. "Yes . . . I do."

Michael Baldwin looked over at the jury for a brief moment, then he turned his attention back to his witness.

"Now, Mrs. Evans, you came all the way to this court not only to testify of your close relationship with Joletta and of your knowledge of her involvement with the Carruth brothers, but to present to this court proof that Joletta Anderson was fearing for her life those last days when she was still alive. Is that correct, Mrs. Evans?"

"Yes, that's correct."

"And by proof, I'm referring to tape phone conversations between you and Joletta during those last days when she feared for her life. Is that correct?"

"Yes."

Michael Baldwin turned and looked up at Judge Foster. "Your Honor, I would like to be granted permission to play certain taped phone conversations between Ms. Yolanda Evans and Joletta during the last remaining days before Ms. Anderson was murdered."

"You have the tapes to present before the court now?" Judge Foster asked.

"Yes, we do."

"Then so granted."

Terrence's lawyer retrieved a tape recording device from the defense table and placed it on a mobile cart in the middle of the courtroom. The bailiff assisted as he took the microphone from the witness stand and placed it on the cart right up against the tape recorder. With everything in order, Michael Baldwin pressed the play button to the tape recorder as the tape began to roll.

After thirty minutes of listening to several tapes of phone conversations between Joletta and Yolanda during the last week that Joletta was alive,

Michael Baldwin seemed confident that the jury, and the entire courtroom, had heard enough to convince everyone that Joletta feared for her life that treacherous last week that she was alive, and that the Carruth brothers, for financial motives, had her killed on the morning of May 30th. Feeling that he'd taken away the guilty spotlight that had shined so brightly on his client since the apprehension of Terrence for murder on that fateful Memorial Day weekend, Michael Baldwin finally rested his case.

The prosecution, however, quickly rose after the defense counselor rested his case and attacked the validity of the tapes, calling them circumstantial in nature and lacking firm concrete evidence that the Carruth brothers had murdered Joletta on that fateful early morning nearly six months ago. With her skill and legal wrangling, she was able to shine the guilty spotlight right back on Terrence as the culprit who'd murdered Joletta Anderson.

Chapter 37

Sunday morning Frances sat in the choir stand, along with the other choir members, half listening to Reverend Speight's sermon. She had a lot on her mind, and the more she thought about it, the heavier it weighed on her mind. When court ended Friday, both sides had given their closing arguments and had rested their cases. With the case now bound over to the jury, Terrence's guilt or innocence was now in the hands of twelve Atlanta citizens who'd give their verdict at any day now. Frances was naturally worried about the outcome of the verdict and the consequences that could lay ahead for Terrence if he were convicted.

Everything seemed to be moving at a spinning pace and Frances didn't know if she could keep up with everything swirling around her. With Terrence's pending verdict looming, coupled with the bomb threat to her home, and Travis' uncertain condition, made for a nerve-racking week. Frances knew she was hanging on only by a string, and it certainly wouldn't take much for that string to finally stretch and break.

When service finally ended, Frances hung around for awhile as she talked with some of the members of the church. By now, everyone had heard about the bomb threat to her house and wanted to know a firsthand account of what had happened. Frances gave out the same details of that harrowing night so many times, that she'd finally grown weary of talking about it.

After she'd finally finished talking to the tenth person about her traumatic experience, she headed out of the sanctuary as she began to make her way out of the church. When she saw Reverend Speight on the front steps of the church as he finished greeting the last few members filing out of the church, Frances decided to stop and say a few words to the reverend.

Since Reverend Speight didn't stand by her when Brother Fitzpatrick declined to let her sing in the annual gospel festival, Frances had pretty much avoided Reverend Speight and had carried an on-going grudge against her pastor. Over the last few weeks, however, Frances had slowly begun to let her grudge go. She came to realize that what was already done, couldn't be changed. More importantly, as she was about to enter this critical time and juncture, she realized that she needed all the support and guidance that she could get.

"Why, hello, Sister Jackson," Reverend Speight said as Frances approached him. "We haven't had the chance to talk in a good while, have we?"

"No, we haven't, Reverend," Frances responded.

"I heard about the bomb threat to your house this week. I wanted to get in touch with you, and I called several times and left messages. But I know you've been all tied up with everything that's been going on with the trial, and your restaurant, and what happen to your grandson, Travis. I know it's been quite stressful for you."

"Yes, it's been a very traumatic week," Frances answered slowly.

"Ernestine been doing alright?"

"She's been going back to her rehab classes, and she's progressing fairly well. She's taking it one day at a time."

"And Willie Joe?"

"Same as Ernestine. He's taking it one day at a time."

It appeared that Reverend Speight could feel the tension between them when they became silent as he suddenly seemed nervous and ill at ease by the sudden silence.

"Sister Jackson, I think that you and I need to do some mending," Reverend Speight finally said earnestly as he looked at Frances. "I believe we've both been somewhat avoiding one another since what went down between us concerning the gospel festival. And I just want to say that I was wrong for not standing by you. I should've overruled Brother Fitzpatrick at the time. You should've been the one who represented our choir with your solos at the festival. But I guess I'm only human, Sister Jackson," he said with a sigh.

"I let all the negative talk and the things swirling around about your family affect my thinking, and I just didn't want the church to be seen in a bad light," he said as he continued. "But I've come to realize that I was wrong. We as a church should've been behind you all the way, and I as the pastor should've been the one out front making sure that this church was supporting you. But I didn't and I was wrong . . ." he said in a heartfelt voice. "I was wrong, Sister."

"Well, it did upset me for a while, Reverend," Frances said candidly. "But I prayed and got over it. Just like I'm praying now for the rest of my troubles and burdens to be lifted from me. And I still believe deep in my heart that God will make a way."

"Then if you believe God will make a way, then He will, Sister," Reverend Speight said wholeheartedly. "God *will* make a way for you. You just keep on believing that."

"And I'm going to keep on praying for it too, Reverend."

"That's good, Sister. Because a faithful warrior's prayer will always be answered," he said encouragingly. "And Sister Jackson, you're the strongest warrior I've ever known."

"And I'm a warrior who's going to need the full support and prayers of her pastor in these next coming days, too," Frances said as she looked sharply at her pastor.

Reverend Speight laid a comforting hand on Frances' shoulder and looked deeply into her eyes. "And you shall have it, Sister. Without a doubt, you shall have it."

Frances and Reverend Speight had a few more words for each other, then they parted.

When Frances finally got into her car and drove away from the church, the thought of her demolished restaurant suddenly began to weigh heavily on her mind. Since the night that her restaurant burned to the ground, she'd avoided going by the site of her destroyed establishment, not wanting to see the destruction and the utter ruin of what she'd worked so hard over the years to build. But somehow today she couldn't avoid it any longer. Something inside of her began to pull her to that sacred place that she'd held so dear to her heart and soul for all of these years. Today something inside of her wanted her to finally face the ugly pain that had tormented her since that night she watched those rising flames destroy a part of her soul.

When Frances arrived at the site of her demolished restaurant, she parked her car and slowly got out. She walked a few paces from her car, then suddenly stopped as she took in the sight before her.

The twisted beams and charred bricks that were piled high and scattered in every direction on the night that her restaurant burned to the ground, had now been hauled away. There was nothing left now but an empty lot. Frances stood there and stared at the empty lot with a vanquished look on her face.

Even as she stood there and stared at the space where her once thriving business once stood, she still couldn't believe that it was really truly gone. But the utter emptiness that lay before her was certainly no mirage. In one fateful, burning, smoldering night, her place of dreams had *in fact* been reduced to nothing but mere ashes. Frances couldn't help but to remember the pain and hurt she felt that night as she watched her restaurant go up in smoke. It was a pain that she'd never forget, and no doubt, one that would certainly be slow to fade away.

Now as Frances stood there staring at the empty vacant space, the only thing that she could think about was the evildoer that did this wicked, treacherous deed. The longer Frances thought about his evil destructive deed, she became more and more determined. She realized that her resolve and her supreme faith in God wouldn't allow her to just lie down to defeat. She finally realized that in the end, ultimately her tormentor would be the one brought to his knees.

Chapter 38

At 7 a.m. Wednesday morning, Frances' alarm clock sounded off its loud, morning greeting. For nearly ten minutes, Frances didn't move. She lay riveted to her bed not wanting to get up. The sunlight streaming through her window began to gleam brighter on her face, and Frances knew she couldn't lay riveted to her bed forever.

Finally, Frances rolled over and shut off the alarm clock on her night stand. She slowly got out of bed as she slumped to her knees and said her prayer for the morning. Every morning, Frances prayed a heartfelt zealous prayer that would want to make the birds sing with joy, but today she prayed a soul, wrenching prayer that literally made Heaven open up its gates.

Today was finally the day that the city of Atlanta would get its verdict. After several days of deliberating behind closed doors, it was announced that the jury had reached a decision. Frances had dreaded, and at the same time, had longed for this day since fate had flung her family into this nationwide scandal. She got dressed today believing that justice would prevail, and that her family would finally get its vindication from the nightmare that it had been mired and stuck in for the last couple of months. But even if justice somehow didn't prevail, and even if her family wasn't vindicated from the nightmare that it found itself mired in, Frances now believed, more than ever, that she had the spiritual power and the strength to keep right on fighting.

By eight o'clock, everyone had arrived at Frances' house. Willie Joe, Patricia, Carolyn, along with Ernestine, sat silently in the living room. Soon Reverend Speight, Ermma, and Earl, from down at the restaurant, had joined the group in the living room as everyone waited for Frances to appear. When Frances finally emerged from her bedroom and entered the living room, everyone stared silently at her. Frances, dressed in her finest Sunday gray outfit, looked solemnly around the room at her family and friends. Nervous anxiety literally filled the entire living room.

"Well . . . let's not be late, folks," Frances finally said as everyone got up and followed her out the door.

WHEN FRANCES AND HER crew made it to the courthouse, the throng of reporters camped out in front of the building quickly besieged them. Frances and her family ignored the rapid flow of questions and the cameras as they went up the steps of the courthouse and entered the building. They entered the main courtroom as they all sat together on the front row directly behind the defense table.

The packed courtroom quickly shot glances over at Frances and her crew as they sat in their seats. Frances, who sat on the end closest to the aisle, couldn't help but to notice the stares. Directly across from her, as usual, was Mayor Anderson and his people, and many others around the courtroom whom Frances had come accustomed to seeing since the start of the trial.

When Frances suddenly saw the face of Skip Hughes, it almost made her cringe. He sat in the far back of the courtroom waiting, like everyone else, for today's verdict. When he caught Frances' eye, he flashed a wicked smile in her direction. Frances knew he was just itching and waiting for a guilty verdict. She knew the assault he had in store for her family would be vicious if Terrence were found guilty. From the look on his face, she could almost see tomorrow's headlines, and the bold black letters he had in store for his column, were far worse than he'd ever produced before.

Not long after both the defense and the prosecution entered the courtroom and took their seats, Judge Foster took the bench. The courtroom quickly became dead silent. As Judge Foster prepared to address the courtroom, Frances stared at the back of Terrence's head as he sat at the defense table as she prayed a quick prayer. She could detect, even from staring at his back, that Terrence was nervous. Frances now could only hope that her last lonesome little prayer would be enough to deliver her grandson.

"Is the jury ready?" Judge Foster finally said in the direction of the bailiff.

"Yes, they are," the bailiff answered.

"Very well. Bring in the jury."

The entire courtroom watched in a strange silence as the twelve members of the jury came into the courtroom one after another as they had a seat in the jury box. Everyone in the courtroom was glued to the white piece of paper that the jury foreman held.

"Members of the jury, have you reached a verdict?" Judge Foster asked.

The jury foreman rose from his seat. "Yes, sir," he answered slowly, "we have."

"Please hand it to the clerk."

The clerk took it as she handed it to Judge Foster. He studied it carefully, then nodded.

"Will the defendant please rise," Judge Foster said as he looked down at Terrence sitting at the defense table.

Terrence and his lawyer rose slowly from their seats. Fear and tension gripped the entire courtroom. The place was so silent that not even a cough or a sniffle could be heard. Everyone was anxious, listening, and waiting. It seemed like an eternity as Terrence, with his lawyer at his side, stood obediently waiting for the reading of the verdict.

The anticipation was like a magnet and everyone seemed drawn to it. The entire Jackson family was glued together in that nervous magnetic tension. Frances continued giving up her prayers as she watched and waited; Ernestine, who sat next to her, lowered her head as she couldn't bear to watch; Willie Joe stared straight ahead with pure fright; Patricia bit her lip as she tried to control her shaking as Carolyn held her hand; Earl, seeming to feel the pressure of the moment, wrung his hands over and over, while Reverend Speight clutched tightly the Bible he carried as he quoted the 23rd Psalm softly. The entire place was in agony, and only the reading of the verdict would finally release the tension.

Judge Foster finally handed the verdict back to the clerk. "Please read the verdict, Madam Clerk."

The clerk unfolded the paper and faced the defendant. "As to the count of murder in the first degree," she read slowly, "we the jury find the defendant, not guilty."

Terrence immediately turned and grabbed his lawyer as they engaged in a bear hug celebration. The place erupted with a mixture of cheers and burst of disgust as the not guilty verdict created an uproar among the divided courtroom. Terrence quickly released his lawyer as he went straight to the railing and embraced Frances as they hugged one another. Frances had tears of joy coming down her face as she squeezed her grandson tighter and tighter.

"Thank you, Franny," Terrence said over and over. "Thank you."

"Thank the Lord, child," Frances said as she wiped her tears from her face. "Thank the Lord."

Judge Foster finally banged his gavel and returned order to the courtroom. Terrence released Frances as he returned to the defense table as he and his lawyer sat smiling.

"Mr. Jackson, you have been tried by a jury of your peers and found not guilty," Judge Foster said as he looked at Terrence. "You are a free man. If there is nothing further, court is adjourned."

When Judge Foster banged his gavel and adjourned court, Terrence immediately got up and went straight over to his family once again. He was smothered by not only Frances, but Ernestine, Carolyn, Willie Joe, Patricia, Reverend Speight, and Earl all surrounded Terrence and gave their hugs and embraces as their joy and relief quickly turned into a happy family celebration. Terrence's lawyer soon joined the celebration and was also smothered with warm hugs and embraces.

With the thrill of victory and freedom glowing from their faces, Terrence and his family headed out of the courtroom. When they made it out of the building and began to descend the steps of the courthouse, a horde of reporters quickly surrounded them as they shouted and pelted them with their many questions. Terrence, the center of the media's attention, seemed more than happy to answer their questions.

"Terrence, how do you feel now that you're a free man?" a reporter yelled.

"I feel great." Terrence smiled as he and his family continued walking as the reporters and cameras followed their every step.

"Did you think that the jury was going to acquit you?"

"I didn't know" he said as he kept smiling, "but I was certainly praying that they would."

"Terrence, what are your plans now?"

"I don't know. I just want to go home with my family."

"Mrs. Jackson," another reporter yelled, "does the not guilty verdict by any way dispel the jinx that has held your family entrapped for all of these years?"

Frances suddenly stopped dead in her tracks as the rest of her family stopped likewise. The reporters stood patiently as they waited for her to respond. Frances, however, was in no hurry. She looked straight into the cameras with the most serious face that a person could ever have.

"That what you have called a jinx has been nothing but a mirage," Frances said slowly. "But now that the mirage has finally been exposed to the light, my family can now walk freely. Because we as a family will walk by faith and not by sight."

"What exactly does that mean, Mrs. Jackson?" a reporter quickly shouted.

Frances slowly turned and looked at the reporter.

"It means that God has made a way."

While the reporters still seemed confounded over the meaning of her parable, Frances and her family headed on about their way. The reporters, still anxious for more information, quickly followed them and besieged them with even more questions. However, Frances and her family weren't about to answer any more questions. They'd had enough invasion of their privacy for one day.

Chapter 39

Frances turned off the motor to her car and slowly got out as she stood near her Lexus and watched the men at work. The weather had turned cold and the sky was overcast, but Frances couldn't feel any better than she felt today. It was five days before Christmas and Frances had received the best Christmas gift she could imagine. Before her eyes, lay the foundation of her restaurant slowly being rebuilt. Brick by brick, her place of business was being erected and restored to its former self. It was still a good ways away from completion, but Frances could tell that it was going to be even better than before. She could feel it in her bones that her restaurant would once again become a major success.

Since Terrence's trial ended five weeks ago, everything had moved at a fast pace. After Mayor Anderson lost his bid for congress on election night to his opponent when the scandal of Joletta's involvement with the Carruth brothers destroyed his chances of winning, the focus around Atlanta quickly shifted to the capture of Daddy T.

Shot down in a blaze of gunfire one night by the police when he was tracked down and tried to flee from arrest, the story made big news around Atlanta when it was discovered that Daddy T. had not only set ablaze Frances' restaurant, but had abhorred tens of young runaway girls and had distributed them throughout the nation in a major sex trade. As the story continued to grow, word of the girls that Frances helped to get off the street and away from Daddy T.'s abusive control soon began to circulate.

With the story gaining not only local but nationwide exposure, Frances was once again sought after by the national media to tell of her harrowing, heroic acts of saving young girls from the streets. Frances, more than anyone, was thrilled that Daddy T. had finally gotten his due justice and wouldn't be able to lead astray any more young, innocent girls, but after months of dealing with the media blitz over the course of Terrence's trial, Frances had simply had enough of the cameras. Her one and only focus since the end of Terrence's trial, was mending back her broken family.

Mending back her family had still been slow and somewhat frustrating, but Frances was patient and confident that true love would *indeed* exist between the members of her family. Willie Joe and Ernestine were still holding on strong, and with each passing day, they left their former addictions further in the past. However, the bitterness and resentment between family members still festered in their family like a disease that was hard to cure.

The animosity between Ernestine and Carolyn, Carolyn and Willie Joe, between Terrence and Ernestine, and Ernestine and Trinika continued to be a roadblock to the love needed to reconcile the differences in their family. The matriarch of the Jackson family was determined to somehow, some way, remove that roadblock and bring about harmony to her family.

Frances, however, realized that her *own* animosity toward Travis hindered the reconciliation process that she so much yearned for her family to have. She prayed that her soul would be cleansed of any hatred she still had harbored for Travis. Now that he was being released from the hospital today, Frances knew that those ill feelings she had for him could resurface and cause her to hate all over again. However, with Travis paralyzed from the waist down and permanently stricken to a wheelchair for the rest of his life, Frances knew that he needed someplace to stay and someone to care for him.

With Ernestine already living with her—and at times causing an emotional drain on her—was enough to deal with in itself. Certainly, adding Travis to the household could bring on more added pressure. In spite of that, Frances believed in her heart that she must take that chance. If nothing else, for the sake of her family, she had to give it a try.

Chapter 40

By 4 p.m., everyone had arrived over at Frances' house. Christmas Day dinner was almost ready for serving and everyone was ready for the feast. There was only one other time that the Jackson family had gotten together for any kind of holiday feast, and that one time had ended in such a quarrelsome, bickering fracas that no other family get-together had ever been arranged. This year, however, Frances thought it would be best if the entire family got together and celebrated Christmas. She thought that it was time to once and for all end the festering animosity tearing their family apart.

While Frances was busy in the kitchen putting the final touches on her Christmas Day dinner, the rest of the family relaxed in the living room and watched television. Everyone carried on a light conversation with someone.

Trinika, who'd just returned home last night from her stay in Buffalo, sat with Terrence as they talked. Frederick and Bethany, home for the Christmas break from Morehouse and Spellman, sat with Carolyn as they conversed. Willie Joe, Patricia, and Ernestine sat together on one couch as they talked to Reverend Speight, who Frances had invited over to join their family Christmas get-together. The only member of the family who wasn't socializing with anyone was Travis. He sat all alone in his wheelchair staring pensively at the television.

When Frances came into the living room with her kitchen apron still tied around her waist, the light conversation suddenly went silent. She looked over everyone in the living room as if they were at a police line-up waiting to take their places along the wall. The look on her face was more serious than anyone in the family had ever seen.

"Someone turn off that TV," Frances finally said.

Willie Joe grabbed the remote from the stand next to the couch and turned off the television set. When the television went off, everyone in the room stared silently at Frances.

"Before we go into the dining room and eat Christmas dinner, I believe it's time that we once and for all clear the air of all the hatred, envy, and bitterness that has been festering in our family," Frances said as she looked around at everyone. "I'm tired of this family back-stabbing one another and it's time for it to stop. I know we've all had our grudges with one another, and now that we're all here, we can finally voice our dislikes and grievances face to face. Now . . . who'll be first?"

Everyone looked at each other with hesitant looks. It seemed that no one had the nerve to speak the first word.

"Alright, I guess I'll have to be first then," Frances said as she boldly stepped in the middle of the room. "Travis, you've been nothing but a thug and a hoodlum," she said as she looked over at him. "You've disgraced yourself and this family by selling those drugs. I hated that you sold those drugs, but in the process of hating those drugs that you sold, I began to hate you also. But I've come to realize that my hate for you was wrong. I don't hate you Travis, you're my grandson and I love you."

Travis looked at Frances as he held back his tears. "I love you too, Franny," he said slowly as he looked around at everyone. "And I'm sorry that my activities have disgraced the family."

Frances went over as she kneeled down and hugged Travis as he hugged her back. When she finally released him from their embrace, she moved aside and let whomever wanted the floor to have it.

"Well, anyone else?" Frances said as she looked around the room.

The room remained silent as everyone avoided looking at one another, as if fearing the slightest eye contact would cause them to confront the person they looked at. Frances could see and sense the tension on everyone's face, but she knew this had to be done.

"Ernestine . . . Carolyn," Frances said as she looked at both of them. "Y'all have anything to say to one another?"

Carolyn and Ernestine slowly looked over at one another as their faces showed the awkwardness of the situation.

"She don't have to say nothing to me." Ernestine flipped her hand as she turned her eyes from Carolyn.

"And you don't have to say nothing to me." Carolyn quickly shot back.

Frances stared down at both of them, then she stormed out of the living room. When she came back, she had her .38 revolver in one hand and a bullet in the other.

She flipped open the chamber as she placed the bullet inside. When she put the bullet into the chamber, she closed it back then spin the chamber around several times. Everyone in the room stared at her with stricken fear. Frances ignored their frighten stares as she yanked Carolyn up by the arm, then reached over to where Ernestine sat and yanked her up also by the arm. Carolyn and Ernestine stared across at one another with fear in their eyes.

"Here, take the gun," Frances said as she glared at Carolyn.

"What . . ." Carolyn said with fear in her voice as she eyed the gun that Frances held for her to take. "I'm not taking that gun."

"Take the gun *damnit*!" Frances blared.

Reverend Speight seemed too scared to care about the spiteful harsh words coming from one of his sisters of the church. At the moment, he seemed too preoccupied staring at Frances' gun, and so did everyone else.

"Here—take it!" Frances demanded as she shoved the gun toward Carolyn.

Carolyn nervously took the gun from Frances as she held it limply.

"Now, point it over at Ernestine and pull the trigger."

"What!" Carolyn said in a flabbergasted voice.

"Do it, I said!"

"This is crazy, Franny," Carolyn said as she gave the gun back to Frances. Frances took it and handed it over to Ernestine.

"Well, then you take it and point it over at Carolyn and pull the trigger."

"Franny, this is going way too far—"

"Shut up!" Frances roared as she glared over at Willie Joe as he was about to intervene.

"Take it!" Frances yelled as she shoved the gun at Ernestine.

Ernestine slowly took the gun from Frances as she held it limp in her hand. She couldn't raise her eyes to look over at Carolyn.

"Well, what you waiting on?" Frances roared. "Take the gun, point it at Carolyn and pull the trigger, and let's see if it'll go off!"

"Franny—this is crazy!" Willie Joe shouted as he jumped to his feet.

Frances stared at both Ernestine and Carolyn as they stood in the middle of the floor avoiding looking at one another. When she saw that neither one would rise to the bait she'd given them, she slowly reached down and took the gun away from Ernestine. She opened the chamber and took the bullet out of the gun as she carried the gun back to her room. When she returned to the living room, she approached her two daughters still standing two feet away from one another as they avoided looking into each other's eyes.

"I'll tell you what's crazy," Frances said as she looked at both Ernestine and Carolyn. "What's crazy is that I have two grown daughters who act like children who don't know how to forgive and love one another. They'd rather hold grudges and keep on hating one another than settle their differences like sisters are supposed to. You two are family, and it's time for this envy between one another to stop," she said as she glared at both of them. "Now, you two can stand here however long you feel like it, but neither one of you ain't leaving here until you settle your differences."

It seemed like an eternity had passed when Carolyn finally raised her head and looked over at Ernestine. Ernestine appeared to have felt Carolyn's eyes staring at her as she slowly raised her own eyes and looked over at Carolyn.

"Sometimes I get mad at you for no reason," Carolyn said slowly. "Maybe it's cause the way you've walked over Franny all of these years."

"And I'm tired of you always being so damn judgmental and a bitch," Ernestine replied.

Frances kept her silence as she let her daughters work it out.

Carolyn glared over at Ernestine, but it seemed that the anger smoldering inside of her began to quickly subside. "I know there've been times when I've been judgmental towards you," she said slowly. "But it never meant that I didn't love you. I just thought that you could do better for yourself."

Ernestine slowly began to soften. "And I guess even though we've often fought one another," she said slowly, "I guess I never stopped loving you either."

"Well . . . uh . . . maybe we can stop fighting one another and just learn to help each other."

"Maybe so," Ernestine said slowly.

The two looked at each other, then slowly came together and embraced. It was a short embrace, but Frances knew that it was a start.

When Carolyn and Ernestine began to sit down, Frances reached out and pulled Ernestine right back up.

"You might as well keep right on standing," Frances said as she looked over at Trinika. "There's some more work in this room that needs to be done."

Trinika appeared surprised that she was suddenly put on the spot, but after a couple of seconds, she slowly rose from her seat and faced Ernestine. The two looked at each other for a long minute. They both seemed tense and nervous.

"I know. . . uh . . . I abandoned you when you needed me all those years," Ernestine said as she looked at her daughter. "And I knew you grew up hating me for it, too. But I can't change the past. The only thing that I can do . . . well . . . is to try to make the present a little better and a little bit easier for the both of us," she said slowly. "I . . . well . . . I just hope that you're willing to give it a try, too."

Trinika seemed to slowly let go of all the pain, the hurt, and the hatred she'd felt toward Ernestine all of these years. She slowly walked over to Ernestine as the two embraced for what seemed like five minutes. When they finally let go of one another, they both had tears streaming down their faces. Neither one said a word, but it seemed that a bond had just developed between them, a bond that mere words couldn't explain.

When Trinika went back to her seat on the couch, Terrence had replaced her on the floor. Ernestine was too busy wiping tears from her eyes to notice Terrence standing in front of her, but when she finally looked up to see that her son waited to greet her, she slowly began to smile.

"I hope the same goes for us, too," Ernestine said as she looked up at Terrence. "I hope you'll give us a try, too."

Terrence embraced Ernestine. "Yeah, the same goes for us too, mama," he said warmly. "The same goes for us."

When they released from their embrace, Ernestine and Terrence sat back down on the couch. The floor was vacant of any participants as Frances scanned the room for someone else to take the floor. She quickly laid eyes on Willie Joe and Carolyn and motioned for them to take the floor.

"I believe you two have some mending to do also," she said as her eyes beckoned for them to rise and make peace.

Willie Joe and Carolyn rose slowly from the couch and faced one another. Neither one seemed eager to confront the other, but both appeared willing to give it a try.

"We just going to stand here looking at each other all night?" Willie Joe finally said as he broke the ice.

"No . . . we don't have to," Carolyn said slowly. "We can bury the hatchet between us once and for all, and become the brother and sister that we used to be."

Willie Joe looked at Carolyn and slowly nodded. "Yeah . . . I'd like that."

They slowly came together and embraced one another. There was no more hostility between them, just genuine love between brother and sister.

When Willie Joe and Carolyn sat down, Frances gave everyone around the room a pensive look as if she were reflecting over something tugging at her heart. She finally got up and left out of the living room as everyone watched her curiously as she left. With her absence, the silence around the room soon grew heavy; but no one would dare move or say a single word.

Five minutes later, Frances came back into the living room carrying an old, large picture frame of her late husband, William. Everyone watched her curiously as she reached high over the mantel piece and hung the picture of her late husband up on the wall. No one said a word, but everyone's eyes were glued to the picture of their father, grandfather, father-in law, William Jackson.

"I want everybody to get up and take hold of somebody's hand," Frances said as she looked around at each person in the room.

Everyone slowly got up and took hold of the person's hand standing next to them. Frances held Travis' hand as Travis held Terrence's, Terrence held Ernestine's, Ernestine held Trinika's, Trinika held Bethany's, Bethany held Frederick's, Frederick held Carolyn's, Carolyn held Patricia's, Patricia held Willie Joe's, Willie Joe held Reverend Speight's, until the circle of hands came back around to Frances' other hand. Frances looked around at everyone in the circle and couldn't help but to feel pride for her family. Her heart was filled with joy and her soul brimmed with mirth.

"I want everyone in this room on this day, and on all the days to come, to feel proud of who you are," Frances said in a resounding voice. "We are William Jackson's family. The world has fought us, has despised us, and even we as a family have fought one another. But today, and every day from here on out, we stand together as a family. God has made a way for this family to come together, and we as a family will never be torn apart again. We'll meet whatever challenges that may come our way, but we'll meet them together as one united family," she said as she slowly looked at everyone. "Now if I may ask Reverend Speight to pray for us on this special day, we can adjourn to the dining room to enjoy Christmas together."

Reverend Speight gave thanks for the day that had brought everyone together and prayed that not only this day, but many more like it, would bring the Jackson family and the entire world together.

When he finished giving his thanks, everyone adjourned to the dining room and began to enjoy the huge feast that Frances had prepared. The food looked scrumptious enough to make a king's mouth water with envy. The baked ham, turkey, mashed potatoes and gravy, macaroni, green peas, candied yams, cranberry sauce, and a rainbow choice of pies and cakes were enough to feed an entire army.

Frances and her family enjoyed their Christmas feast like a real true family. Plenty of laughter, joy, and conversation went around the table, and there wasn't a silent voice among the entire group. Whenever this night ended, everyone would know that love truly existed in their family. No one, however, was in a hurry for this night to end, because everyone knew that this Jackson Christmas feast, was one that would always be remembered.

Don't miss out!

Visit the website below and you can sign up to receive emails whenever Vincent Armstrong publishes a new book. There's no charge and no obligation.

https://books2read.com/r/B-A-IWNV-ZRSCC

BOOKS 2 READ

Connecting independent readers to independent writers.